MURDER
AT
FIRST BLUSH

MURDER
AT
FIRST BLUSH

A COSMETIC CRIMES MYSTERY

ARLENE KAY

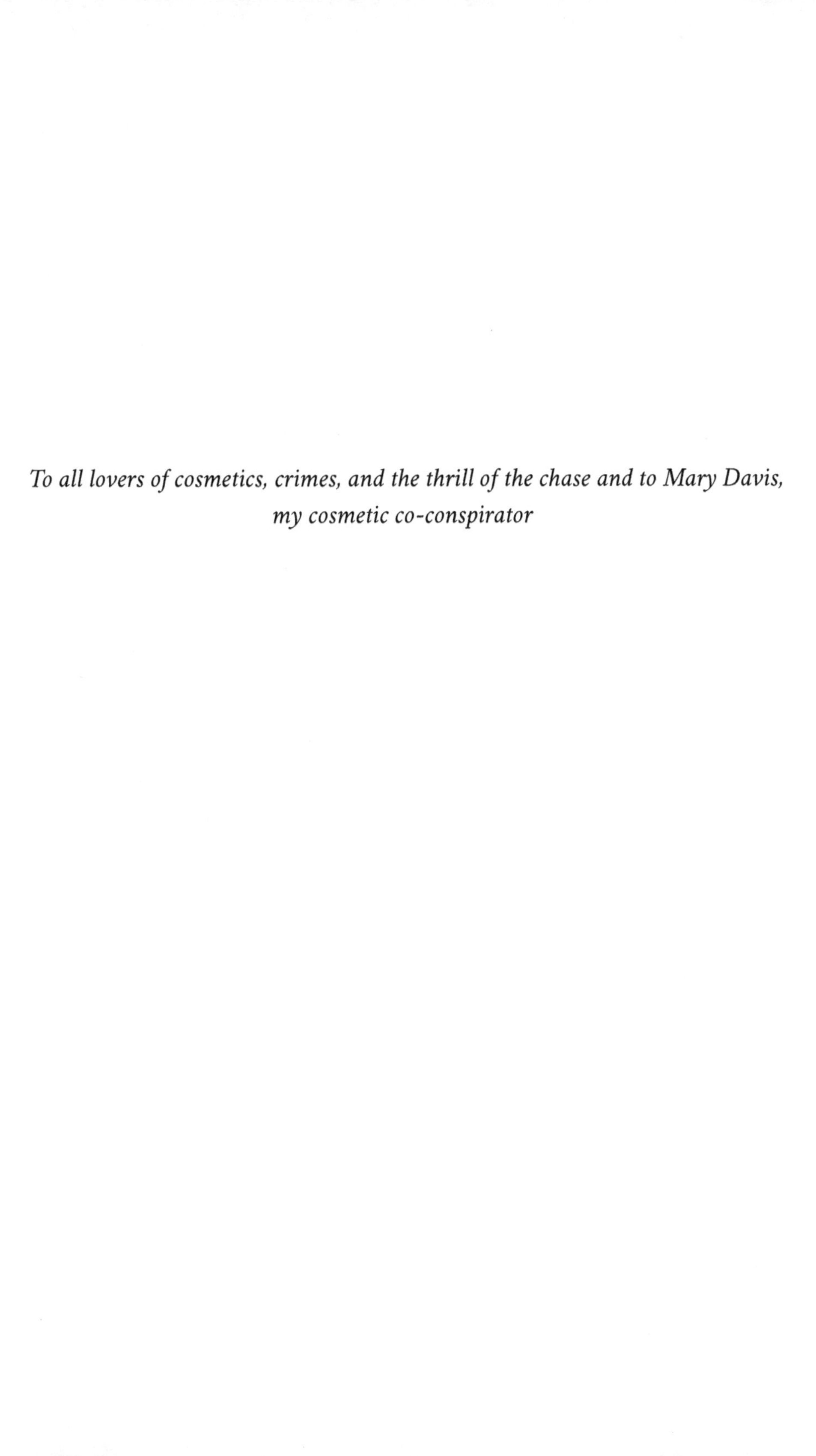

To all lovers of cosmetics, crimes, and the thrill of the chase and to Mary Davis, my cosmetic co-conspirator

Praise for Murder at First Blush

"What fun! As a sleuth, Marky hits the mark. And her sidekick, Gemma, is a real gem. Life is grim for the town's former golden girl, but Arlene Kay offers up a rich and lively journey home. This high energy story streaks along and the ending is unexpected and satisfying."—Lane Stone, *The Collector, Big Picture Trilogy*

"Arlene Kay brings her usual wit and humor to the first book in what promises to be a winning series. The charming small-town setting includes a cast of quirky (and potentially murderous) characters. Her intrepid and not-so-perfect-after-all heroine makes a terrific sleuth in this appealing and clever cozy. Perfectly delightful—a must read for fans of the genre!"—Carol Bugge (C.E. Lawrence)

Chapter One

I stood on the steps of the Art Institute of Chicago, savoring my last look at the street below. I was six years old when Aunt Violet took me on my first expedition to that magical place. She held my hand and carefully explained that the Art Institute deserved reverence and awe. The treasures it held included a vast reservoir of beauty and culture that had thrilled museumgoers for over a century. Sixteen years later, I still vividly recalled each element of that trip. Perhaps I was a tad spoiled, strutting about in a bright crimson coat with black velvet collar and patent leather Mary Janes. But Violet made me feel special. We enjoyed high tea at the Drake Hotel and spent the rest of the day communing with the culture gods.

My aunt was herself a renowned artist, but to me, she was so much more. Few adults listened to a child, but Violet led me to the impressionist wing and asked me to scrutinize each treasure and describe the emotions it evoked. She shared insights about the artists that made them spring to life. A severed ear, a life cut short, all those elements nurtured my obsession with painting and fueled my determination to become an artist. Alas, I later learned that sometimes desire alone was simply not enough.

Michigan Avenue, that Magnificent Mile, was bustling with life—businesspeople, tourists, and commercial vehicles flooded the vital city I had grown to love. Chicago had lured me into a fevered four-year relationship, then spurned me like a faithless lover.

Don't be a drama queen, I told myself. You've been spoiled. Stop the pity party and get on with your life. Be grateful. I had plenty of time to take stock of things during the trip to O'Hare Airport and my flight home to

Harbor Bay, Michigan. After all, at twenty-four years of age, I was in the prime of life. I'd earned a BFA from the Art Institute, for heaven's sake. That counted for something, didn't it? Besides, Marketta Davis was no quitter. I had always been a fighter. People even called me plucky. Failure was foreign to me. Those slogans were my mantra until very recently. Now they rang hollow as reality struck. Perhaps that bit of hubris was also the problem. I'd led a charmed life filled with calm seas, no squalls. High school valedictorian, promising artist and finally, a dream come true—a scholarship to Chicago's Art Institute. I'd thrown myself into painting with every fiber of my being, and for a time, all had gone well. Memories of Harbor Bay and my life there gradually receded into the background with one notable exception—my Aunt Violet.

She was my role model, a gifted artist and cosmetics entrepreneur who had conquered the European market. I didn't often see her because she flitted around to various exotic locations like Paris, London, and Rome. That made Harbor Bay low on her to-do list. Still, I treasured each letter and hoarded the generous product samples she sent. Much to my mother's chagrin, every doll I owned bore witness to my experiments with lipstick, blush, and eye shadow. Aunt Violet was everything I aspired to be and as far from the humdrum existence of Harbor Bay as one could ever get. Now, like it or not, that bourgeois bastion would once more be mine.

When my advisor and secret crush Claude Winslow assessed my portfolio, he delivered the bad news gently. My painting was "adequate" but not inspired. I would make a fine teacher but not a gifted artist. Bottom line: my application for the institute's MFA program was denied. I was out on my ear and headed back where I came from. With limited prospects and a dwindling bank balance, I fled the Windy City.

* * *

My parents tried mightily to cushion the blow, but word soon spread in our close community that Marketta Davis, the golden girl of Harbor Bay, had fallen flat on her face. My sense of self-worth plummeted to new depths.

Forget Kubler-Ross's five stages of grief. I was firmly stuck on depression. When my parents jetted off to New Zealand for a six-month sabbatical, my final layer of insulation from reality vanished with them.

Most folks were kind. Oh, how I grew to hate that word. Ladies brought casseroles, and several of my former friends invited me to social events that resembled wakes more than parties. Conversations were stilted and even the best-intentioned tiptoed around the elephant in the room. As the pachyderm in question, I dreaded pasting a bright smile on my face and radiating specious sunshine. Talk of husbands, babies, and church suppers bored me silly. I ached for the passionate debate about art, politics, and literature that had fueled so many evening sessions in Chicago. Excuses and recriminations were pointless. It was my own fault. These were good decent people who were content with their lives while somewhere in the process, I had become an elitist snob who simply didn't fit in. Success wasn't guaranteed to anyone, even Marketta Davis, the belle of Harbor Bay.

* * *

I put on a brave public face.

Count your blessings, I told myself. Nobody likes a whiner. Most people would gladly trade places with you.

One sunny afternoon, I strolled down Main Street, reliving the familiar scenes from my past. The Soda Spot, our high school hangout, still stood, looking somewhat the worse for wear, but the Harbor Bake Shop had been replaced by a sleek edifice that boasted fresh croissants, espresso, and bagels. Sign of the times, I supposed. A sense of nostalgia overwhelmed me as I recalled the innocence of those simple childhood pleasures I had discarded. Life in Harbor Bay wasn't exciting, but it had provided me with security and comfort. Too bad my bid for the brass ring had fizzled out so spectacularly.

It took a chance encounter with an old high school pal to administer a healthy dose of reality and tough love to me. Gemma Watts, a vivacious redhead with a bellowing laugh, slapped me on the back and stated the obvious. "Okay. Stop moping around. You struck out. Now that you know what it's like to be normal, what's next? You've always had it way too easy. Blonde hair, blue eyes, perfect skin. You never even had one pimple during high school. The rest of us had to claw and scramble for everything we ever had. It's your turn now. What's your game plan?"

What indeed? I pondered this question as I assessed the business climate in Harbor Bay during my survey of Main Street.

"Things have changed in Harbor Bay over the past few years," I observed. "Lattes, yoga studios, and hair emporiums all around us. Maybe this town is ready to accept something new."

Gemma nodded. "Lots of upscale houses being built around the waterfront. Gentrification, they call it. Good for business but kind of sad too."

"How so?" I asked. "Isn't that part of progress?"

Gemma shrugged. "Maybe. I kinda miss some of the old things, though. You know, the soda counter and the penny candy store. The people are still the same, though. A pretty nice bunch overall."

Maybe that's what I had missed in Chicago. Big cities are exciting, but they can be lonely too. Aunt Violet succeeded in conquering Paris. Unlike me, she was fearless. Perhaps a smaller stage suited me just fine.

My parents urged me to teach art for the local school district, an underwhelming prospect at best. An entrepreneurial spirit stirred within me, but a lack of capital put paid to that idea.

Even my college mentor admitted that I had a flair for color. During art school, I earned extra cash by working the cosmetic counters of some of Chicago's premier specialty stores. That allowed me to gain expertise in their product lines and burnish my customer relations skills. My list of grateful clients included some of the city's prominent matrons and trendsetters, many of whom summered in Harbor Bay. Why not capitalize on those talents and connections? It wasn't the Art Institute, but it was artistry of sorts.

"Ask your parents for some help," Gemma said. "Lord knows, they could spare a few bucks for their only child. What's wrong with running a cosmetics store anyway?"

"A beauty emporium, my dear. So much more upscale. Think of my Aunt

Violet's empire. Even she started with a single store." I was teasing Gemma, but considering the empty storefronts I'd just seen, there was a grain of truth to it. Aunt Violet might be the answer to my prayers. When it came to business acumen, Violet had few equals. If anyone could assess the prospects for success, it was Violet.

I crossed my fingers and called Violet at her office in Paris. Seeking advice was easy but asking for money was unfamiliar and somewhat humiliating. After listening to my ideas, Violet immediately switched to business mode.

"Harbor Bay has real potential," she said, "especially with that summer crowd it draws. Quaint stores are a big draw in a place like that, and it doesn't sound like you'd have any competition."

Before I summoned my courage, Violet beat me to it. "How are you fixed for capital, Poppet? Most small businesses fall flat on their face due to start-up costs."

I confessed that my funds were limited, in fact, almost non-existent.

My aunt chuckled and said something in French that I didn't quite understand. "Looks like you need an investor. Would I do? Sometimes I still miss Harbor Bay, believe it or not. The people. The sense of community. Those things are hard to replicate, even in a glamorous place like Paris. Don't ever discount them, Marky."

I could barely believe my luck. Good fortune had smiled upon me, and suddenly, I'd found my future right in the very place I'd once abandoned. Gemma's reaction was priceless. She slapped me on the back and did her version of a victory dance.

"I knew you'd make it," she whooped. "Marky Davis, the star of Harbor Bay."

I immediately enlisted her as my partner. Gemma was a certified aesthetician and a natural salesperson who never met a stranger. Plus, her local connections were far stronger than mine.

"Are you serious?" she asked, shaking her auburn curls wildly. "It's like a dream come true. I don't have any money to contribute, but I swear I'll work my fingers to the bone for you."

I hugged my friend. "For us, you mean. We're partners. Fifty-fifty. Even

Stephen. You know the drill."

Together we brainstormed an appropriate title. I opted for APHRODITE, a Temple of beauty, but Gemma nixed that right away. "You've got to be kidding," she said. "Way too artsy-fartsy for our crowd. You'll scare away most potential customers who haven't studied Greek." She suggested something homey instead. "Not too homey," I groused. "We're trying for something friendly but different."

Once again, my aunt came to the rescue. She had always called me Poppet. Poppet a friendly, affectionate term that made me smile. It was perfect for a shop like ours that stressed beauty with a light touch.

"Face it," Gemma said with a smirk. "Half the women in town think lipstick is something exotic. Probably call you a hussy behind your back for lining your eyes."

That was sobering news. I'd always seen myself as the wholesome type, not some femme fatale. Still, Gemma had a point. I'd asked her mother to quiz her friends about the issue while Gemma surveyed the under-thirty crowd. The results jolted me but helped to inform our business plan. Women in Harbor Bay, even those with generous incomes, were intimidated by approaching a "fancy" place. "They don't want to be judged," Gemma said. "You know how off-putting some of those snooty places are. Who needs that? A name like Poppet sounds welcoming."

"No problem luring the summer crowd into the store," I said. "They'll love it."

"Yeah, but what about the other six months of the year?" Gemma asked. "Gotta get the locals involved too."

We needed advice from someone in the beauty biz, and I knew just who to call.

Aunt Violet came to the rescue once more. "Look Marky," she said. "European women care more about skincare than face paint. Facials, eye creams, massages, and the like. Emphasize that to lure the crowd in, then show 'em how a touch of makeup can change their outlook. Oh, and once you get established, hire a mature woman too. Works like a charm."

After we hung up, my head was swimming with ideas, advice, and fear.

The vacant storefront directly on Main Street that I'd scoped out was the perfect location. If only the price was right.

* * *

The stars aligned for us. That property was available at a reasonable price and included a bonus feature of a loft apartment that would suit my living needs perfectly. Gemma warned me that the reason that the reason the rent was reasonable was because the location was considered a jinx. Apparently, several previous retail ventures had failed within six months. With fingers crossed and all the optimism of youth, I sealed the deal and embarked on my great adventure. "Poppet, the Spot for Beauty" would succeed. It simply had to.

One day as I clambered up a ladder to stock the shelves, an unexpected visitor arrived.

"Hey, Marky," he said. "Watch yourself with that ladder. Doesn't look too sturdy to me. Here. Let me hold it."

I knew that voice from a thousand late-night phone calls and a few high school dances. Blaike Harrington, my long-ago steady beau had once again entered my life. I carefully climbed down the ladder and faced him. Blaike was twenty-six, older than Gemma and me but remarkably unchanged. Still a blue-eyed, sandy-haired hunk with plenty of muscles and a thick crop of hair. Because our coloring and features were similar, people had always teased us about being long-lost siblings instead of a couple.

His gaze was direct and personal. "I couldn't believe it when I heard you'd come back. Welcome, Marky. You look wonderful." We shook hands rather awkwardly, but I still managed to check out his left finger, just in case. No sign of a wedding ring.

"I'm ready for a break," I said. "How about an espresso at Bucky's?"

* * *

Somehow sharing a table at the town's favorite bakery seemed less daunting than facing this man in my unfinished store. Our parting had been fevered and painful. I had my eyes firmly focused on Chicago; he was mired in romance. Blaike offered me an engagement ring and a future, but it wasn't enough. He was expendable, and with the callous indifference of youth, I broke his heart.

For the next hour, we played catch-up. Blaike had finished college, gotten his MBA from the University of Michigan, and joined his family's investment firm.

"Pretty impressive," I said. "That's a really great credential. Why come back to Harbor Bay?"

He smiled. "I could ask you the same thing. Besides, I never really left. Life here is pretty tame compared with the Windy City, I suppose."

I bit my lip. "Plans changed. No danger of my becoming the next Mary Cassatt or Georgia O'Keefe. I got a big-time reality check at the Art Institute."

Blaike nodded. "You have everything going for you— looks, brains, talent. That hasn't changed. You're still the superstar of Harbor Bay."

I pointed toward the gold and cream sign across the street. "That's my dream now. Poppet. Poppet, the Beauty Spot." I gulped. "I hope Gemma and I can make a go of it."

Blaike hesitated before responding. "You and Gemma, huh? Sounds like a winning formula. You two were quite a team before." We exchanged glances, both of us unsure how to proceed. Finally, he said, "Look. I'm not trying to push my way in, but I'd be glad to review your business plan. Maybe I can offer some suggestions. Just tell me if you want me to back off."

My mouth felt dry despite the double espresso I'd just drained. Blaike was a good guy. I'd expected him to avoid me or be neutral at best. We hadn't spoken in four years, but it felt like only yesterday. Right now, he also seemed like the answer to a prayer. "I'd appreciate that. I've got plenty of ideas, but numbers were never my strong suit. See what you think." We toasted our alliance with pottery mugs and the promise of more to come.

Chapter Two

"Unbelievable," Gemma screeched when I told her about Blaike. "I figured he'd never come near you after the way you treated him. You broke that boy's heart. He moped around town for months after you dumped him. Wouldn't even look at another girl. Most guys would hate your guts."

I didn't argue with her. Better to let the storm subside and bow my head. Besides, she was right.

"Did he tell you what he does? Blaike Harrington is a big noise in Harbor Bay these days. Town council, Chamber of commerce—the works. Works for his daddy's investment business and makes a bundle."

That didn't surprise me one bit. Both Blaike and I were always ambitious. That was one of the things that scuttled our romance—we were way too competitive. I tiptoed around the burning question. "I suppose he's married by now. Couple of kids too."

Naturally, Gemma wasn't fooled for even a second. "Nope. Guess that guy was pining for the love of his life. I don't think he's even seeing anyone." She grinned. "I could ask you the same question, Marky. No husbands or fiancés lurking in the shadows? Come on. Fess up. Remember, you're talking to an expert on bad boys." Gemma looked away as though this was a painful memory.

Discussing my love life was out of bounds. Naturally, I'd dated in Chicago, but painting had been my true obsession, and serious romances simply hadn't interested me. I quickly changed the subject to business. After a few more jabs about lost love, Gemma got serious and agreed that free business advice from someone like Blaike was too valuable to ignore. We arranged a meeting.

Sometimes a woman must swallow her pride and accept help. That's what I told myself when we met with Blaike. It wasn't his attitude that rankled, or his detailed analysis of our business plan, because Blaike's suggestions were sound and his focus strategic. I couldn't detect even a hint of personal interest—and that's what bothered me. I told myself to chill. A lot of time had passed since Marky Davis had been prom queen and the toast of Harbor Bay. Lots of water under that bridge. Could be that he simply wanted to be a friend. That hurt my pride, even though it was probably for the best.

Blaike suggested that we expand our offerings beyond products into services such as massage, facials, makeovers, and pedicures. Private consultations and special event planning were also moneymakers that would boost our bottom line. Both Gemma and I readily agreed to his ideas. We left the meeting buoyed by a surge of optimism for the future of Poppet and its owners.

We envisioned a fantastic opening night event that would put our name on everybody's radar. Poppet's watchword was FUN. Nothing stodgy, just a tranquil oasis where customers would feel valued and welcome.

That was not the case with the town council. Small-town politics had always befuddled me, especially after getting a taste of large-scale shenanigans in Chicago. In Harbor Bay, the system was painfully personal, built on a complicated web of social and familial connections.

I'd known Mayor Zachery Thanos all my life. Although he was now retired, Dr. Zach had served as the town dentist for three decades. He was an amiable sort who gifted his young patients with an endless supply of bromides, toothpaste, and floss. I recalled his habitual warnings about eating too many sweets or failing to keep appointments, all delivered with a warm smile. In his role as mayor, he managed to keep peace among the town's fractious elements by brokering compromise and projecting an air of goodwill. He was seated at the front desk dispensing forms, directions, and advice to anyone who approached him.

"Marky Davis," exclaimed the mayor. "Haven't seen you in ages. Still keeping up with that floss, I hope. Wouldn't want you to spoil those pretty teeth."

I was accustomed to Zach's folksy ways and would never hurt his feelings. Gemma, on the other hand, rolled her eyes and turned aside. Patience had never been her strong suit. After exchanging pleasantries with the mayor, we completed the permit process and left city hall.

On the outside steps, we encountered Harbor Bay's resident novelist Tilda Egan.

"So, you're our newest business owner," Tilda said, fluttering heavily mascaraed lashes "Good luck to you both. This town needs a little glitz." Tilda herself was a glamour puss, at least by local standards. Her raven locks were expertly styled, and the pantsuit she wore had a definite designer flair. Despite her literary claims, no one in town had ever actually seen or read anything she produced. Tilda lived extremely well for someone without any visible means of support, and many residents marveled at this.

"How Tilda Egan wangled her way into town government, I'll never know," Gemma groused. "She's got more moves than a centipede. Twice as deadly too."

"Ah, come on," I said. "Aren't you being a bit harsh?"

She folded her arms and glared my way. "Nope. The way that woman manipulates men is criminal. Boardroom or bedroom, it's all the same to her."

"Gemma!" No need to start a blood feud with a potential client, especially one who used cosmetics. "Admit it. Tilda is what passes for a sexpot in Harbor Bay. She obviously takes care of herself."

"Plays a mean game of golf, too," Gemma said. "Better than half the guys in town."

According to Blaike, Tilda Egan favored massive commercial development in our little town. Big box stores, chain stores, anything that brought in a buck. That was troubling. I'd seen the pernicious effect of that approach in other communities. It changed the character of the local landscape and inevitably led to the demise of small businesses. Needless to say, it also aroused controversy.

"Fine." Gemma then offered to spearhead our grand opening event, a complimentary Spa night for local dignitaries. "Pampering appeals to everyone," she said, "but with this crowd the watchword is *free*. Hard for anyone to turn down that kind of deal."

One council member had balked at the concept. Lionel Stevens, retired attorney and zoning commissioner, railed against the frivolity of what he termed a "group grope." I'd never met him but according to Gemma, Lionel was a crusty soul who spent any free time on his boat in the company of anyone other than his wife, Kim. He regarded her as an acquisitive nuisance who refused to rein in her spending.

I wondered if there was more to their saga than that. Relationships, especially marriages, were complicated affairs.

"Don't fret," Blaike said after the final council meeting. "Peer pressure won out. Lionel reluctantly agreed to attend the gala. Just don't expect him to enjoy it. He complains about everybody and everything, including his wife."

"Especially his wife," Gemma hooted. "Poor Kim. She's not a bad egg. Not that smart but good-natured. What she sees in Lionel, I'll never know. Security, I guess. He's loaded, you know."

Blaike frowned. "I remember her. Kim was quite a few years ahead of me in high school. She tried for a modeling career, but things turned sour, so she left New York and came home."

"Surprised everyone by marrying Lionel," Gemma said, "but they've been together for a while now."

Another failure like me, I thought. *Maybe we should start a loser's club.*

"What about Philippa Gordon?" Her credentials were formidable—a former school principal, ardent environmentalist, and chair of the Board of Review. During my high school years, Principal Gordon had terrified me, although she was a tough but fair administrator. Under her steely-eyed gaze, many a truant had wilted, confessed his crimes, and begged for mercy. Although I was the original goody-two-shoes, she never warmed up to me. Even now, I detected a faint whiff of disapproval whenever we crossed paths. I found that hard to understand. Though I'd struck out in Chicago, I still considered myself an upstanding citizen. Her attitude wounded my pride.

You're pathetic, I told myself. *After all these years, you still crave approval. Grow up.*

"Principal Gordon and Tilda Egan are polar opposites," Gemma said. "Philippa uses facts, not flirting, to sway votes. Realistically she's the power player in town."

"How so?" I asked.

"Think of it. The Board of Review grants or denies final approval to all land use and commercial projects. Philippa takes that post very seriously. Nothing gets by her. Believe me. Sparks fly if any shoddy proposals pop up."

I hunched over my computer, reading the Harbor Bay website, looking for people to add to the invitation list. "Who's this councilman at large? I never heard of Paul Prentis before."

Gemma's normally sunny disposition suddenly turned sour. "Lucky you. Not one of my favorites," she said. "Another case of family connections gone awry." Gemma snorted. "What a slimeball that guy is! He looks good and knows it. Too bad what you see is not what you get."

"How come I don't remember him? He's about our age, isn't he? The name Prentis sounds familiar, but I don't recall him."

"Paul went to prep school. Cranbrook Academy all the way, baby. No need to mix with riff-raff like us." Gemma gave her mile-wide grin, but I detected an odd note of sadness in her. Cranbrook Academy was an extremely pricey prep school located in one of Detroit's most affluent suburbs. If Paul boarded there, it's no wonder I never met him.

Blaike curled his lip. "Apparently, business ethics isn't part of their curriculum. Paul has already stiffed several local investors here and made plenty of enemies. He won't be joining us next week because he's out of town. You should be thankful for that small mercy."

After such a buildup, I was disappointed that this bad boy of Harbor Bay would be absent. On second thought, Poppet had enough challenges to surmount on opening night without dealing with a tricky trust fund baby.

* * *

As opening day approached, I declared myself officially exhausted. Gemma and I spent hours customizing products and services to suit each guest and agonizing over sample bags and other goodies. We interviewed our potential customers to zero in on their special needs. For example, Mayor Zach had back problems, some of which could be addressed by Gemma's specialty, a deep tissue massage. Lionel admitted that he often had difficulty sleeping, so a Trigger Point Therapy was an ideal solution. Both ladies had very different preferences and needs. Tilda wanted the works—facial, makeover, and manicure. I thought that since she was open to almost anything, she'd be fun to work with despite her superior attitude.

Aunt Violet had shipped a full range of French products to us, and I had targeted an adventurous client like Tilda for them. A different approach was needed with Philippa, whose modest request centered around skincare products rather than cosmetics. Since she was a teetotaler who followed a strict fitness regimen of tennis and running. Philippa sought a routine that would shield her skin from the elements. I noted that exposure to the sun was probably responsible for the premature aging of her complexion. On the other hand, perhaps it was simply the effects of her poisonous personality.

As opening night drew near, both Gemma and I suffered a major case of jitters. We apportioned space to accommodate privacy and comfort for each client, but the list of possible omissions haunted me.

"Did we order enough champagne?" I asked. "I'm never sure how to figure the servings. I suppose the snacks will be okay. No one complained of any particular allergies that I'm aware of."

Finally, Gemma held up her arms in surrender. "Enough! Chill out, or you'll never make it to opening night. This place is amazing. Wait 'til word of mouth spreads the good news. We'll capture the entire Traverse City area."

She had a point.

My plan was to lure corporate events to our store and align with upscale hotels to do bridal parties and other celebrations. Everything depended on our initial launch. I wasn't much of a gambler, but both of us had bet all our chips on Poppet, the Spot for Beauty.

Chapter Three

Gemma had no qualms at all about our big night. Her sunny outlook was one of the things I had always loved about her. Life had given her some hard knocks, but they hadn't quenched her optimism. Her father was but a distant memory, and for most of her childhood, Gemma and her mom had cobbled together just enough income to survive. That made our venture even more crucial. Gemma's hopes and dreams were inextricably linked to Poppet's success.

I recalled Aunt Violet's advice about including a mature woman on our staff, and Gemma's mother seemed like the perfect fit. Like her daughter, Mandy Watts was a genial redhead who had an easy manner that charmed everyone she met. We agreed that Mandy would greet our guests when they first arrived and work the front counter of the store. Although that allayed some of her concerns, I sensed that she still was nervous.

"I've never worked retail before," Mandy said, shrugging. "Done a ton of waitressing, though, so I can handle the drinks and goodies, no problem. Plus, I know everyone in town. Some of them too well!" She winked to show that it was no problem. "Pretty good at stocking shelves and tidying up too."

Blaike tapped on the front door, dressed in faded jeans and a torn University of Michigan sweatshirt. "Reporting for duty," he said with a snappy salute. "I'm yours to command."

Gemma immediately directed him to the stock room, where heavy boxes needed to be unpacked. "I love a man with muscles," she teased. When Blaike turned to look at her, she added, "Especially one willing to work for free. Come on. Let's party!"

Gemma turned on a rock oldies station, poured beverages, and made good on her suggestion. The countdown to opening passed quickly.

I found myself enjoying what could have been a soul-searing experience until someone rapped loudly at our door.

"Who's that?" Blaike asked.

"Obviously, someone who can't read." I'd painted a sign touting our grand opening the next day, along with a gentle reminder that the store was closed for a private party this evening.

Our unwelcome visitor ignored the drawn shades as well as the sign and knocked even louder. When my nerves could stand it no longer, I bowed to the inevitable and unlocked the front door. After all, it might be an unexpected delivery or an emergency. Turned out it was neither. A tall, tanned stranger strolled into the store as if he were the rightful owner of the place. He flung off his sunglasses and grinned, showing perfect teeth, expertly styled hair, and plenty of attitude.

"You're Marketta Davis, the painter," he said triumphantly as if he had clinched the Final Jeopardy question. He was quite handsome and obviously knew it.

I answered him politely but firmly. "Actually, I'm the proprietor of this store. We're closed today, but please come back some other time."

My response puzzled him. Obviously, he expected a warmer welcome, maybe even a curtsy.

He glared at me as if I had missed a step on the evolutionary scale. "My name is Paul Prentis, and I'm also your landlord." He eyed the paintings that lined the walls of our shop. They were some of my best works, and I was proud of them. They had drawn accolades at the Art Institute but despite that, something inside of me hoped this snarky stranger would praise them too. No such luck. Our lease specified "Prentis Properties," but so did half the real estate in Harbor Bay. An attorney handled the details, and the name Paul Prentis had never been mentioned. No wonder he had sailed into our store with all flags flying. Our families moved in very different social circles, so it was no wonder that we had never met.

The appearance of Gemma and Blaike spared me from embarrassment and allowed time to assess Paul Prentis. So, this was the Councilor at large, town bad boy, and overall reprobate. Gemma described him as a prep school scamp who had never quite reached adulthood. Watching him go toe-to-toe with Blaike, I could understand why. Money and privilege can have a corrosive effect on some people. I recalled the famous Lord Acton quote about power corrupting and absolute power corrupting absolutely.

"Your office said you'd be gone until next week," Blaike said. His tone was brusque and distinctly unfriendly.

Prentis yawned. "Plans change. I wouldn't miss your little party for the world." He spoke with a prep school drawl, which was both unpleasant and pretentious.

Gemma brushed up against him with her duster. "Oops! Better make a getaway while you can, Paul. Otherwise, we'll put you to work."

They exchanged looks, communicating something, an emotion that I couldn't put my finger on. He gave her a knowing grin, but Gemma continued sprucing up the aisle and said no more.

I gave Paul my best social smile. "Nice meeting you. We'll expect you at the party tomorrow night."

With that, the bad boy of Harbor Bay nodded sharply and vacated the premises.

* * *

Gemma and I agreed to dress down by wearing black leggings and t-shirts, but Mandy opted for a lovely black silk dress that was her go-to garb for special occasions. When I told Gemma that her Mom was a hottie, I got a sharp rebuke from my partner. "Wake up, Marky, don't be patronizing. She's forty-eight. Hardly ready for the scrap pile. Think of Mandy as our target customer and go with it."

Once again, Gemma was right. I needed a major attitude adjustment if Poppet were to succeed. I soothed my spirits by spending an hour at my easel painting a floral abstract with vibrant colors. *This venture will succeed* I vowed. *You can do it.*

"What's the story with you and Paul Prentis?" I asked Gemma. "I sensed some tension there."

She shrugged, and for a moment, an unexpected look of vulnerability crossed her face. "We have history. Leave it at that for now. Some day when we have a minute to breathe, I'll fill you in. It's not a pretty story."

Everyone needed a zone of privacy around them and their life, and Gemma was no exception. I gave her a salute and dropped the subject.

Our guests, except for Paul Prentis, arrived promptly at six o'clock. His tardiness didn't surprise me one bit because he appeared to be the type of person who enjoyed making a grand entrance. 'Show boater' my grandpa would have said. *Jerk*, I said. After we'd uncorked the champagne, I proposed a toast to Poppet and my hometown of Harbor Bay. Blaike hoisted his flute and added one more thing: a salute to coming home and new beginnings.

After a few more pleasantries, we guided our guests to their treatment rooms. I knew from experience that women appreciated privacy for makeovers and product applications. Men wanted to relax and enjoy their massage without interruption. Manicures and pedicures could be provided in open cubicles without any problem.

As Gemma whisked Mayor Zach into a treatment room, the games began. Tilda perched on a stool and engaged me in a detailed discussion of our products and their usage. We were joined by Lionel's wife, Kim Stevens, a stunning brunette whose knowledge of cosmetics was encyclopedic.

So, this is the former model.

Her toned body was a testament to hours spent in the gym. An unlined face and perfect features suggested that the hand of a skilled surgeon had been at work.

Both women sampled new products and dove into the goodie bags I had assembled for them.

Meanwhile, Philippa and Mandy bonded over a love of natural products and organic food, while Blaike engaged Lionel in a discussion of condominium proposals.

Thirty minutes later, Mayor Zach emerged wearing a broad grin. "Gotta hand it to you, ladies. My back never felt so good. Sign me up as a regular."

After some persuasion from his wife, Lionel Stevens took his turn on the table. The crusty attorney's expression hovered between a snarl and a sneer. "I warn you. I've been to the best spas in New York and Chicago, and none of them met my needs."

That put Gemma's skill as a masseuse to the test in a very public way. Fortunately, her deep tissue massage changed Lionel's attitude, and he grudgingly admitted that it was a positive experience.

Our guests seemed to be enjoying the program until Paul Prentis sauntered into the store. Everyone exchanged minimally polite greetings with him as they warily watched him embrace the ladies and nod to the gents. Tilda turned her back to him and continued testing products, but Kim Stevens froze in place. *Was there some history between these two as well,* or was Kim merely anxious to avoid conflict with her husband? Age may have been a factor. She was at least two decades younger than Lionel and far livelier. Then again, according to Mandy, Lionel made most corpses look animated.

Philippa Gordon sipped Perrier and moved to the end of the counter. Paul noticed the snub and immediately targeted her. "Ah. Principal Gordon. Not toasting our hosts with champagne. Surely you can indulge this one time. You used to be more fun."

Philippa tightened her grip on the Perrier but ignored the odious Paul.

I admired her for that. It didn't make her more likable, but it showcased her dignity and toughness. I knew for a fact just how tough the woman was. Her glare could pierce a three-inch steel plate. I'd been the recipient of it enough to know that.

Nothing deterred Paul Prentis when he was on a mission. He ignored the reaction of his peers, claimed center stage, and demanded immediate attention. "Let's get this show on the road, girls. I'm a busy man."

Gemma shook her head and ignored him. "Wait your turn, Paul." She continued folding towels and tidying up the massage area, much to Paul's chagrin. "Come on, Gemma," he sneered, "You know I always go to the head of the line. Give your landlord a little love. That's one of your talents, as I recall."

That rude remark shocked the entire party.

Gemma blanched but remained silent.

Her mother chose to act. Mandy Watts clutched her champagne glass and threw the contents in Paul's face. As he sputtered and wiped his face, Blaike moved between Paul and Mandy, grabbing his arm. "Time to leave, buddy."

I detected the strong scent of alcohol as Paul drifted by. The confrontation with Blaike sparked even more hostility from our councilman at large.

"Get your hands off me, Harrington. I'm not your buddy. Never was. Never will be." Then, he whirled around and pointed his finger at Lionel. "Don't look surprised, Stevens. You've got your own problems at home. Ask little Kim to fill you in if you're interested. She's told me all about it."

Kim Stevens gasped and dissolved into tears. Meanwhile, Lionel charged across the room, fists at the ready. "I warn you, Prentis. I was light-heavyweight boxing champion at Yale."

Paul yelled a vulgar epithet and faced Lionel. "In what century? Besides, I never fight with old men. No challenge."

Blaike interceded once more by grabbing Paul's arms behind him and propelling him toward the exit. Products flew across the room in our beautifully arrayed showroom. soon became a wasteland. I didn't weep, although it took every molecule of my strength to avoid doing so. Just in the nick of time, a surprise guest appeared. My Aunt Violet entered the fray and immediately restored order. At first, I couldn't believe my eyes. Was this an apparition or the answer to a prayer? No monarch could have looked more regal than my aunt with her flawless makeup, perfect coif, and Chanel cape. She clapped her hands and said in a steely voice, "Stop this nonsense immediately."

I flew into Violet's arms and embraced her, inhaling the subtle scent of Creed.

Mayor Zack quickly seconded the motion. "Come on, guys. Let's be civilized. 'Tomorrow's another day."

"Funny you should say that, Mr. Mayor," Prentis sneered. "Your days in charge of Harbor Bay are numbered. Trust me on that."

Lionel mumbled an apology and nudged Kim toward the door. I noted that despite the upheaval, Tilda Egan had managed to remain above the fray.

She stayed perched on a stool, carefully reapplying lipstick and blush. Her green eyes glittered with either excitement or malice.

After what seemed like an eternity, Gemma, Violet, and I were finally alone, surveying the damage to our dream. Mandy had offered to help clean up, but to spare her frayed nerves, we sent her home.

"I wanted to surprise you," Violet said ruefully. "Apparently, I succeeded."

"You're like a gift from the gods," I said. "An avenging angel." Gemma joined me in embracing my aunt.

"You should have seen the look on Paul's face," she said. "Sheer terror. It was priceless." She brandished a broom and saluted Violet. "Oh well. Time to play janitor."

Two solid hours of mopping, cleaning, and polishing restored a modicum of order and helped to calm our jangled nerves.

"Nothing like manual labor to work off stress," Gemma joked.

I tried to find some way to comfort my friend, but I was stumped. Paul's behavior was designed to humiliate her in front of her clients and erode her confidence. It was the same old rich kid vs. poor kid story that was standard in many high schools. Gemma had experienced it all her life. But things had changed. Gemma was no longer the girl from the wrong side of the tracks. She deserved respect for the person she now was, and I vowed to reinforce that.

"I'm so sorry about tonight. Paul is a jerk!"

Gemma patted my back. "Forget it. I can take whatever he dishes out. I'm used to it from him. Bring it on, Frat Boy. Like Violet says, we will thrive!"

"We can leave the rest of that stuff until tomorrow," I said, but Gemma shook her head. "Tomorrow's a big day for us, partner. I'll handle this if you rearrange our displays."

She fastened the trash bags and dragged them out the back door to the alley. They were heavy, and I helped her load them onto a trolley.

Tomorrow! That thought gave me a surge of confidence. I told myself, just make it through this horrific night, and all will be better tomorrow. I spent some time daydreaming, chatting with Violet, and envisioning our grand opening the next day. We were certain to draw a crowd of curious townspeople, and I planned to personally greet everyone.

I checked my watch and saw that Gemma hadn't returned yet.

That alarmed me. The alley was dark and narrow, the perfect haven for muggers or rodents. I reached under the counter and grabbed the powerful flashlight I'd borrowed from our tool chest. *Better safe than sorry.* Not an original thought but one worth considering.

We'd purchased a large metal dumpster from the local disposal company that would endure all kinds of weather. At the time, I'd considered it a bargain, not a tomb. I crept toward the dumpster, carefully avoiding the trash that had blown in from the street. Gemma was nowhere to be found. I called her name in a reedy voice that I barely recognized as my own. My mind dredged up every horrific scene from the mystery novels I devoured.

Buck up, I scolded myself. *Show some courage.*

My attitude changed when I made a grisly discovery. The body of Paul Prentis was sprawled across the narrow alleyway with a violet extension cord wrapped snuggly around his neck. Violet. How ironic. We'd chosen that color as a tribute to my aunt. Now it seemed like a macabre joke. A trail of blood snaked down the side of his head, suggesting that his assailant had delivered a mighty blow before strangling him.

The dead man wasn't alone. My best pal and partner Gemma hovered over him, mumbling something incoherent.

"I didn't touch him," she sputtered. She was shaking, shivering despite the evening heat. "I swear he was already gone when I found him." Gemma gagged, and I fully expected her to faint or vomit.

Words failed me. I gulped and leaned against the dumpster to steady myself. Before I could speak, flashing lights and a shrieking siren announced the arrival of a Harbor Bay police cruiser. Who in the world had called them?

Chapter Four

Chief Gideon Hall was a solidly built middle-aged man who had kept order in Harbor Bay for two decades. There was something comforting about him. His massive shoulders and corded arms reminded me of a California Sequoia, sturdy and unyielding. A firm but fair manner of policing balanced the competing priorities of status, commerce, and equity and made him a popular figure in town. No one seemed to care or notice that he was a Native American man in an overwhelmingly white town. I'd never had much contact with him before, but that was about to change.

He leapt from his patrol car, gun drawn, moving quickly for such a big man. A lanky deputy brandishing a flashlight accompanied him. "Police. Hands up, ladies. Stay where you are."

No danger of my making any sudden moves or any other kind. I was firmly wedged between the dumpster and the side of my building, paralyzed by fear and barely able to stand. Gemma fared even worse. She babbled something incoherent and collapsed on the ground in a dead faint.

"Marky," Gideon said as the flashlight caught my face. "Marky Davis? Good Lord, girl, what in the world happened? And Gemma Watts?"

I seldom cry. My dad always called me a tough nut who refused to crack. But opening night, a free for all, and a dead body proved to be my undoing. Instead of weeping, I heard myself wail something nonsensical. "Paul Prentis! My God! Is he dead? He can't be. We just saw him tonight."

Gemma's gaze was unfocused as she struggled to her feet and stared silently at the corpse. Paul was a stranger to me, but apparently, she had known him well. Too well.

Gideon Hall quickly assessed the situation and holstered his gun. "Okay, ladies, calm down. I want you to back away from the crime scene and go into your shop." Gemma immediately staggered toward the door, but I was frozen in place, unable to move. "She's in shock," Hall told his deputy. "Help her in."

He was gentle as he took my arm and guided me through the side door of Poppet. I recognized the deputy as Benny Soto, a kid a few years behind me in high school. His parents owned the local bookstore, and he had been known as the quiet, studious type. His manner was more assertive now. Earning a badge and gun had apparently given him swagger and confidence. I limped toward one of our wing chairs and plopped down with all the grace of a platypus. Gemma was leaning against the counter, shielding her face with her hands as if to ward off a bad dream or a blow. Neither of us said anything until we faced Aunt Violet.

"Marky? Gemma? What's going on here?" She folded me into her arms and hugged me so tightly that I could hardly breathe, let alone speak. Violet glanced at Benny and immediately anticipated his next move. He stood, hands on hips, with his fingers brushing the holster at his side. Another time I would have scoffed, but the world was different tonight. This was Deputy Soto, the lawman, not our high school pal. One false move might be our last.

"It's Paul Prentis," I stammered. "He's dead. Murdered. We found him in the alley."

Benny started firing questions at us until Violet intervened. "Hold on. Take a deep breath. If a crime's involved, I assume you've read them their rights, Deputy."

Benny sputtered and stuttered, unsure of his next move. My aunt folded her arms, unyielding in the face of his bluster. That confounded him. Suspects were supposed to cower and confess. "Chief Hall will decide that," Benny said. "He'll be right in."

I pondered the tough decision I had to make— involve Gemma or withhold evidence from the authorities and risk my own future. She was no killer, but she had some connection to the odious Paul Prentis that might cast suspicion her way. She despised the big creep, but from what I'd witnessed tonight, Gemma was hardly alone in that. Somewhere in the deep recesses of my mind, I recalled that there were penalties for aiding and abetting a criminal. Still, the decision was easy. My partner was no criminal, and I would aid and abet her to the very end. I gulped, considering that my career choices were rapidly expanding from failed artist to entrepreneur to jailbird.

Violet navigated the row of partially drained bottles pouring each of us a glass of Perrier. "Here, girls. Sip this and try to relax. Gideon will help us sort things out."

I'd forgotten that my aunt knew Chief Hall and just about everyone who counted in Harbor Bay.

I longed to quiz Gemma about her relationship with Paul, but Deputy Soto's big ears were attuned to our every utterance. I settled for taking several long sips of Perrier instead. Gemma's eyes had a feverish glow that suggested incipient hysteria or too much caffeine. I suspected door number one was the culprit. My mind turned to more practical matters, such as the direct impact of the murder on Poppet and our grand opening that morning. In exactly eight hours, our doors would swing open, and the good citizens and neighbors of Harbor Bay would stream in. That wasn't surprising. Murder was a ghoulish topic, but excitement was at such a low ebb in our little town that even sensible souls would welcome a respite. Besides, Paul Prentis was a prominent, if not popular, citizen with plenty of baggage that would fuel speculation. I planned to capitalize upon that. Sooner or later, suspicion would turn to Gemma, and any tidbit I might glean that worked in her favor would be critical.

"We can still open tomorrow, right?" Gemma stared pointedly at Soto.

He jumped back as if she had slapped him. "Uh, yeah, I guess so. You're really talking about today, though." He checked his watch, an oversized timepiece favored by cops everywhere. On his gangly wrists, it looked out of place, as if a child were wearing his father's jewelry. Maybe not," he said, using a stern, official voice. "After all, this is a crime scene. Forensics have to check it out."

Gemma had recovered her composure and was unimpressed by authority.

She frowned and pointed toward the pristine interior of our shop. "Look around you. The murder didn't happen in here. We're sure of that. Your so-called crime scene is out in the alley."

Despite cheering for Gemma, I felt a twinge of compassion for him. Soto had the intellectual edge, but when it came to tenacity, Gemma was miles ahead. He wilted under her withering glare and started to stammer. Only the appearance of his boss spared him from an ignominious retreat.

Gideon stood in the doorway, blocking out the streetlights and the horrific scene in the alley. His eyes swept over us with the practiced look of a career lawman. After twenty years in Harbor Bay, this man knew his town and the people in it. I suspected that he had few illusions about either.

He nodded to Gemma and me, but his gaze was focused on Aunt Violet.

"It's been a while, Violet. Too bad we had to meet like this. You haven't changed one bit." His words were banal, but I sensed something special in them. Had the chief been among my aunt's conquests?

Naturally, she kept her composure. I believe the French term is "sang-froid." However, a faint blush rose in her cheeks. "Nice to see you again, Gideon, even under these tragic circumstances. These young ladies are still in shock. Please be gentle with them."

"Understood." He nodded and turned my way. "So, you had a big shindig here tonight. Why don't the two of us have a chat while Gemma gives my deputy a list of your guests. He motioned toward one of the treatment rooms. "That should be private enough. You can join us, Violet."

I gulped but meekly followed his lead. In most detective novels, the police zeroed in on a suspect early in the process and proceeded to railroad the unlucky soul into jail. Gideon Hall was an intelligent, fair-minded person, but he was still a cop. Caution was my watchword. I vowed to suppress my natural impulse to babble nonsensically under stress.

"Do I need an attorney?" I asked. My voice sounded weak and weedy, even to me.

He glanced down at me and chuckled. "I get it. You're probably a fan of Law and Order and those other crime shows. You're welcome to an attorney, but that would just delay things. You're not a suspect, Ms. Davis. Not yet, at least. Besides, your Aunt Violet will protect your interests."

I forced myself to meet his gaze. "Okay. Do I get a Miranda warning or something?"

"Sure. Why not?" He was teasing me, something I considered unseemly under the circumstances. Gideon pulled a tattered card from his wallet and slowly recited the familiar litany of rights that every real or suspected criminal received. Despite the somber occasion, I rather enjoyed being part of the process. That didn't make me a monster, did it? My mind raced with fear. If he probed more deeply into the scene in the alley, I would probably fold like a cheap fan. My mother always knew when I was hiding something, and unlike Gemma, I tended to defer to authority figures. I had to speak with Gemma before committing myself.

"You were alone when you found him? Except for Gemma."

I faked a cough, stalling for time. Since Gemma was already on the scene, I wasn't alone. After convincing myself that it was a technicality, I answered. "Not really. I stayed inside while Gemma emptied the trash. When she didn't return, I got worried and went to find her. I didn't see anything at first. It was dark, and I remember thinking we needed to install lighting." I stifled a sob.

"You didn't touch him?" Gideon Hall raised an eyebrow. "Most people would have checked his pulse or something. Natural reaction."

Violet frowned and squeezed my hand. "Don't be timid, Marky. Tell Gideon what you recall."

Something about her attitude activated my courage. "That cord was wrapped around his neck in a bow, and his eyes bugged out. No way was he still breathing. I couldn't force myself to go near him."

Hall hadn't finished with me just yet. He slouched against the wall and tried a casual approach, apparently his version of the good cop routine.

"Funny thing about that cord. Pink, wasn't it? Don't think I've ever seen one in that color. Kind of girly. Like something you'd find in a beauty shop."

"It looked like one of ours," I admitted. "Violet, not pink. We thought of my aunt when we saw them at the Home Depot. We bought several."

"They sent me a picture of it," Violet said. "As a tribute."

That evoked a grin from the Chief. "Ah, yes. You're Marky's aunt. I almost forgot. Gumption must run in the family." He switched tactics without warning. "Prentis was a big guy. Not everyone could take him down."

"He was under the influence," Violet said. "Unsteady on his feet. If someone whacked him on his head, he couldn't offer much resistance."

Picturing that grisly scene made me shiver and aroused either the chief's compassion or caution. Most men fear scenes with hysterical women, and apparently, he was one of them. I was glad that he didn't press me any further about that cord. It looked identical to several we had purchased for Poppet. Surge protector, three feet of braided cord-the whole megillah in living, breathing pastel. Gemma had accompanied me on that shopping excursion, and we'd laughed about it. Some joke.

"Okay, Marky. Why don't you describe your party? You know, guests, activities, anything out of the ordinary."

He whistled when I recited the names. After all they were the crème de la crème of local society or what passed for it in Harbor Bay. He was less interested in the spa services each of my guests had received. I didn't mention the fracas between Paul and Lionel. Someone else was certain to cover that.

"Mr. Prentis came late, you said. Made a grand entrance, I bet. That was his way." I got the strong impression that Chief Hall was not a fan of the deceased.

"As my aunt said, he'd been drinking. A lot. I didn't know him, but he seemed obnoxious, like he was some entitled prince or something."

"Not surprising. His family has big bucks, as you probably heard. Paul got used to having things his way." He shook his head ruefully. "That kind of attitude can lead to trouble, especially in a small community. Folks resent it."

Hall acted as if Paul's murder was not unexpected. On the other hand, if every obnoxious fool in Harbor Bay was mowed down, our population would decline dramatically, especially during the tourist season. Wealthy visitors could try the patience of saints and sinners alike.

"That'll do for now, Marky. Stop by the station tomorrow and give a written statement. Gemma too." He folded his arms, suddenly morphing from avuncular pal to stern lawman. "Who knows. You might just recall some details that you forgot to mention. Happens a lot in my experience."

He studied my aunt. "Anything to add, Violet? You never miss a trick."

Her smile was enigmatic. "I also arrived late. Just in time to witness a fracas between Paul and Blaike Harrington. Lionel was involved too." She shook her head. "I'm afraid I was quite severe with them. Grown men acting like little boys."

Once again, Gideon chuckled. "I'll bet you cooled things down in a hurry. You always had that effect on troublemakers."

With that, he tipped his hat my way and exited the room.

Gemma was alone when I found her. Deputy Soto had hastily followed his boss out the door, thrilled to finally escape from her clutches. At least that was Gemma's take on the situation, and I could hardly dispute it. Soto had looked a bit green around the gills after going mano a mano with my partner.

"You were alone out there," I said, "but I didn't tell anyone."

Her eyes widened. "Alone. You mean, except for Paul? Don't get spooky on me, Marky. Dead bodies don't count. Besides, he was dead when I got there."

I lowered my voice to a whisper. There was no one else around, but it seemed prudent. "I'm talking about another living, breathing being. When I got out there, you were standing over Paul's body. You'd been gone quite a while. Was anyone else around?"

For once, Gemma was speechless. She finally managed to eke out one word. "What!"

I nodded. "You heard me."

"You're crazy. I can't believe you suspect me. I wouldn't kill anyone, even a turd like Paul Prentis. I couldn't." Gemma poured herself another slug of Perrier and hastily gulped it down. "What did the chief say? You told him, didn't you?"

When it came to interrogation techniques, Gemma was a champion of the third degree. No wonder criminals hired attorneys. I hadn't felt that much guilt since my mom caught me smoking in eighth grade. "Just the bare bones. Not before talking with you again. I need to hear your side of the story. You told me that you hadn't even touched Paul, and I believe you. Now trust me enough to tell the whole story." I glared defiantly at Gemma, prepared to do battle. But there was no need. She threw her arms around me and gave me a fierce hug. "Unbelievable! Little Miss Goody Two Shoes finally rebels. You did the right thing—the only thing worth doing. I'm innocent. We're in this together now."

I forgot that there was another person in the store. Aunt Violet sighed loudly and emphatically. "Need I remind you two that this is homicide we're involved in? Don't underestimate Gideon Hall for even a moment. Perhaps we should consult an attorney. Someone who knows criminal law."

I'd never fancied myself a detective despite inhaling every mystery tale from Holmes to Christie. Perhaps I had learned a thing or two from them that might help Gemma. "Why bother with lawyers. Lionel is the only one that I know, and he wouldn't be much help. We're innocent," I wailed. "Not even close to real suspects. Gideon Hall is a sensible man. Maybe we should just tell him the truth and trust him."

Gemma snorted in disgust. "Truth! That Paul humiliated me and provoked my mom. Maybe you should mention that I was out there alone with him doing who knows what. Don't get weak on me now. Everyone from the Governor of Michigan to the Prentis family will be breathing down his neck. Gideon Hall is a good man, but he's only human. I might get railroaded right into prison unless we find something." She grinned. "Besides. I bet I can get Soto to spill his guts. We had a connection."

My head was spinning from too much alcohol and way too much trauma. I felt the telltale signs of a migraine marching toward my brain with hobnail boots. Sleep. Blessed sleep. Maybe that would clarify everything or at least allow me to think coherently. Gemma had way too many connections to suit me. Why was she so secretive about Paul Prentis? His comments sounded very personal, and it wouldn't surprise me if they had "dated" at one time. Gemma's fate was inextricably linked to mine and Poppet's.

"I think it's wise to just sleep on things for the night," Violet said. She shooed Gemma out the door and left for my parents' house while I staggered up the stairs to my loft. Before my weary head touched the pillow, my cell phone beeped, and Gemma's clear voice rang out.

"I'll tell you everything tomorrow, Marky. My life depends on finding the truth."

Chapter Five

Gemma wasn't exaggerating. Harbor Bay was a small community, and news spread fast to the surrounding towns in northern Michigan. Reputation and integrity still meant something here. Even a whiff of scandal or hint of dishonesty could be fatal to someone who dealt with the public. Murder was beyond the pale. Anyone from the poor side of the tracks was automatically a suspect, and Gemma deserved my help or at least a chance to explain herself. After tossing and turning for several minutes, I switched on the lamp and checked the clock. One a.m. Not much chance of sleeping anyway.

A sharp, persistent rap on the front door startled me into a panic. I leapt out of bed so quickly that I barely had time to salvage my robe and slippers. I was wracked by indecision, terrified to open the door but curious about my visitor. Good sense dictated that I ignore the summons. After all, a murderer was somewhere in Harbor Bay roaming free. Once again, my cell phone buzzed, identifying Blaike Harrington as my caller.

"Let me in, Marky. I can't stand outside all night."

Poppet was locked up tight, so I spent precious moments deactivating the alarm, switching on the coffee, and unlocking the front entrance. Blaike was the picture of innocence. He'd discarded his rumpled clothing in favor of a crisp white oxford shirt and slacks. His hair glistened with water and smelled shower fresh. I reminded myself to be cautious. After all, Blaike was twice my size and, friend or not, might well be guilty of a heinous crime. He lowered his eyes and spoke slowly, cautiously.

"Benny Soto called and told me about Paul. I didn't want to leave you alone here in case you were scared. I'll leave if you want me to. That scuffle with him was inexcusable, and it ruined your party. Now it really complicates things."

I held my ground and said nothing. He was right. There was no excuse for his behavior, although there were probably reasons, and I might find out something useful from Blaike. Still, I refused to make things easy for him. Instead of comforting him, I filled a mug and offered him coffee. He once was a coffee snob, a trait we both shared. This brew was Nespresso's high-octane blend, a fragrant, tempting escape into caffeine paradise.

He accepted it gratefully and took a sip. "Ah. Fantastic. I needed this." After draining his mug, Blaike finally came to the point. "Chief Hall—what did you tell him? I don't blame you for anything. Enough people will fill him in. I hated Paul Prentis, and it was no secret."

Blaike had always been a strong, self-confident man. I hardly recognized this weaker version of him. Insecurity was an unattractive trait in a man. It aroused the bully in me.

My response was neutral, neither friendly nor hostile. "Don't worry. I kept you out of it. For now. He cut me some slack because of the circumstances. But tomorrow, when I sign a statement under oath, things may change. He already suspects something. He's nobody's fool."

"Face it, Marky. Paul was a maggot. A festering mass of evil. No one will miss him or really care that he's gone. I circled back to your shop, thinking you and Gemma might need some help cleaning up. When I saw the police cruisers, I left."

Sounded reasonable enough if he hadn't fled like a felon. Everyone, even Blaike, was on my suspect list now."

"Didn't you wonder why they were there? Why run off?

Once again, he hesitated. "I guess I didn't want to get involved. You know how rumors spread in a small town. I was afraid you or Lionel had called the cops about our dust-up. Sounds awful, doesn't it? Paul Prentis was a thorn in my side—in everyone's side. Pushy, arrogant, and dishonest. The guy was a nightmare, Marky. If anyone deserved to die, he did."

"Maybe, but he didn't have to die in my alley." I flashed back to the party.

Blaike had really mixed it up with Paul, but it was Lionel who threatened him. Mandy threw the drink in his face, Kim was driven to tears, and Gemma bore the brunt of his crude remarks. Just about everyone there had reason to loathe Paul Prentis, but murder was a different matter entirely. He was a big guy who looked strong, not easy for a woman to take down, much less strangle. And that cord—something bothered me about that extension cord. We'd purchased six of them.

"Wait a minute," I said. "You remember those violet cords we got a couple of weeks ago?"

"Yeah. So what?"

I hastily scanned the area and located three. When I stepped into the storeroom, I saw two more, sitting innocently on the shelf in pastel splendor. Suddenly what had seemed like a touch of whimsy looked more like harbingers of doom. That cord was no weapon of convenience. The killer deliberately used it as a macabre joke.

"Marky. Are you okay?" Blaike touched my shoulder, causing me to rear back against the shelf. Our storeroom was a narrow space. That made me acutely aware of his presence.

"Paul was strangled with a violet extension cord," I said. "Probably one of ours."

He gasped and backed away. Obviously, Benny hadn't shared that bit of news.

How had the killer found that extension cord and spirited it out of Poppet? None of the guests accessed the storeroom during our gathering, but it was open while we prepared the room. Gemma, Mandy, and I knew where everything was, of course, and one other person. Blaike Harrington. He helped stock the shelves. If anyone grabbed that extension cord before our gathering, that spelled premeditated murder.

"Yeah. I'm fine." I scooted past him out into Poppet's main floor. "Look. I really need to rest. Chief Hall expects me to show up first thing and give my statement."

"What about the opening? Maybe you should delay things for a day or two."

I considered our preparations and plans for the big day. Blaike might be right. Festive banners, treats, and prizes seemed woefully out of place so soon after a tragedy. Violent death was always a tragedy, no matter who the victim was. Paul Prentis was not beloved but ignoring his murder seemed cavalier and callous.

"I have to check with Gemma and Aunt Violet first." I pressed my hand against my forehead, hoping to stave off that migraine for even an instant. My skin felt warm and clammy to the touch, a sure sign of trouble to come.

"I'll check back with you after you meet with Hall," Blaike said. "Don't worry. I have nothing to hide. Tell him everything you remember about the party. Time for me and all the others to face the music. Whatever tune it is." He strode out the door, leaving me alone with my thoughts.

Despite the fears that plagued me, as soon as I locked up, I immediately fell into a deep slumber. Coma was a more accurate description as I snuggled in the arms of Morpheus.

* * *

It took a persistent battering on my door combined with the shrill ringtone of my phone to rouse me. Gemma rarely was deterred by anything, least of all a sense of propriety. I should have known that she was the culprit.

"Wake up," she chortled. "Good Lord, girl, I thought you were a goner."

My sense of humor thoroughly deserted me. "Not funny, Gemma," I growled, pulling my robe tightly across my chest. "What time is it anyway?"

"Seven. Rise and shine. We've got a big day ahead of us. Here." She thrust a double shot of espresso at me. "Come on. Down the hatch."

She ignored my scowl and prowled around the area, straightening shelves and folding towels. "Mom thinks we shouldn't open today. Unseemly is what she called it."

Once again, I knew that Violet would instinctively know the right thing to do. My parents would have charged down here immediately and demanded that I decamp to their house. Not an option for a struggling business owner trying to entice the public into her shop. We'd billed Poppet as a temple of calm and tranquility, not a den of death.

After weighing the pros and cons, Gemma and I decided to postpone the grand opening until the weekend. I posted a sign that expressed sympathy for the Prentis family and said that out of respect for them, Poppet would remain closed until after Paul's funeral. In truth, I resented that big creep more in death than I had in life. His boorish behavior had caused someone to strike him down. Why in the world choose Poppet as the site for his last hurrah? It seemed so unfair. I decided to keep those sentiments to myself, especially when dealing with the authorities. They did me no credit, even if they were justified.

Once again, Gemma came through with the ideal solution. She urged me to ask Aunt Violet for advice. As luck would have it, that lady soon joined us. She looked camera ready even though she, too, had gotten very little rest. She had once told me that no true lady would appear in public, even in an emergency, without having first paid attention to her personal grooming. Although she was a woman of a certain age, my aunt looked at least a decade younger than her fifty-five years. Her raven locks were flawless, and by either nature or art, her complexion had been spared the ravages of time. After a quick update on the murder, we plunged immediately into measures for damage control.

"I don't recall this Paul Prentis," Violet said, frowning, "but of course, I've been gone for thirty years. I went to school with a Phil Prentis, though. Probably his daddy. A slick operator and very aware of his social status. Pushy bordering on obnoxious if my memory banks are right."

Gemma nodded. "You got it, Violet. Prentis Properties Inc. Still the big dog in Harbor Bay. Our landlord, can you believe it?"

I mentioned our decision to defer opening for a few days, and Violet heartily approved. "No sense in giving people something else to gossip about. You want to distance Poppet from this murder. Otherwise, it could tarnish our brand."

Violet laughed when I mentioned the chief. "Good old Gideon. We used to date back in the old days, you know. He's one very sweet man. Sharp too. Don't try to put anything over on him, or you'll regret it."

Talk about food for thought. I recalled his keen eyes that seemed to bore into my soul. Good thing I planned to spill everything before he gave me the third degree. At my aunt's prodding, Gemma provided an entertaining and surprisingly accurate account of our private party, sparing no one, including her own mother.

"Wow," Violet said. "Lots of fireworks and plenty of folks with motive and opportunity. A word of caution for you both. Tell the truth but don't volunteer anything extraneous. Now about this Blaike Harrington. Weren't you two high school sweethearts, Marky?"

"Yes. But that was over long ago. He's just a friend now."

Gemma hooted loudly. "You should see them together, Violet. Just like Romeo and Juliet."

I bit my tongue and refrained from mentioning that fate had been most unkind to both the Capulets and the Montagues. Why spoil my partner's illusion?

Violet sighed. "Gideon will be feeling heat from all sides to make a quick arrest. Could be dangerous for you, Gemma, or anyone else with a motive."

"Oh no," I said. "Everyone at that party tangled with Paul. It isn't fair."

"Fair? When did that ever matter? Well, Ms. Marky, what are you going to do about it? Sounds like we should give the police some help."

I was aghast at the very thought. After all, I was an artist, not some bumbling detective. Gemma, however, leapt at the idea.

"Way cool, Violet. We can poke around. Stir the hornet's nest a bit. Always wanted to be a gumshoe like on tv."

"Fine, that settles it. I'll give the matter some more thought and see what I can do. After all, renewing old friendships makes sense, and word spreads fast in Harbor Bay."

* * *

I wore a modest silk shirtdress for my date with destiny. Red was a color that defined and flattered me, although in retrospect, it bore an unfortunate resemblance to blood. Gemma made no concession to either the occasion or the company. Her artfully torn jeans and form-fitting sweater announced to all the world that she was a fearless woman ready to stand her ground. My aunt wore a cream-colored pantsuit that bespoke dignity and class.

After ushering us into the chief's office, Deputy Soto planted himself against the back wall with his arms folded. If that was his version of machismo, it failed miserably. To me, despite that gun in his holster and his practiced sneer, he would always be Benny Soto, bookworm. Gideon Hall rose when we arrived and motioned us to two chairs in front of his desk. We declined the offer of a beverage and sat silently, awaiting his next move. Frankly, I found his genial manner off-putting. Fictional lawmen used swagger and steely glances to intimidate their prey. This man killed us with kindness.

"Okay, ladies. Let's review everything that happened at your soirée. I know we discussed things last evening, but this is for the record." He turned toward me. "Try to be specific and don't leave anything out." He glanced at a printed sheet on his desk and reeled off a host of names. "You listed these folks as your guests. Any additions or deletions?"

Like bobbleheads, we nodded in unison.

"Okay. Let's see here. Did any of them mix it up with Paul Prentis? He was the kind of guy who enjoyed conflict. Thrived on it."

Gemma stayed silent while I stuttered a response. "At first, everything went fine. We showcased our products and gave each guest a personalized treatment. Free gifts plus plenty of wine relaxed even some of the stuffier ones. That changed when Paul showed up.

"Oh. How so?" Gideon Hall inched forward like an alligator stalking supper.

I mentioned Paul's insistence on being served first and the insulting remarks he made. Gemma interrupted me and laid her cards right on the table.

"Hell, Gideon. I was one of his first targets, but I wasn't the last. He insulted me, then attacked Kim and almost everyone else in the store. Except Tilda and Philippa. They ignored his little show." Gemma then provided chapter and verse on each incident at Poppet, including Mandy and the wine glass.

"No kidding. Your mom did that? Spunky little thing, isn't she. And Lionel, ready to fight! Good thing you were the adult in the room, Violet, not that it mattered in the end."

He stretched his arms in a long, languorous gesture, then went in for the kill. "What about afterwards when you found the body. Anything else come to mind, Marky?" Despite his genial manner, something about the chief frightened me. I stammered a not very convincing reply that neither he nor I fully believed.

"I've been thinking about it. I did see someone else in that alley. Just a blur, nothing I could actually identify." My voice stayed steady, but I twisted the tissue in my lap until it shredded.

Gideon Hall played along, although I was certain that he knew I was lying. "Was this blur masculine or feminine? You're an artist, so I expect you'd notice things like that."

"Oh, definitely male. Even though he was wearing a hoodie, I could tell that. But seeing Paul like that…, I'd never seen a dead person before."

He nodded. "Right. Most folks haven't. Sounds like you were in shock. Not surprising. One more thing before you leave. That purple cord bothers me. Any idea who could have grabbed it?"

Gemma shrugged. "We stacked them in the storeroom. It's next to the loo, so I guess someone could have prowled around there without being noticed."

"Kind of obvious, wouldn't you say?" His question was pointed, his tone rapier sharp. Benny Soto noticed the change too. He hunched forward as if he were on red alert.

I recalled that both Kim and Tilda used the lavatory to freshen up. Dr. Zach too. He complained about the effects of age on his bladder, not a subject I was eager to pursue. Lionel and Philippa stayed around the buffet table, although I couldn't swear to that. Both Kim and Tilda carried sizable handbags capable of concealing an extension cord. Philippa had only a clutch purse.

Gemma plunged right into the fray. "That smacks of premeditation, doesn't it? Surely Paul's murder was spontaneous."

"Maybe. He might have arranged to meet someone after the party. Started a fight and paid the price. Couldn't have put up much resistance if he was drunk. Even a woman could handle him then." Despite his folksy manner, the look in Gideon's eyes was dead serious. He rose and gave each of us his card. "Okay, ladies. Go with Deputy Soto, and he'll print up your statements. I must excuse myself. Another witness to interview. Blaike Harrington. Funny thing. Seems he insisted on coming in." Gideon's words were perilously close to a taunt. I forced myself not to react

After we left the police station, Gemma exploded. "Brrr. That was scary. Not Soto, of course. That boy couldn't scare my grandma. Especially my grandma. I'm talking about the chief. He knows something or thinks he does."

She was right. I hoped that Blaike was prepared for the grilling that awaited him. Harbor Bay was a sleepy coastal town, but Gideon Hall was no rube. Once again Aunt Violet's judgment had been spot on. My vague description of a hooded figure might give Gemma cover if she needed it, but sooner or later, the truth would emerge.

"Who do you think did it?" Gemma clutched my arm in a grip worthy of a wrestler. "I'm not saying it was someone we know, but it's possible. Face it. Paul Prentis was headed for a bad end. Someone would have sent that boy to his grave sooner or later."

I shuddered at the possibility. Murder was an ugly word that seldom intruded on the peaceful life in Harbor Bay. The last violent crime I could recall involved two tourists who got into a drunken brawl. Nobody cared much about that incident, but this was different. Paul Prentis was a troublemaker and a creep, but he was one of us. So was Gemma, for that matter. Before long, townspeople would take sides, and the waters would roil. Would Poppet become one of the casualties in an internecine feud?

Gemma had the same thought. "Listen, Marky, I hate to be selfish, but we've got to consider our business. Best to leave this alone and focus on Poppet."

I stared her down. "You've certainly changed your tune, Missy. Last night you were all hot to trot about being—a gumshoe I think you called it. What changed?"

Gemma stammered a reply. "I'm selfish. Okay, I admit it. Poppet is the first real break I've ever had, and I don't want to risk it." Her voice wavered. "You've always had everything go your way. School, talent, looks. Remember which side of the tracks I'm from, Marky."

I patted my friend on the back and said no more. We had a business to launch and a murder to solve. Surely, we could accomplish both without destroying our future.

After Gemma calmed herself, we formulated a plan of action. Each of our guests was a potential murderer, and with a bit of luck, we might narrow down the suspect list. Our best tactic was to ask for advice. Everyone, particularly a town dignitary, enjoyed being flattered. We planned to double-team them—with one exception. Philippa Gordon thoroughly cowed me. Had ever since I was a child. I knew that she would see right through me and reduce me to a blubbering fool with a few cutting remarks. Not so, Gemma. She was fearless and up to the challenge. "No problemo," she said. "Principal Gordon dragged me into her office all the time in high school. So many lectures. Blah, blah, blah. That woman never let up on me. I guess I was her pet project or something."

Tilda Egan was first on our list. Instead of discussing the murder, we planned to discuss our product lines and ease into Paul's death. Cosmetics were one topic upon which our town writer was an acknowledged authority. Gemma hinted that Tilda might also be an authority on Paul Prentis.

"Are you sure?" I asked. "After all, an attractive single woman in a small town spawns gossip. Maybe it's just jealousy."

Gemma folded her arms and smirked. "Marky, my dear, you are either hopelessly naïve or dense. How do you think she got that house of hers? Prentis Properties, that's how. My friend Ida did all the paperwork. Tilda got a particularly good deal on a prime lot."

Since both of us were physically fit, we decided to join Tilda's morning yoga class. It was well known in Harbor Bay that, unlike many of us slackers, the woman was a zealot who never missed a session. This seemed like a less contrived way to meet her.

"I'll bet being supple is an asset in her line of work," Gemma said with a straight face. "Writing, I mean. Need to flex the old muscles."

"Cool it, kiddo, or she'll shut you down. Remember, every potential customer is golden. Focus on our mission."

We arrived at Belle Yoga just in time to see Tilda waltz in and claim a center spot. Despite the early hour, she was a model of perfection, from coordinated gear to her matching yoga mat. Gemma and I chose less stylish apparel. We waved at Tilda, then settled down to an hour of exhausting hot yoga. Despite being a decade younger than Tilda, she left both Gemma and me in the dust. Afterwards, we limped into the locker room and hit the showers.

"I'm getting a smoothie," Gemma growled. "Screw the calories."

Tilda stayed in front of a lighted mirror, calmly applying a coat of mascara and a dab of lip gloss. I observed that they were both high-end products featured at Poppet and competing stores. She flashed a superior smile our way. "Not everyone's cut out for this. Better stick to massage, Gemma."

I faked a laugh before my pal erupted. "You're an expert, Tilda. That's obvious. Hey, if you have a minute, can we run something by you?"

Her response was guarded and unenthusiastic. "I suppose so. I don't have much time."

I explained our quest for customer reaction to Poppet's products. "Feedback is essential, especially for a new business. I noticed the brands you just used, and they're the kind of upmarket products we stock."

Praise sweetened Tilda's attitude. "When will the store open? I saw a closed sign on it today when I passed by."

Gemma explained the postponement with a shrug. "It seemed like the right thing to do. He was our landlord, after all."

"Suppose so." Tilda's response was grudging at best. I saw an opening and seized it.

"Let me offer my condolences."

She narrowed her eyes. "Whatever for."

People often tell me I have an innocent face. Now it was put to the test. "Oh, forgive me. I understood that you and Paul were close."

"I bet you heard we were lovers too." Tilda moved within a few inches of me, close enough to strike if she chose to. Our temporary rapprochement ended abruptly. "Well, don't believe everything you hear, little Mary sunshine. Paul was a business acquaintance. Period. And by the way, my sources say that your boyfriend is the prime suspect, and he's not the only one." She stared brazenly at Gemma. "Everybody knows Blaike and Paul hated each other. Always have." She swung her bag over her shoulder and stalked out the door leaving me deflated. Some detective I was. Hercule Poirot could rest easy. Miss Marple could go back to her knitting.

"That went well," Gemma smirked. "Gideon Hall will really appreciate your help. Tilda ate your lunch, kiddo. Let's hope we do better with Kim."

Violence solves nothing. I suppressed the urge to decorate my business partner's yoga mat with a strawberry smoothie and settled for a civilized snarl instead.

"Maybe we should pay a visit to city hall. Mayor Zach always loves to chat. Let's get his take on things."

Gemma nodded. "We can play up the angle about bad publicity. Ask for his advice. Old guys love that kind of stuff." She finished her smoothie and discarded it in the nearest trash barrel. "He was always sweet on my mom, you know. If we need reinforcements, she can pry something out of His Honor. One way or another."

We agreed to regroup outside City Hall after freshening up. Mayor Zach was a man of decided habits who ate lunch every weekday at the Cozy-Corner pub and, according to rumor, even ordered the same items: tomato soup and grilled cheese on wheat with a dill pickle. The more I thought of that, the hungrier I grew. No need to feign an appetite.

I hastily dressed in jeans with a Poppet t-shirt, and leather jacket. My eyes were enhanced with neutral shadow and a double coat of mascara. I was treading a fine line between sensual and slutty, a distinction that was important in a small community. Still, most townspeople would forgive my excesses since their view of artists, especially big-city ones, was somewhat jaded. Gemma had no worries. She was a known commodity in Harbor Bay. Her choice of outfits, which often bordered on the bizarre, was considered part of her identity and ignored.

The Corner, as most natives referred to it, was dimly lit and densely populated. It was a popular spot in and out of the tourist season, celebrated for low prices and generous portions. I spotted his Honor immediately, seated at a choice table and hunched over a bowl of soup. He was a tall man, well over six feet six, with a skeletal frame and beak nose that accentuated his resemblance to a stork. That image consumed me whenever the man came into view. As teens, we had always joked that in view of his appearance, Zach's ideal profession was obstetrician, not dentist. Today his eyes were focused on our daily newspaper, a throwaway that usually featured local happenings and society gossip. Today the headline was anything but normal. It screeched in bold black letters, "Prominent businessman murdered. Police stumped."

"Mind if we join you, Mayor?" Gemma's high-wattage smile lit up the room. "We need your advice."

Zach was a gentleman of the old school. Deference to ladies and courtesy were his watchwords. He stood until we were seated, removed his reading glasses, and folded his newspaper. "Well, well. This is a pleasant surprise. Two lovely ladies. What can I do for you?"

I bowed my head slightly. "You know about the murder. Will customers stay away from Poppet because of it? Will they blame us?" Just mentioning it ratcheted up my anxiety level tenfold. I had much to lose if this business venture failed.

He patted my hand. Mayor Zach at his most avuncular. "Now, Marky, you just settle down. When you were just a little girl, you acted the same way in my dental chair. Remember what I told you then?"

"To close my eyes, take a deep breath, and think about kittens."

He grinned. "Still good advice. Now Gemma here—she knows the score. Frankly, most folks loathed Paul Prentis. His whole clan is just plain unpleasant. Plenty of dry eyes at his funeral. You can bet on that."

"We figure he had tons of enemies," Gemma said. "As drunk as he was, Paul was easy pickings."

Zach frowned. "Enemies? I'm not sure of that, but he was no picnic to deal with, I can tell you. City council meetings got contentious when he showed up. Sometimes I thought that boy loved to scrap just for fun. But he was sharp as a tack. Yes indeed. He had a parcel of land south of the town that he planned to develop come hell or high water. Every obstacle we raised never even fazed him. Profit Paul, they called him, and it stuck."

"Paul always had a mean streak," Gemma said. "Seemed to know everyone's weak spots, and he wasn't shy about exploiting them." She grimaced. "I should know."

"No one paid him much mind, honey," said the mayor kindly. "You handled him just right by ignoring that nonsense." He laughed. "Course, your mama put him in his place. When she threw that drink in his face, I nearly died laughing."

Zach glanced guiltily around the room where several of his constituents were seated. "Guess it's not respectful to speak badly about the dead. What's that Latin phrase, *nihil nisei bonum?*"

"Gideon thinks one of our guests killed him." I shivered just thinking of it. "But I can't believe it. "

We paused as our lunch orders arrived. Gemma chose seafood stew, but the grilled cheese called out to me. Zach's eyes studied me as I took my first bite.

"Yum! Just as I remembered it. That pickle makes it perfect."

"You and Blaike were an item at one time," Zach said.

"In high school," Gemma jeered. "She dumped him big time."

I aimed a kick at her shins. "Ancient history. We're just friends now."

After finishing his soup, Zach dabbed his lips with a napkin and asked for the check. "My treat, ladies. Just remember one thing, Marky. People can change, and not always for the better. I've seen it happen way too often. As for your business, don't worry. This town needs bright, energetic young people like you. They'll mob your store. Wait and see." He paid the cashier and strode into the sunlight.

* * *

We spent the balance of the day at Poppet, checking inventory and obsessing over each detail. According to Mandy, Paul's funeral was scheduled for Saturday, three days away. His family had reserved the glitziest room at the country club for the reception that followed, and most of the townspeople of Harbor Bay had been invited to pay their respects.

He'd like that. Showboating to the bitter end. I'd only met the man a few times, but he'd left an indelible impression on me—all negative.

"No way I'm joining that freak show," Gemma said. "I'm no hypocrite. The world's better off without him in it."

She changed her tune after I reminded her that it was a perfect opportunity for snooping. Liquor and lies tended to flow freely at these events. Occasionally even a hard truth surfaced. Besides, since Paul's final appearance was at Poppet, it would look churlish not to make at least a token showing.

"Will Blaike be there?" Gemma asked. "What's your guess?"

Blaike had avoided me since his midnight visit so I had no idea. Gideon Hall hadn't charged him, Gemma, or anyone else with anything but that might change at any time. I'd heard from several sources that he was under pressure to name someone—anyone—as a suspect. Paul Prentis had enemies aplenty. What puzzled me was the use of that violet extension cord. It smacked of premeditation and something else. Malice. That weapon had a direct link to Poppet. This was no random crime of passion. By using a girly item as a weapon, the killer had made it both perverse and personal. Surely that fact alone should exonerate Gemma. She had far too much to lose.

Our grand opening was rescheduled for Monday, just five days away. I'd purchased a discrete ad in the *Harbor Bay Herald* announcing the big event and listing the heavily discounted services we planned to offer. Already several customers had booked appointments online, including Kim Stevens. I took that as a very good sign. Our local bakery agreed to supply mini-cupcakes, biscotti, and a large sheet cake in the image of a spunky sprite named Poppet. Mandy was handling arrangements for all the treats and leveraging her contacts to secure the best prices. We hoped to cement relations with our peers by patronizing local businesses. Quid Pro Quo all the way.

If only my parents were there to join in. I was happy that they forged ahead with their own plans, but I missed them. Gemma had Mandy to confide in, but I was a bit of an orphan. Thank heaven for Aunt Violet. No one could ask for a better, more accomplished ally.

Chapter Six

In a bit of wish fulfillment, I opened the door to my loft apartment, and there in all her splendor, stood Aunt Violet. She epitomized understated European chic: French twist, flawless face, and subtle jewelry. When she embraced me, folding me into a swirl of the softest Italian cashmere, I detected the faint hint of scent, probably one by Creed.

"Marky, I hope I'm not interrupting." Violet craned her neck and surveyed the room.

"Are you kidding?" You're an apparition. The answer to a prayer. How does it feel to come home again?"

"Home? Seems strange to use that word. Harbor Bay was an alien world to me for so long, but now it feels just right."

She had arrived with only one suitcase, a compact Louis Vuitton roller bag. "Not much luggage for a long stay," I said.

Violet laughed. "Don't worry, dear. I shipped the rest. Old habits die hard, and I always overpack. Be prepared is my motto. After all, I have my image to protect."

We stepped into the living room and settled on the sofa. There wasn't much room to maneuver with my artist supplies and easel dotting the landscape. My loft was austere, ill-suited to hosting guests as particular as Violet. She must have read my mind.

"Relax, Poppet. I've already started to get settled house-sitting for your mom." She paused, "But tonight, I'm taking a break to talk murder."

I warmed two snifters of brandy, prepared a platter of cheese and fruit, and shared everything I knew, suspected, or feared with her. In so doing, I managed to clarify several points about Paul's murder that had plagued me.

"There's no way around it," I said. "The killer must be someone at our party. How else do you explain that extension cord?"

She nodded. "Strangling is so up close and personal. This person wanted to humiliate him too. Tell me again about the cast of characters."

One by one, I mentioned their names. Violet knew most since they were longtime residents of Harbor Bay. Kim was the exception.

"Tell me about Kim. A frustrated model, you said. She's very lovely. That much I saw for myself."

I described Kim and the speculation that she and Paul might have had an affair. "That's rumor, of course. You know how small towns are. Even if it were true, would that be enough to murder someone over?"

Violet considered her response. "Maybe. I recall Lionel Stevens. Not very popular. He was a stuffed shirt even in high school. Always tattling on the other kids. Butter wouldn't melt in his mouth, according to your grandma." She frowned. "Does he have money? He must."

Violet was right on target once again.

"So, I hear. They say he's the second richest man in town, after the Prentis bunch. Lord knows he seems tight with a buck, but wealthy men often are."

Violet frowned. "Kim probably likes that financial security he gives her. Modeling, even successfully, is a cruel profession for a woman. What about this son of theirs? Killed in an accident, I heard."

"Yeah. I don't know the details, but it was a tragedy. Hit and run. I heard he was a good kid. Their pride and joy."

Violet squeezed my hand. "Just like you are for me and your parents. Life can test the strongest of us."

I laughed ruefully. "Kind of like painting, I guess. Cruel and remorseless."

Violet patted my knee. "You just cut it out." She pointed to several canvases I had on display. "Very nice, especially that nude. You have talent, girl, and don't you forget it. Talent and tenacity—two things every successful artist needs." She stretched her arms toward the ceiling.

"Maybe I'll consider painting Kim. Most people fall for that right away. The chance to be immortalized by the renowned Violet Davis." She winked as she said that. "A touch of humility never was my strong suit.

Violet Davis was a listed artist, business mogul, and international celebrity. Anyone, particularly an ex-model, would be thrilled. Marky Davis was nothing but a failed art student.

Violet's frown was a thundercloud. "When will you ever really see yourself? You are a talented artist, my dear. Never doubt that. I've seen your work, so believe me. Kim's ego has taken a battering. She'll be flattered by the attention."

I mentioned Lionel again. If Paul tangled with him over business matters, he might strike out. Money and reputation meant a lot to Lionel. Risking his life to avenge his wife's honor was another thing entirely. Lionel was too clever to murder Paul directly after a confrontation. Violet agreed.

"Remember, he thinks like a lawyer. Cautious. Sneaky. And Paul would have been on his guard no matter how drunk he was."

Violet suddenly yawned. "Pardon me, honey, but I'm exhausted. Jet lag, you know. Let's pick this up after I take a nap."

* * *

While Violet napped, I dashed over to our local bakery to stock up on supplies. My aunt's good opinion meant a lot to me, and I was determined to impress her. As I exited the bakery laden with bags, I barreled right into Mandy Watts. That encounter elevated my guilt level to its zenith. She was fiercely protective of her daughter and would eviscerate anyone who even suggested that Gemma had a violent streak.

"Whoa, Marky," Mandy said. "What's the hurry?" Her tracksuit told me she had just completed her morning run. No wonder the woman was in such stellar shape. I mentioned that the treats were a surprise for my aunt.

"After, we'll be at Poppet."

"Want me to join you later? Violet might have some marching orders for us."

After we agreed on a meeting time and parted company, I quickly buzzed Gemma's number and shared my plan. Shouts of jubilation mixed with several hoots and hollers as she promised to join us immediately. Gemma called our meeting a council of war. I termed it a strategy session.

A surprise visitor awaited me when I arrived home. I found Violet entertaining another suspect in Paul Pruett's murder—Blaike Harrington.

He apologized so effusively for arriving uninvited that I was embarrassed for him. While I arranged our spread, Violet slipped away, but. Gemma arrived soon after, sporting her trademark distressed t-shirt, jeans, and fringed jacket. It occurred to me that I was the outlier in this eclectic group, bumbling about with zero style. Aunt Violet had every hair in place, her makeup was perfect, and the suede pantsuit she wore was impeccable. I had much to measure up to.

"Don't get flustered, Poppet. You have youth and beauty on your side." Violet grinned as we shared the bathroom mirror. "Besides, young Blaike seems totally captivated by you. Don't argue, I can tell these things."

I braided my hair, applied a light cosmetic touch. In times of stress, most women have a favorite outfit that they can rely upon. Unfortunately, I had none.

They were gathered around the makeshift card table I had cobbled together, chatting like old friends. Violet had a gift for relaxing people, and Gemma never met a stranger. Once the niceties had been observed and the gods of good manners appeased, Violet, turned to Blaike. "Where do you stand with this murder charge? Gideon Hall is methodical but determined. Don't underestimate him for a minute. If he builds a case, it'll be airtight."

My aunt's burst of candor had obviously floored him. Blaike gulped. "I'm not quite sure. My attorney said they have no proof, but circumstantial evidence can be damaging too." An uncomfortable silence descended upon us. "My reputation is my brand, and in a small town, even a whiff of scandal can sink a business." Blaike bit his lip, looking glum. Gemma bowed her head and, for once, remained silent.

I broke the impasse by sharing the results of our session with Tilda and Mayor Zach. Nothing earthshaking had emerged from either one, although I was curious about the land deal that Paul had been pushing.

"Oh yeah," Blaike said. "He made a big thing out of that. Wouldn't shut up about it. Some waterfront parcel, very pricey. Prentis Properties planned to build upscale condos there. Retail shops too."

Gemma's eyes brightened. I knew she visualized the upscale customers it would generate and the impact on Poppet. Unfortunately, there might be adverse effects, too, such as environmental issues.

"Where does Philippa stand on all this," asked Violet. "I can't see her prostrating herself before the gods of commerce. They used to call her a tree hugger in her younger days. In any event, she was always very levelheaded. Dull even."

Blaike shrugged. "She's pretty strict. Still acts like a school principal half the time. Throws a scare into us, I can assure you. Funny thing, though. At last month's meeting, she seemed less opposed to that land deal than before. Paul acted pretty cocky about the whole thing."

Philippa Gordon yielding to a bully. The very idea was sobering and even shocking. She was unlikely to succumb to bribes or other inducements from a scoundrel like Paul Prentis. I was positive of that. Still, everyone had a breaking point. Maybe Philippa was lonely and craved male companionship or had some secret vice. Visualizing her in the brawny arms of Paul Prentis totally creeped me out. *Unrequited love?* Not her style from what I recalled of that stern, puritanical schoolmarm but a crime like embezzlement was always possible. She didn't fit the mold for a killer, but I could always dream.

Gemma curled her lip. "Lionel mixed it up with Paul. Why isn't he on the griddle? Just because he's rich doesn't mean he's innocent. Let's face it, Kim acted very guilty around Paul. I think she had a thing with him. There was plenty of talk around town about the two of them. Of course, folks around here gossip about almost everyone."

No one could argue with that, but in my view, Lionel's pitiful spat with Paul left the lawyer humiliated and thoroughly cowed. I doubted that Lionel would sneak back to the alley for another round after that.

"Looks like we need an action plan," I said. "Not that I want to step on Gideon's toes necessarily. Consider us his helpers. We can do things unofficially without arousing suspicion. Let's assign roles. You know. Divide and conquer. That memorial service sounds like the perfect opportunity for some sleuthing."

Blaike reacted differently. "Just for the record, I had no part in Paul's death. He was scum, and I certainly don't mourn him, but I didn't touch him."

We exchanged the type of tight smiles that mean nothing. Blaike didn't seem homicidal, but anyone could be provoked to violence. I knew that when the local newspaper linked the violet cord to Poppet, it would arouse the community's suspicions. That was something we wanted to avoid.

Gemma and I cleared the table while I asked Violet to list our tasks. She whipped out her iPad and began. Gemma agreed to broach Philippa. Blaike would research any areas of dispute within the council and find the particulars of that land deal. I was assigned to Kim, and Violet agreed to tackle Lionel. He was almost a stranger to me but based upon my cursory dealings with him, Lionel might respond well to flattery or asking his advice. Since our initial approach to Tilda was a spectacular failure, someone else needed to ingratiate herself with the town novelist. Someone like my aunt who was better equipped to worm information out of her.

Gemma suggested that Mandy could cozy up to Gideon Hall. "He's always been sweet on her, you know. Personally, I think he's kinda hot for an old guy. And my mom can be sneaky as hell, let me tell you. Mandy the man eater, they used to call her."

No one knew how to respond to that. Picturing a mom—anyone's mom—as a seductress was truly uncomfortable. Fortunately, Blaike broke the silence.

"Maybe you should sit this one out." Blaike stammered as he said that. "I'm used to fighting my own battles, and this thing could go south in a hurry. You have your own interests to protect, and dealing with a killer isn't one of them."

Blaike was known as a stand-up guy, someone who embodied good values. When I thought of our tangled relationship, I'd often wondered about the road not taken. Things might have been very different if I hadn't treated him so cruelly. He had absolutely no reason to care for me anymore.

Water under the bridge, Marky. Get over it. Blaike will never be more than your friend.

Just then, Gemma jumped up, grabbed her purse, and stared him down. "Hey. This is no charity thing. Like it or not, Poppet's part and parcel of this whole mess. We can't afford to fail. The longer this murder goes unsolved, the worse for us all."

No one could argue with that, and nobody tried to. We left unspoken the role Gemma might have played and the likelihood that Gideon Hall would pursue it. Each of us had a vital role to play in this drama. One of our acquaintances, colleagues, or friends was a murderer. There was no way to sugarcoat that fact or wish it away. I shivered as I considered the implications. What possible skills did a failed artist, a masseuse, an entrepreneur, and a businessman have that trained police lacked?

Violet must have read my mind. "You're wondering what each of us brings to the table, aren't you, Marky?"

I nodded, ashamed that I was so transparent. People always said I was a dreadful poker player whose face gave her away. This was one of those times.

"Look, Poppet. Each of us approaches things differently. Gemma uses candor, I use stealth, and you project that air of naïve charm. It totally disarms your opponents. One thing we all have in common is determination."

Blaike furrowed his brow. "Hey. What about me? I have a stake in this, you know. A big stake."

Violet patted his hand. "You, my dear boy, are Captain America. Truth, justice, and the American way. No one can seriously suspect you of cold-blooded murder, even Gideon."

She wagged her finger at us. "Just remember, subtlety is our watchword. Trust no one out of our little circle here. Everyone is a suspect and a potential murderer."

Despite mixing Super Man with another action hero, Violet's observations were on target. We had no official standing, and in this instance, that was a plus. No one would lawyer up around us or take us seriously, for that matter. Some of my literary favorites, such as Miss Marple or Harriet Vane, had maximized those same advantages. There was a downside, too, of course.

Someone who had murdered once might ruthlessly eliminate any person, professional or amateur, who posed a threat. That meant that any of our merry band who got too close could be targeted for death.

* * *

Harbor Bay Country Club was the ritziest place in the county. Yearly dues were astronomical, and the initiation fee for those fortunate enough to be sponsored was designed to weed out undesirables. As such, it was the mother ship for the monied classes like the Prentis and Harrington clans. I'd visited it before during my time with Blaike, although my parents had neither the desire, money nor social cachet to qualify. Aunt Violet was the exception. As a town luminary, she had received an honorary membership and a free pass to all club activities. The only times Gemma and Mandy had graced the sacred portal, they had been serving drinks or assisting the kitchen staff. Very upstairs, downstairs.

The edifice itself was impressive, situated overlooking Grand Traverse Bay, with enough brick and limestone to satisfy the most demanding taste. On the day of Paul's memorial, a sizable gathering from the town, including all my party guests, streamed in. For many, this was their first and only entrée into the world of privilege. They wouldn't miss it on a bet.

A staff member greeted us as we entered, directing us up a sweeping staircase to the main ballroom. A supersized portrait of Paul looking young, confident, and handsome rested on an easel outside the entryway. The airbrushed version camouflaged any flaws, but it couldn't disguise the smirk on his face. How astonished he must have been to suffer such an ignominious end. Each of us received a tasteful brochure highlighting the achievements of his brief time on earth. I scanned the narrative, willing to overlook the hyperbole. Loving parents had earned the right to embellish the life of their offspring despite the inconsistencies.

I turned my attention to the seating arrangements. Mayor Zach led a delegation from the town council that, to my surprise, included Blaike Harrington. They sat upright, like stock players in a community theater farce. The men wore the typical sober suits, but the ladies showed glimpses of style. Kim's long, lean silhouette was elegant in a navy suit with big gold buttons. I'd seen that outfit or one very similar in the pages of *Vogue*. Tilda's choice of attire was more daring. She wore a black sheath that was anything but funereal. In a wink to propriety, the plunging neckline was tempered by a mere hint of lace trim. True to form, Philippa's shapeless garb resembled a shroud more than a dress. Somehow it suited her perfectly. Predictably, Aunt Violet put all of us to shame. Her *Chanel* suit, subdued jewelry, and court shoes added just the right touch of understated chic to the proceedings. Mandy, Gemma, and I were merely bit players and glad to be spared the limelight.

After a brief prayer, Paul's father addressed the gathering, sharing reminiscences of his son's childhood, youth, and adulthood. It was an understated tribute that was curiously touching as well. Although his pain was visible, Mr. Prentice kept his grief well in hand. Several work colleagues and Paul's college roommate also added their memories. The remarks were positive, but they were also sterile and devoid of any real emotion. The formalities ended with an invitation "to partake of the comestibles," as Mr. Prentis phrased it.

Time to circulate," Aunt Violet said. "Listen to everything like the proverbial fly on the wall."

I needed no encouragement to mingle with the crowd. My first quarry was our own police chief, who stood ramrod straight on the fringes of the crowd. I'd read that the culprit frequently lurked around his victim's funeral gathering and wondered if Gideon Hall had the same thought. We greeted each other cautiously but courteously as the big man offered me his hand.

"Marky, nice of you to come. Shows proper respect for the deceased."

I scrutinized his expression, searching for any signs of sarcasm but Gideon was far too experienced a player to betray his feelings.

"Paul was my landlord and a guest at our opening. It seemed only right." I looked him straight in the eyes, glad that my own skill in prevarication had grown.

He chuckled. "Not playing detective, I hope. That's a dangerous game for amateurs."

Not wanting to push my luck, I hastily changed the subject. "Who's that guy over there?" I pointed to a tall, gangly redhead who strongly resembled a giraffe. He was engaged in what seemed like a heated exchange with Lionel Stevens. Gideon shrugged. "Beats me. Don't recall ever seeing him before. Seems like he's got Lionel all steamed up, though. Why don't you amble over there and find out? Pretty girls can usually diffuse tensions."

I forgave him for being sexist. After all, cop culture was inherently male from everything I'd ever read. And truthfully, that scene had piqued my curiosity. "Maybe I'll just check it out," I said. "He might be a potential customer."

Gideon's sardonic grin gave him away. He didn't believe me for even one minute. I summoned my dignity and approached the two combatants. Lionel's face was flushed, and his hands were curled up into tight fists. Despite his age, he seemed to fancy himself as a pugilist who could confront opponents many years his junior. Reliving his glory days from Yale, no doubt. Either way, the redhead didn't look impressed. He folded his arms and loomed over Lionel.

"Greetings, gentlemen," I said in my friendliest voice. I turned to the stranger. "I'm Marketta Davis. I don't believe we've met."

He inspected me as if I were some noxious insect buzzing about. "Jonathon Crane." Without saying another word, he headed toward the bar and ordered a drink.

"Well! He's certainly curt. Who is he?" I hoped Lionel would calm down and say something—anything—to provide information, but that didn't happen. Instead of speaking, he snorted something vile, turned on his heel, and stalked away. My store of girlish charm, such as it was, had obviously been exhausted.

"What's your secret?" Gemma said, edging up to me. "Pepper spray?"

I snarled a response that was totally inappropriate for a funeral, but Gemma found it hilarious. "That's the spirit, girl. Stand up to these stodgy slugs." She admitted that giraffe man was a stranger to her as well. "Not bad looking, though, if you like the stringy types.

I scanned the crowd and saw that Blaike had joined the group. Despite the occasion, he looked perfectly at ease. Not surprising. This was his tribe, the monied upper reaches of Harbor Bay society. He raised a hand in greeting, but before he could join us, Jonathon Crane sidled up to him. From the frown on Blaike's face, I got the idea that he was neither a stranger nor a friend.

"The plot thickens," I hissed to Gemma. "That guy is like a viper in the nest. Find out who he is. "

"No problem. I'll ask my mom. She knows everyone." As Gemma scurried away, I noticed that Jonathon Crane had moved on to Philippa's side. He engaged in some small talk before handing her what looked like a newspaper article. Philippa's back was turned away from me. I couldn't gauge her expression, but her body language spoke volumes. She stiffened as if a bolt of electricity had shot through her. Only the timely arrival of Mayor Zach Thanos allowed her to escape. Zach was at his most avuncular as he slapped Crane on the back and guided him toward the exit. Only an onlooker like me was likely to notice anything amiss. Talk about the specter at the feast! That stranger was a prescription for disaster.

"Enjoying yourself, Marky?" Blaike gave me a smile that tingled my toes. "I guess enjoyment is probably in poor taste. Still, old profit Paul would have enjoyed this display."

"I saw you talking to that stranger. That tall redheaded guy. Who is he?

Blaike's response was noncommittal. "Oh him? He's nobody. Believe me." Gemma joined us just then. That allowed him to make his escape before I could question him further. "Talk later," Blaike said, sprinting toward the exit. Mayor Zach was there sipping what looked like wine.

"I'm ready to leave," I said. "First, let me round up my aunt." I searched the room and finally located her chatting with Tilda Egan. Tilda was somewhat of a pariah in the rarified circles of Harbor Bay. Men avoided her if their wives were within earshot, and wives avoided her on principle. Violet had no inhibitions whatsoever. Anyone in her path was fair game when it came to information gathering. She acknowledged my wave and, after a few parting remarks, left Tilda.

"Hussy!" I turned abruptly, colliding into a mountainous mound of female flesh. Josephine Soto, mother of Benny and bookstore proprietor, peered down on me from on high. I recalled visiting her shop, Novel Approach, with my parents and attending some of the activities she had sponsored. In those days, Mr. Soto was part of the package, but according to Gemma, he had decamped for parts unknown with a summer visitor. Although she had always been somewhat solemn, Mrs. Soto was now monosyllabic. She snorted something unintelligible and hurriedly moved past me with her eyes firmly fixed on the departing redheaded stranger. I collected my aunt and slipped away, leaving those who remained to swap stories and mourn Paul Prentis.

* * *

Gemma and I were proud and a bit nervous when we unveiled Poppet to my aunt. Mandy joined us and immediately established rapport with Violet. Clipboard in hand, she approached each aspect of our shop with clinical precision. Good curb appeal," she noted. "Clean and uncluttered. Invites a customer to come in." She examined our shelves, made several suggestions about placement, and surveyed our product listing, nodding as she observed the array of brands we featured. Our treatment rooms got high marks for privacy and comfort, but the lighting displeased her. "Way too bright, ladies. Unflattering to anyone, particularly your older customers. Remember you're selling illusion as well as services."

We discussed price points and techniques for luring new customers and retaining regulars. I was thrilled when my aunt suggested featuring my paintings to decorate the walls. It was something I had considered but felt too timid to implement. By the time we concluded, I was exhausted but exhilarated too. In three days, my dream would become reality, assuming, of course, that another leading citizen didn't bite the dust.

That evening, Violet, Gemma, and I had dinner at Harbor Bay's most elegant spot, The Velvet Claw. We donned our fanciest duds and prepared to do a bit of proselytizing while we were at it. The proprietor was a newcomer to the area but not adverse to recognizing a local celebrity. He immediately greeted Violet, plied her with complimentary goodies, and took innumerable selfies with her. Gemma and I were part of the scenery and happy to be on the back burner. Naturally, the grand opening of Poppet figured prominently in the conversation, and owner Chester Morel received a personal invitation to join us. After we ordered, a familiar party of two was seated behind us. Kim and Lionel Stevens slipped silently into their seats without greeting anyone. She looked lovely but tense in a sapphire velvet dress and cape. Lionel was the picture of respectability in his bespoke suit, although his grim visage was off-putting. Their hopes for anonymity were dashed when Gemma glided over to their table and greeted them. Despite a tepid response from Lionel, she insisted on including Violet. I watched my aunt with admiration as she proceeded to charm both. Kim glowed when Violet referenced her former career as a model and mentioned a desire to paint her portrait. Even Lionel exhibited faint signs of animation when his lawyerly skills were touted and deferred to.

"I have some pressing legal matters to attend to," Violet told him." Perhaps I can make an appointment to discuss them with you. If you accept new clients, of course."

Lionel puffed out his chest. "I kept only a few select clients, but I would be honored if you, my dear lady, were among them." He handed her his card and settled back in his chair, surfeited with almost orgasmic delight. Score one for Auntie.

When we left the Velvet Claw, our appetites for food and information had both been satiated.

"Things looked pretty tense between them," Gemma said. "Probably the legacy of the delightful Paul Prentis. That man destroyed everything he touched. Who could blame Kim if she strayed off the straight and narrow? She's a beautiful woman, and Lionel is such a big sour puss." Whatever their issues, I knew that Violet would unearth them. After this evening, Kim and Lionel would both be captivated by my aunt. People confided in her whether they meant to or not.

Gemma dropped Violet at my parents' home, and I headed gratefully for my loft to dream away the events of the day. As a business owner, I had finally crossed the threshold to adulthood. No more dreams deferred or childish fantasies. This was real life replete with pleasures and perils.

* * *

The next day I resolved to spruce up for the big event by trying some of my own products. I scooped up *Kiehl's* restorative hair pack, an exfoliating scrub, and a soothing gel masque by *Dermalogica*. While waiting for the magic to work, I sat at my easel and completed an unfinished charcoal sketch. The subject was a male figure, blanketed in darkness and turned away from onlookers. I called it "ambiguity," and it represented to me the conflicting emotions I felt about the murder itself and the victim. Paul Prentis made many enemies, but the gap between hatred and homicide was enormous. Most citizens in Harbor Bay abided by the law. Even minor offenses like speeding were frowned upon. Murder, the ultimate societal taboo, was unthinkable. My knowledge of psychology was limited and provided very little insight into the subject. Gideon Hall might know but probably wouldn't share much with an interfering amateur. I'd read any number of articles that police repulsed such efforts with all the vigor of a body fighting infection.

So be it. That obstacle won't deter me. There was simply too much at stake. The guests at our party were upright citizens. The cream of the Harbor Bay crop. Yet I knew with every fiber of my being that one or more of them were guilty. Their names flashed before me in a blur: Mayor Zach, the kindly dentist; Lionel, the stiff, unyielding lawyer; Tilda, the enigmatic literary star; Philippa, the pillar of moral rectitude or lovely Kim, imprisoned in a gilded cage. Truth compelled me to add Blaike, Gemma, and Mandy to the list, although my effort was half-hearted. I refused to even consider Gemma as a suspect. She had no motive other than the slings and arrows that Paul had flung her way. Hardly enough to incite violence.

By all accounts, Paul Prentis was a bottom feeder determined to achieve his ends at any cost. Everyone has secrets that he or she preferred to hide. I scoured my mind to find my own, but they were fairly innocuous. Failure at the Art Institute was the bane of my existence, something that was both humiliating and devastating. Initially, I'd tried to conceal it, but word soon spread like a virus around Harbor Bay. My failure was nothing criminal, and I had very little to lose except self-esteem. That had been painful, but life would go on, and people would soon forget. Gemma even suggested that failure made me more "relatable," something to which I had never aspired. I worked feverishly on my sketch, wondering all the while which vices could destroy the lives of those outwardly upright souls if Paul Prentis disclosed them. The answers to that were the keys that would ultimately unlock the puzzle.

Promptly at nine, Gemma and Mandy arrived, eager to hang the grand opening banner and make final arrangements. We planned to ply our customers with punch, petit fours, and pleasantries. No discussion of the murder or any grim reminder of Paul Prentis would be allowed. Mandy assembled gift bags while Gemma and I brainstormed strategy and practical matters such as snagging email addresses and doing demos.

At lunchtime I took orders and dashed across the street to Bucky's Biscotti. The shop was deserted except for the long, lanky figure of deputy Benny Soto. *Carpe Diem*, I told myself. Let's see what information he's willing to share.

"Hey. Everything quiet in Harbor Bay?"

He jerked up his head and blushed. As I recalled, that was de rigueur for the lad who had earned the nickname "blushing Benny" in high school.

'Oh, Marky. Yeah sure. I'm taking my lunch break before things heat up." He straightened up to his full height and tapped his nightstick. The chief wants what he calls a visible presence on the streets. Makes citizens feel safer, you know."

I lowered my voice and tried to appear properly awestruck. "Understand-able. Since the murder, everyone's probably on edge."

He surveyed the room for eavesdroppers and nodded. "You wouldn't believe the calls we've gotten. Every strange noise makes some old lady jump out of her skin. But don't you worry. We'll be making an arrest soon. Very soon."

My heart sank as I pictured the likely scenario. Gemma handcuffed and being led away in disgrace. I tried a different approach. "Our grand opening is tomorrow, you know. Keep your fingers crossed that everything goes well. No excitement."

"Everyone's excited that your aunt is back in town. Don't remember her myself, but my mom is a big fan. Thinks she's some kind of movie star."

"Thank your mom, and please invite her to the opening. I'm sure Aunt Violet would love to see her again." I gave him a brochure and made my escape. If he was right, the police might well be building a case against my friend and business partner. He had no evidence, but that wouldn't stop a determined lawman. It also made the success of our venture even more essential.

Gemma gasped when I told her. Knowing and proving were two distinct things when it came to crime. She nudged Mandy and gave her marching orders. "Time to trot out your feminine wiles, Mom. Tell Gideon you're nervous or something."

Mandy smiled. "Don't worry. I'm sure I can think of something. You girls stay here while I have a little chat with him. A woman living alone is so vulnerable, you know."

Her helpless act didn't deceive me for a second since I knew for a fact that Mandy owned several weapons and was a crack shot. Still, I had every confidence that she would play her part with aplomb and that Gideon just might take the bait.

Our preparations were perfect, but I was still a bundle of nerves. Gemma sized me up and suggested an outing. "Are you a gambler, Marky?"

"Obviously. Why else would we be here?"

"No. I mean a real gambler. The casino is only a half hour from here, and they have great entertainment. Let's lock up and try our luck."

After citing the many reasons why it was irresponsible and impossible, I finally weakened. "Okay. But I can't stay late. Let me call my aunt."

Violet declined my invitation. She'd made plans to join friends at the local country club for drinks and dinner. Nothing major, she swore. Just an intimate gathering. Apparently, the local women's club was angling for donations for their forthcoming charity auction, and Violet was considered a prize catch.

Gemma hooted when I told her. "Your aunt's got more moves than either of us. I bet she'll get some hot news while she's there."

* * *

We hopped into Gemma's Jeep and sped toward the casino at warp speed. I'm a cautious driver, but Gemma is a daredevil. When we reached the exit for the Grand Traverse Casino, I breathed a sigh of relief. Gambling with my life was not on my personal agenda. This was my first trip to the casino, but my pal was apparently a well-known and popular fixture there. She was greeted enthusiastically by the doormen and ushered into the main gambling parlor. I am no risk-taker when it comes to gambling. Losing on the twenty-five-cent slots is fun. Anything more alarms me, and I can ill afford to indulge a gambling habit. The floor manager was apparently a pal of Gemma's who gave us passes to the show and stopped to chat. While I visited the ladies' room, he and Gemma swapped stories from their misspent younger days.

When I rejoined them, I noticed a peculiar look on Gemma's face, a look of shock and excitement. "Follow me," she said, vaulting toward a vacant seating area. "You'll gag when you hear this."

Her build-up was so labored that I longed to shake her like a rag doll. "Spit it out, for crying out loud. What happened?"

"Guess who runs up a huge tab at the craps tables all the time? Someone we both know."

I shrugged. "Not, Blaike, I hope."

Gemma frowned. "Blaike. Not everything concerns your beau, Marky. We were searching for motives, right? Well, according to my friend, our esteemed mayor is a constant and unlucky regular here and at the other casinos too."

"Zach? Zach Thanos?" I couldn't believe my ears. How could a kindly dentist turn into a rogue gambler?

"You got it, girlfriend. We were looking for motives, and he's got a gold-plated one. Folks in Harbor Bay wouldn't look kindly on a mayor with an unlucky streak. Sort of makes you nervous about your town's future."

I was reeling from the news, unable to process it. "Gambling's not illegal you know. If he likes to play the slots, big deal."

Gemma scoffed. "Slots? Zach's into the big time. Table games, big stakes. Could make him vulnerable to a lizard-like Paul Prentis, especially if he owed him money."

Suddenly our little excursion had turned sour. I had an urge to go home, bolt the door, and hide under the bedcovers like I had as a child. Detective work was far more interesting in novels where the suspects were strangers, and the victim deserved his fate. *Think strategically*, I told myself. Council minutes were part of the public record. *Evidence.* If Zack agreed to any proposals that favored Prentis Properties, those minutes would prove it.

"Let's get out of here," I said, "before we learn any other unsavory secrets."

Gemma pouted but finally agreed. "Okay. But next time, I want more of an outing. And don't you be so squeamish, princess. We want to save my skin, and if that means getting down and dirty, so be it."

I couldn't argue, so I didn't even try. Fictional heroes always triumphed over danger, but our situation was more perilous. This murderer acted decisively to stop Paul Prentis and might do so again. Aunt Violet and Mandy faced potential danger also. If we were to solve the crime and safeguard our own lives, caution must be our watchword.

Chapter Seven

I didn't disturb my aunt that evening. There would be plenty of time to tell her the grim news on opening day. Sleep would have been hard to come by, but I warmed a cup of milk and quickly swallowed the magic potion. I drifted off, still fearing what other unsavory secrets we might uncover. I'd known most of these people for years. They were upright pillars of the community who had always been revered and admired. Everything was topsy-turvy now if one of them had taken a life. My sleep was plagued by visions of Dr. Zach wielding a scalpel and a leering Tilda Egan dancing madly around a recumbent Paul Prentis. I tried to warn him, but my voice didn't work. I awakened to the shrill call of the alarm clock.

We'd agreed to convene at eight a.m., and that demanded a polished version of my better self. I wracked my brain, trying to recall the Yoga techniques for creating a calm, placid exterior. After all, as co-owner of a new business, I needed to project confidence. Aunt Violet had taught me that. I tiptoed down the stairs and surveyed my domain. The interior of Poppet resembled a beautiful bride, redolent with promise, perfumed and ready for adventure. I stood in the shadows for a moment, breathing in this realization of my dreams. The weather outside was perfect, crisp, clear, and inviting. I attached the welcoming banner to our flagpole and sighed with contentment. In three hours, my destiny would begin.

The arrival of Gemma and Mandy broke the spell. Both Watts ladies beamed with pride, excitement, or something very like it. Aunt Violet followed closely on their heels. This was old hat for her, but she showed as much enthusiasm as the rest of us.

"Sit on that stool, Ms. Marky, and let me make you even more beautiful." I hadn't paid much attention to my makeup, but as usual, Violet was right. We were all ambassadors of our brand and had to reflect the products we sold. In short order, I received a touch of foundation, blush, and special emphasis on my eyes. "They're your best feature, you know. Lovely hazel eyes just like my dear sister." The results spoke for themselves, and I pirouetted around the aisle feeling like a princess. Gemma claimed the chair as soon as I vacated it. "Okay, Violet. Do your best." My aunt used fewer products on Gemma. "Less is more, darling. You have incredible skin that must shine through."

Mandy sipped a latte and grinned at us. "I have some info if you're interested. Straight from the chief himself." She immediately captured all our attention.

"I told Gideon the truth—mostly. Maybe I fibbed just a bit, but it was in a good cause. He was always a sucker for a needy woman."

Violet laughed. "Don't keep us in suspense, Mandy. What's the scoop?"

Mandy recounted her episode with the chief in a remarkably cogent fashion. According to Gideon Hall, the investigation was still "ongoing," whatever that meant. He assured her, however, that she needn't fear some marauding murderer out for blood.

Violet's gaze sharpened. "Sound like he's got someone in his sights already. Not good." She looked away from Gemma.

"I'm not sure about that. At first, I thought it was Blaike Harrington, but Gideon's known Blaike since he was a boy. Coached him in little league." Mandy wrinkled her brow. "I got the idea that there are others in the mix too. Gideon is the slow, methodical type of man. Doesn't jump to conclusions."

If only that were true. Violet then added her findings from last evening to the mix. "My friends were circumspect until Tilda Egan swanned into the dining room. Then they became quite chatty. Plenty of opinions about that lady, especially from the married women." She grinned. "Actually, the consensus was that she is no lady."

Mandy leaned in, eager to hear every word. "Tell me. How did she look, and was she alone?"

"She looked quite lovely. All in black with just a touch of gold. And yes, she was alone. She ordered a martini and ate a salad at the bar." Violet's eyes sparkled. "Dues at that club are high. Stratospheric, in fact. I mentioned it to my friends. Asked them if she got special consideration as a resident author."

"And…" Gemma curled her lip.

"They scoffed at the suggestion and even at the notion that Tilda was a writer. Apparently, she pays the full freight. No discounts for impecunious artists."

There was more to it. Aunt Violet was withholding something vital. "What's the punchline?" I asked her. "Come on. Give."

She hesitated. "Naturally, at the tony clubs, money alone isn't enough. You have to be sponsored by another member." After sipping her latte, Violet continued. "I fished around until they mentioned Tilda's sponsor." Violet looked away. "It was Blaike Harrington."

Even though I tried to control my emotions, I gasped. Blaike was an innocent, and Tilda was an obvious hussy who'd seduced him. After a second, fairness forced me to scale back the rhetoric. Femme fatale was a term that more accurately described Tilda. Just as lethal but a less judgmental assessment. Besides, truth be told, I really knew very little about Blaike's predilections. This was no longer high school. He was a man with adult appetites that someone like Tilda could easily satiate. A niggling little voice reminded me that he had yet to even kiss me. Perhaps he regarded me as a friend, not a romantic partner. No man had ever described me as a seductress, more's the pity. Wholesome girl next door was more common, if not more flattering. Lust seldom entered the picture.

Gemma immediately jumped into the fray. "I thought you'd say Paul Prentis seemed more her type."

Mandy slapped her daughter on the back. "Tilda is every man's type. Listen to your mama on this one, darling."

Who could argue with that? I reminded myself that Tilda was a likely customer for Poppet, and as such, it was important to court her, not criticize her. Attitude adjustment was needed for the owner of a successful business.

Our scoop about Dr. Zach stunned both Violet and Mandy. He was such a beloved, almost saintly figure in Harbor Bay that it was difficult for them to believe anything negative. "Gambling isn't illegal," Violet pointed out. "The mayor must pay his debts, or those casinos would cut him off in a heartbeat. Unless somebody else paid for him." She shuddered. "Private detectives have a nasty business unearthing everyone's vices and secrets. Fortunately for me, mine are all out in the open."

Mandy laughed. "Hell, Violet, you turned your vices into virtues. Everyone in Harbor Bay sees you as this glamor puss more French than American. The sky's the limit where you're concerned."

Her words rang true. Many people assumed that exotic behavior was commonplace in Europe's more sophisticated society. In contrast, conventional Harbor Bay, Michigan, was a churchgoing Midwestern town where neighbors were easily shocked.

I expected Gemma to chime in with a comment, but she bit her lip and occupied herself by rearranging the bottom shelf of our *ORIBE* display. Just nerves, I told myself, although I resolved to question my partner more closely after hours. Surely, she had nothing to hide except having the bad luck to find Paul Prentis's corpse.

We had no more time to digress because it was the witching hour—time for our grand opening. Butterflies metastasized in my stomach as the first customer walked through our doors. For better or worse, Poppet was officially open for business.

* * *

Customers slowly trickled in, and after lunch, that trickle became a steady stream. Some wanted only information, but a sizable number bought products or booked spa services. Aunt Violet was the big draw. Matrons edged up to her for selfies and advice, often dragging their reluctant spouses with them. Mandy circulated throughout the room, dispensing hors de oeuvres and chatting up old pals. Gemma staffed a table explaining massage types and techniques. She was especially adroit at calming shy clients who worried about disrobing before a stranger. As for me, I busied myself assembling client information, ringing up sales, and fending off questions about the murder of Paul Prentis. A blend of tact and artful candor satisfied most of the curious, although some of the more persistent ones didn't flinch. They insisted on revisiting the dreadful event and sharing their opinions on the victim.

The consensus was clear: Paul had been a plague on Harbor Bay for far too long and deserved what he got. The name Blaike Harrington was never mentioned, although a few old chums from high school alluded to my close personal relationship with him. I brushed them off with a shake of my head and a reminder that high school ended years ago. A lot of water over that bridge, as Gemma would say. Changing buyers into returning customers was my only goal, so I indulged most of their questions. Toward closing time, when Philippa Gordon buzzed into the store, I was taken aback. Old fears resurfaced, and I found it difficult to maintain my poise. Fortunately, she ignored me. She sped up to Violet, engaging her in a brief though animated conversation. After they exchanged hugs, I saw her slip a card into my aunt's hand and depart.

Same old Principal Gordon. Austere, unapproachable, and unapologetic. The woman gave me the creeps. I couldn't help wondering what secrets she harbored and what she would do to keep them. Frankly, Philippa seemed too programmed and unimaginative to indulge in illegal or scandalous behavior. Even an unpaid parking ticket seemed beyond her reach. Murder was unthinkable. Of one thing I was certain: if she killed Paul, she would have covered her tracks and eliminated any clues. Using the purple extension cord to implicate us would merely be icing on the cake. Nothing personal, just business.

Most shops in Harbor Bay closed at six p.m. in the off-season and we followed that lead. Massages and facials could be scheduled by appointment only for evening hours, and we had several clients with reservations for the week ahead. I was anxious, almost terrified, to review our performance and assess our progress. My anxiety subsided as Mandy poured each of us an adult beverage, pulled down the shades, and locked the door.

"Okay, gang," I said. "How did we do?"

Gemma retrieved her iPad and shared the number of services she had booked. It was impressive, although not overwhelming. I told myself not to obsess. Progress would be incremental, not a tidal wave. Besides, I had budgeted enough to tide me over for six months. After that, Poppet would have to stand on its own.

"You and Philippa were mighty chatty," Mandy said to Violet. "That's not like her. Pretty standoffish normally, at least with most strangers." She blushed. "Not that you're really a stranger here, Violet. No offense."

My aunt patted Mandy's arm in a no harm, no foul gesture. "Really? We're going to meet for lunch tomorrow. She's interested in upping her game a bit. Nothing too radical, just judicious use of a few products." Violet and Philippa were of an age, but that's where the similarities ended. My aunt's creamy smooth skin and shiny hair stood in stark contrast to Philippa's drab appearance. That made me wonder. Was sensible Philippa Gordon, pillar of respectability, trying to enhance her image or expand her social life? Pretty slim pickings in Harbor Bay, although Mayor Zach and a few others were available.

Gemma rolled her eyes. "Plenty of talk about Paul Prentis but not much sorrow. That boy had a talent for rubbing everyone the wrong way. Benny Soto's mom dropped in, and she said Paul threatened to double her rent if she didn't toe the line. Called her place a dump and an eyesore."

That bookstore was an institution in Harbor Bay, a charming space with nooks for reading and wide aisles for browsing. It operated under the outdated premise that intelligent readers still existed. Novel Approach tapped the heart of the community but like most of its kind, the profit margins were slender. A philistine like Prentis, blinded by dollars and cents, probably envisioned a marijuana dispensary in the space.

After tidying up, we surrendered to the gods of exhaustion. Tomorrow was another business day. With a pinch of luck, word would spread, and that would draw still more customers. Besides, weekends were prime targets for tourists and summer residents. Most had yet to arrive, but sunny weather always drew shoppers. I designated Mandy as our liaison with the hospitality industry. Plenty of weddings, graduation parties, and anniversary soirées occurred from June on. Poppet could provide the type of spa and professional makeup services these customers expected. Mandy, with her easy-going charm, was just the point person to seal the deal and placate anxious brides.

* * *

After soaking in a warm bath, I planned to spend some time at my easel finishing that charcoal sketch. Several patrons had complimented my paintings and asked if they were for sale. That inspired me to post discreet price tags and mention that custom works could be commissioned. When my iPhone sang its saucy tune, "I Will Survive," I toyed with ignoring it. Good manners prevailed, however, and to my chagrin, I recognized the caller as Blaike Harrington, the same man who had sponsored Tilda Egan for membership in the country club.

"I need to see you," he said. Something about that deep velvety voice moved me more than it ever should have. "I'm outside your store."

I should have rebuffed him. Should have ignored the tremor in his voice and pleaded exhaustion, but I didn't. Something told me to hear the man out. I didn't fear him. He was no killer. Blaike was just a complication I didn't need.

"Give me a minute," I said, hastily grabbing my jeans and a button-down shirt. My hair was my faithful ally, and most of Aunt Violet's makeup still adorned my face. Blaike would have to take it or leave it. I was no match for the wiles of a succubus like Tilda Egan and wouldn't try to compete.

Blaike stood in the doorway, sheltered from the streetlights and passersby. He was not alone. His companion was a lovely rough collie, a blue Merle, whose plummy tail, and wide grin immediately captivated me.

"Who is this?" I asked, bending down to stroke her. "She's beautiful."

He grinned. "This is Fantasia, my mom's dearest friend. When mom passed, I became the guardian of this lovely lady."

My childhood was spent reading tales of *"Lad, A Dog"* and watching reruns of *Lassie."* I love animals and have a special fondness for collies. A charmer like Fantasia was a definite icebreaker, even considering the tense situation that confronted us. I buried my head in her dense fur and found contentment.

"I know you're busy," Blaike said, "but I had to talk to someone. Someone I can trust." His eyes met mine, and for a moment, I forgot that he was a murder suspect with questionable links to Tilda Egan.

"Okay. Sit down while I brew us some tea. Today was the opening of Poppet, so I haven't had much time to relax."

After we exhausted our supply of small talk about the store, he finally came to the point. "Gideon Hall thinks I'm guilty."

"Really? Did he say that?" Paranoia was unusual behavior for a man like Blaike unless, of course, he had reason to fear the chief.

Blaike hung his head. "No, but he keeps dropping in, and that idiot Benny Soto glares at me whenever we cross paths. My lawyer says not to worry, but it's hard to ignore the suspicion, especially in a small town like Harbor Bay."

Gemma had wrangled a copy of the autopsy report through some contacts she refused to identify. As I recalled, it merely stated the obvious. Paul Prentis was manually strangled before that extension cord had decorated his neck. Strangling was an aggressive act, one born of passion and superior strength. But that violet cord was a deliberate, contemptuous act of humiliation for a macho bully like Paul. I handed a copy of the purloined document to Blaike.

"Where'd you get this," he asked. "Hall keeps dragging his feet whenever my attorney asks for it."

I shrugged. "You know how things go in this place. Contacts are everything." Blaike's lawyer was a prominent litigator from Chicago, well respected but a stranger, nevertheless. Locals regarded him with suspicion, and any high-pressure tactics that he might employ were doomed to failure. Gideon Hall merely smiled and deflected the inquiry.

"One thing worth noting," Blaike said. "This says Prentis had alcohol and Rohypnol in his system, plus traces of cocaine. That explains how someone, even a woman, could take him down so easily. After all, he was a pretty big guy. Slip some of that stuff in his drink, and he'd start feeling groggy right away."

"Wait a minute. I missed the Rohypnol part. Isn't that the date rape drug? I thought he'd collapse right away if he ingested that."

Blaike shook his head. "Not necessarily. Our fraternity at Michigan made a big deal about explaining that. Some guys were using just a bit of it in combination with Coke. Moderated the effects, or so they said. Paul might have gotten a small dose or used it voluntarily. Either way, it would have dulled his senses but not knocked him out."

He had a point. Paul stumbled out the door after the fracas. I was so glad to see him leave that I didn't question his condition. If he had been impaired, a woman or someone older like Lionel or Dr. Zach could have attacked him. Prentis arrived at the party under the influence of something. I'd assumed it was alcohol combined with generally obnoxious behavior. If drugs were involved, that would have exacerbated his condition. I wracked my brain, trying to recall who at our party handed Paul anything to eat or drink. Mandy had circulated with a tray of drinks, but anyone could have taken one and offered it to Paul. On the countertop, we'd arranged bottles of Perrier and imported beer. No one was monitoring them, so we had no idea who helped himself. Paul didn't seem the type for sparkling water, but I suspected that exotic beer might have suited his taste.

"Was he known as a drug user?" I asked. "It wouldn't surprise me, but still…."

Blaike shook his head. "Believe it or not, Paul was fairly conservative when it came to illicit substances. His dad would have blown a gasket if he got arrested, and Paul was wary of doing anything that impugned the family name. Prentis's money fed his lifestyle, you know. Harbor Bay isn't exactly a haven for drug use, although I'm sure when the tourists arrive, we get our fair share."

Try as I might, I could no longer deny it. Paul's killer must have been one of those upstanding citizens milling about Poppet that evening. Difficult, almost impossible to believe. I'd known most of them since I was a child. Surely I would have detected homicidal tendencies by now.

"Do you have any suspects?" I tried to be clever but subtle. "What do you know about Tilda Egan? She strikes me as tough enough to do almost anything."

Blaike snorted. "Tilda? I can't see her ruining her manicure, let alone strangling someone. Besides, what's her motive? She's got a pretty good life here."

I used Fantasia as a distraction and was rewarded with a doggy kiss. "I don't believe that Tilda's the serious writer that she claims to be. Not one bit. I think she's a phony. When I asked her what genre she wrote, she gave me this puzzled look and ignored the question. Maybe Paul knew and threatened to expose her and blow her cover."

"Unlikely. Besides, Tilda's not pretending. She's writing a memoir, and it's very steamy. I've seen the first chapter." Blaike waved his arms. "Hot stuff. Makes Harbor Bay into a Midwest version of Peyton Place, complete with love nests and all kinds of perversion."

That news left me flabbergasted, or as the Brits say, gobsmacked. If she was spreading salacious rumors or threatening to spill secrets, Tilda would have been a more likely victim than killer. I tried another tact. "Aunt Violet told me that Tilda's a member of the country club. That's a shocker. They used to be very selective."

"Not such a big deal anymore. Most younger people aren't really into that kind of stuff. Nowadays, just about anyone who can pay the freight gets accepted." Blaike acted nonchalant rather than guilty. Had he sponsored Tilda because he figured prominently in her memoir or hoped to be part of her future research? I wondered.

Before I probed further, my courage deserted me. What if Blaike confessed to some torrid affair with Tilda? Most men would yield to her charms and enjoy her favors, no questions asked. Compared with her, I was a pubescent teenager vying for an invite to the prom.

"Tilda told us that Paul was her friend. Nothing more."

Blaike raised his eyebrows. "Oh yeah? Who knows for sure? Tongues wag in small towns, especially when a woman who looks like that is involved. Other women get jealous, and men exaggerate."

His reaction begged the question: could Tilda have murdered Paul? It also forced me to examine my own conscience. Tilda Egan activated every jealous bone and insecurity in my body. She and Philippa were my preferred suspects, but objectively speaking, I had no evidence upon which to base it. Gemma fell into that category too. She and I needed to have a serious conversation.

"What about the minutes of the city council," I asked. "They're online, aren't they?"

Blaike nodded. "Yeah. Matter of public record. Open meetings law, you know the drill. That land development project was one big deal. Back and forth. Plenty of passion on both sides."

"Did it pass?" I asked. "Hard to find any information about it." *The Harbor Gazette*, a weekly newspaper that fancied itself as an offshoot of the *Chicago Tribune*, featured national news and political commentary at the expense of local events. Their coverage of the Prentis murder had been limited, although I expected that to change. In fact, although the editor had asked to interview me about Poppet, I suspected that he had other motives in mind. The Prentis name was influential in Western Michigan, Chicago, and beyond. The grisly details, especially the violet extension cord, might even titillate readers across the nation.

Our conversation eventually grew stilted, and without the intervention of the lovely Fantasia, it would have totally evaporated. No romantic overtures either. Forget about steamy looks or passion-fueled talk. Blaike perched himself on the arm of my sofa and kept his distance. After a few desultory remarks, he made his excuses, planted a chaste kiss on my forehead, and left for home. Blaike's passivity was curious. He claimed to be under Gideon's watchful gaze but did little to clear his own name. Wimpy men turned me off. Before now, I had never placed Blaike, the high school quarterback and homecoming king, in that category. For pity's sake, Gemma, Violet, and Mandy showed far more spunk! I dismissed thoughts of Blaike, tidied up the kitchen, and prepared for bed. Sleep was my ally that evening. It came easily and gifted me with gentle dreams of sweet success.

Chapter Eight

Aunt Violet was up to something. She sailed into Poppet promptly at nine a.m., dressed for adventure or what passed for it in Harbor Bay. A prim cream-colored shirtwaist highlighted by a flashy Hermès scarf made an eye-catching ensemble that I could never replicate in two lifetimes. Fortunately, she also carried two double lattes and a box of croissants from our local patisserie.

"Up and at them," she said, eyeing my bedraggled appearance. "Good Lord, girl, you need some pep in your step. Can't let the customers see you like that." She poured my latte into a mug and patted the stool next to the makeup counter. "At your age, it won't take much to make you gorgeous. Nature's cruel that way."

"Why are you so perky?" I growled. Her high spirits annoyed me.

She favored me with a smile. "My meeting is in another hour. Wouldn't want to be tardy."

"Meeting?" My synapses weren't all firing just yet. "Who are you meeting?"

Violet gave me a shake of her head as she applied eyeliner and shadow to my naked lids. "Here. This forest green shade should work wonders on those hazel eyes of yours. Always worked for your Mama, as I recall. And try this Chanel mascara. All the rage in Paris."

She was baiting me, and of course, I leapt for it like a hungry trout. "Stop stalling. Who's the lucky guy?"

"Nothing exciting. Just business. Today is my appointment with Lionel Stevens. Legal matters, you know. Can't ignore those."

She'd wasted no time following up on her chat with Lionel last week.

There was a lesson in that for me and especially for Blaike. Carpe Diem, or something equally profound.

"Do you know him well? Lionel, I mean."

"Nope. We moved in different circles when I lived here. He was sort of a nerd, studious but stuffy if you get my drift. And nothing to look at. His lovely wife is a total stranger to me. I was serious about painting her portrait, though. There's an air of tragedy surrounding her that translates well into oils."

Tragedy? I hadn't considered that, but, in many ways, Kim Stevens was an enigma. Aloof but vulnerable. I had very limited contact with her, but somehow, since I was the president of the league of losers, I considered her to be a kindred spirit.

Violet walked over to my easel and studied the sketch "That's very nice, dear. I'd suggest you work on it during business hours too. Point of interest for customers. A great gimmick. Reminds them that you are a true artist in oils and cosmetics. In fact, you might have a contest. You know, name this sketch, or anyone who makes a purchase gets a raffle ticket. It's quite a lure for customers, something different but valuable."

Another nugget from my aunt and something to create excitement and buzz for Poppet and keep my artistic dreams alive.

Gemma bounced in, full of energy. She had two early customers scheduled for massages and several more in the afternoon. Mandy entered the shop and was delegated to visit local hotels and hair salons. We hoped to establish partnerships with both businesses so that when tourists asked for recommendations, Poppet was on the tip of their tongues. She also loaded up her station wagon with plenty of samples and discount coupons to sweeten the pot for the staff. I felt cautiously optimistic about our prospects as long as Poppet was linked to glamour, not gore.

From ten to noon, we had a steady stream of customers. Most were shy about discussing their needs, but several were very knowledgeable. I abhor high-pressure sales tactics, so for the undecided clients, I provided the websites for our vendors and guided them to the computer for a YouTube makeup tutorial. Naturally, they were encouraged to browse freely. I reminded them that Violet had scheduled a Saturday seminar that would focus on skin care secrets. More mature customers identified with that, and to my surprise, several women bought products for their husbands, sons, or partners.

As I prepared to close the store, a slender man of incredible height wedged his way into Poppet. His blaze of red hair easily identified him as the interloper from the memorial service. Although he was a stranger, for some reason, he didn't frighten me. Perhaps it was his skeletal frame so reminiscent of a giraffe or the wide grin that decorated his face. Either way, I returned his smile and asked how I could help him.

"Sorry for the last-minute interruption," he said. "I'm Jonathon Crane from the *Gazette*." He continued when I didn't respond. "We've never met, but I'd like to speak with you."

"Is this an interview, Mr. Crane? I've had a long day. As a matter of fact, we met briefly at the memorial service. Did you know Paul Prentis?"

His grin was infectious and quite captivating, and he wore his reddish-brown hair in what could only be described as a buzz-cut run amuck. To top it off, I heard traces of a British accent in his voice. He ignored my question and pressed forward with his agenda. "I won't take too much of your time." He swiveled his neck around to survey my entire shop. "New businesses usually welcome publicity. Especially when it's free."

I motioned him over to the seating area. "I know a line when I hear it, but you're right. Poppet needs all the buzz it can get. Especially when it's free!"

His first questions were innocuous enough. A bit of my biography and the names of my business partners. Aunt Violet's involvement intrigued him, and he asked several follow-up questions about her. Jonathon Crane was a smooth one, I'll grant him that. He examined my paintings, praised their artistry, and snapped a few photos before launching into the real purpose of his visit: the death of Paul Prentis.

"That had nothing to do with Poppet," I said. "He was found outside in the alley."

Crane raised his eyebrows. "Really? Didn't he attend a social at this store prior to his murder? Maybe I was misinformed."

I felt my pulse racing and grasped the gilt arms of my chair to steady myself. "Many of the local town leaders attended that social. I'll be glad to furnish you with a list if it helps. Mr. Prentis was my landlord, you see. He didn't stay long. Kind of a courtesy call, you might say."

Giraffes are such amiable creatures, not the kind to pounce on unsuspecting prey. I quickly revised my impression of Jonathon Crane. He was far closer to a python, a rapacious reptile ready to strike without warning. Snakes don't frighten me, but I was wary of them. Very wary

"I heard there was a fracas that night. Mr. Prentis was offensive and mixed it up with Lionel Stevens. Something about Mrs. Stevens. And your partner and her mom got involved. Something about champagne in his face." No more Mr. Nice Guy. His face now showed definite traces of a smirk.

I folded my arms and glared. "I don't gossip about customers or guests, Mr. Crane. It's unfair and very indiscreet. You'll have to get your scoop elsewhere. I have a business to run."

We faced off for an instant, but in the end, he acknowledged defeat. He ambled over to the work area and fingered the violet extension cord. "Very pretty. Distinctive, wouldn't you say? How do you suppose one ended up around the victim's neck?"

I took a deep breath and managed a smile of my own. "That's a question for Chief Hall. He knows all the details."

Before leaving, the reporter fired one parting shot. "You and Blaike Harrington were an item once. Too bad he's the prime suspect. Messy. Very messy. And your partner had quite a connection to the victim as well. Small towns can be a jungle."

My composure returned and, with it, a snappy rejoinder. "Come back for a complimentary massage sometime, Mr. Crane. Work out some of those kinks. Your muscles seem rather cramped."

He winked at me as he made his exit. "I just might do that."

* * *

"What a creature!" I described my encounter with the fourth estate to Gemma and grimaced. "Such a sneak! He was Mr. Sincerity until the murder came up. He probably won't even use the material about Poppet except for that stuff about the extension cord."

Gemma hesitated. "Jonathon Crane? Name sounds familiar, but I just can't place him."

"Looks like a rabid giraffe with a faint British accent—probably phony. You saw him at Paul's memorial service."

She gave me a quizzical look. "Can giraffes get rabies? Never heard that before."

I finally lost all sense of patience. "Forget about the stupid rabies and focus. Someone fed that reporter details. Things that could jeopardize our business."

Gemma held up two fingers. "Wait a sec while I make a call." She grabbed her cell phone and stepped into one of the treatment rooms. When she returned, she had the answer and some alarming news. "Okay. Your visitor is a Chicago guy on loan from the *Sun Times.* Works the crime beat and is considered hot stuff. And get this—he was nosing around the Art Institute asking questions about you."

I gulped. "Me? That's all I need. Things must be pretty dull in the Windy City these days if the murder of a small-town chiseler like Paul Prentis sparks their interest."

"There's more. This Crane guy does their true crime podcast. You know how popular those are these days. Could be he thinks this murder fits right in. And don't forget that plenty of rich Chicago folks have summer places here."

I covered my ears, unwilling to hear another discouraging word. That effort was wasted. When Aunt Violet sailed in, Gemma gleefully repeated the entire episode.

"Interesting. Jibes with what I heard today from Lionel. He handles the Prentis accounts, business and personal. Seems like Paul made several risky investments and was desperate for this land deal to go through. Some unsavory types from Chicago were pressuring him. I take it they aren't known for patience."

Lionel Stevens appeared to be the soul of discretion. I was surprised that he disclosed confidential information about a client to an outsider, even one as charming as Violet. When I said that, she laughed.

"Darling, Lionel didn't say a word about Paul. Wouldn't even admit he was a client. Tight as a vault, that man is. As luck would have it, I ran into Kim, and we had lunch at the club. She filled me in on the dirty details. Poor girl. She's terrified that Lionel might think she and Paul were an item."

Gemma's eyes grew huge. "And were they?"

"Apparently not. Just a harmless flirtation. Very common in Europe, but Americans can be so strait-laced about such things." Violet reapplied her lipstick. "Don't worry. I'll get the whole story. I plan to paint Kim's portrait. She's quite lovely, you know. A bit too high strung, but that's understandable."

The upkeep on a lovely woman like Kim might be costly. Was Lionel desperate for funds himself, desperate enough to fiddle with client accounts? I wondered.

I could easily envision Paul Prentis as a blackmailer, even though my concept of blackmailers was based solely upon novels and cable crime shows. In them, the criminal always paid for his crimes by coming to a bad end. Victims frequently struck back at their tormenter, much as someone in Harbor Bay had done.

Violet fluffed out her hair and faced me. "I understand you had a late-night visitor. Two of them."

I'd make a dreadful spy or undercover operative. Blood rushed to my head, and my cheeks grew warm. Confession was my only option.

"Small towns, small minds," I said. "It was nothing. Blaike stopped in for a few minutes."

Gemma and Violet exchanged knowing looks while I fumbled with my comb. I folded easily and described both Fantasia and my conversation with Blaike.

"That boy does sound a tad weak," Violet said. "Hope he has an able attorney. Else wise Gideon Hall will dismantle him piece by piece." She shuddered as she visualized it.

Gemma's complexion turned a whiter shade of pale. "Gideon had Benny Soto nosing around too. He'd love to make a big splash and play the hero."

"Forget about that. I propose a little field trip," I said. "Tomorrow's Sunday. While the faithful gather for services, let's peek at this site that Paul was pushing. Maybe we'll find a clue or some inspiration."

Gemma had a prior engagement, and Violet planned to appear front and center at the Harbor Bay Congregationalist Church. She was a nominal Catholic but subscribed to the ecumenical spirit when it served her needs. Besides, gossip flowed like sacramental wine at the parish socials that followed Sunday services. She suggested, without a hint of irony, that I ask Blaike to accompany me.

Gemma heartily endorsed the idea. "Come on, Marky. Suck it up. Besides, he knows the site. No sense spinning your wheels when you have a guide."

Once again, I folded. To my relief, Blaike accepted my suggestion without hesitation or demur. He also agreed to bring Fantasia and some liquid refreshment.

Tonight was Saturday evening, but unlike in my prior life in Chicago, it was not date night. I was obsessed with Poppet and the thousand little things that could spell success or doom for her. Comfort came at my easel as I fine-tuned the charcoal sketch. It was a somber scene. In fact, the finished product had a distinctly sinister air that wreaked of menace, not joy. The cloaked figure was of indeterminate age or gender, and the backdrop bore a marked resemblance to my alleyway. I realized with a start that the huddled form on the ground was a corpse. No wonder I had named it Desolation.

Chapter Nine

Sunday sunshine illuminated my studio, banishing the blues and making the world a much brighter place. Besides, things were looking up. I had an adventure and a quasi-date with a handsome man to look forward to. When Blaike, Fantasia, and I piled into his Land Rover and sped toward the waterfront, I felt a thrill of anticipation.

"I'm surprised you drive an SUV," I teased. "Very sensible, suburban dad of you. As I recall, you always favored sports cars."

He frowned and brushed off my comment. "Sports cars are for kids or guys on the make. I'm neither of those things. Besides, an SUV is practical. Been driving one for the past five years. More room for stuff and a seat for my little princess here too."

The docks were familiar to me, of course, but I couldn't visualize the plan to erect two hundred condos alongside upscale shops and eating spots. Fishing boats still plied their craft from those piers, and artist shanties, bait shops, souvenir stands, and down-market motels occupied almost every square foot of space. People relied upon those venues for their livelihoods, and many of us believed that they added to the charming fiction that Harbor Bay was merely a humble lakeside town and not a trendy resort on steroids.

"What happens to these places and people if that land deal is approved?" I knew the answer but wanted Blaike to verbalize it.

He shrugged. "Some will relocate farther down the coast but let's face it, making a marginal living is tough in Harbor Bay even now. We planned to preserve the fishing fleet and boat docks. They're money-makers, and tourists expect that. As for these other things—he pointed to a particularly seedy motel—they're expendable. Draw a bad crowd and don't contribute to the tax base. Really no loss."

I held Fantasia's leash and sat down on a bench facing the water. The waves had a hypnotic effect on me, and stroking the beautiful collie's thick coat helped me to temper my remarks. "If your survival depended on them, you might feel differently. Sounds like Paul had you convinced to vote his way."

Blaike tapped his foot. "There's a difference between scenic and seedy, Marky. To answer your question, I hadn't made up my mind yet. The council was evenly split. Two for, two against, one undecided, and one abstention. Before you ask, I was one of the undecided votes. The night of your party, Paul said someone had gone his way, and he had the votes to win. I never knew who that was. Plus, knowing Paul, it might have been false bravado intended to stampede me."

We bought fish tacos at a food truck and enjoyed them in companionable silence. Lake Michigan was famous for its white fish, a delectable treat I found impossible to resist. Fantasia got her share as well. She was far too well-bred to beg, but the look of hope in her lovely eyes forced me to share my feast with her.

"Softie," Blaike teased. "She knows how to play you." He abruptly changed the subject. "Listen, Marky. If something happens—if I get arrested or something—will you look out for her? Fantasia likes you, and she is such a good girl. I wouldn't want to leave her with strangers."

My throat felt dry. "Of course, I'd take care of her. That's the last thing you should worry about. But it won't come to that, will it? Gideon Hall has nothing against you. No motive."

Blaike laughed. "He thinks he does. Circumstantial evidence can still hang you."

I spent a moment processing what he'd said. "You quarreled with Paul. Big deal. That guy fought with just about everyone, or so I'm told. Lionel fought with him, at least he tried to. Seems like he's a more viable suspect than you."

"Maybe. I'm just tying up loose ends in case the worst happens." Blaike patted my hand. To my chagrin, it was more of a fraternal gesture than a romantic one. The story of my life—Marky Davis, everybody's pal, nobody's gal. To lighten the mood, I shared my encounter with Jonathon Crane, the marauding scribe.

"He's a real creep. I didn't like him one bit. And he seemed very interested in you."

Blaike exhaled. "That doesn't surprise me at all. The guy's a muckraker, not a journalist. A friend of my dad in Chicago tangled with him, and it wasn't pretty. None of the allegations were true, but this guy still lost a lot of business. Crane is a conspiracy theorist who doesn't let truth get in his way. He hints but stays just clear of libel. This podcast business is new, though. Leave it to Crane to dredge up something salacious."

As we disposed of our trash and ambled toward his car, I asked one more question. "With Paul dead, where does that leave the project?"

Blaike's smile said it all. "Dead in the water, just like Paul."

* * *

Gemma's Sunday was as productive as mine. She'd attended an author event at *Novel Approach* and managed to chat up Benny Soto in the bargain. From her description, the junior deputy had been putty in her hands. Unrequited love or lust led Benny to spill secrets that no civilian had access to.

"Benny says they've got the motive for Paul's murder. Only problem was he wouldn't tell me what it was. Not at first." She gave me a superior smirk. "After I worked on him a bit, he finally came clean. Course, it cost me a dinner date."

"Skip the chatter and cut to the chase. What motive?"

Gemma cleared her throat. Two seasons of community theater had turned her into a drama queen who tried to milk every scene. "Blackmail! I guess that was Paul's specialty. He'd dig up dirt and use it to his advantage no matter what the cost." She stamped her foot. "That dude was pure evil."

My mind raced as I considered the possibilities. Tilda, Zach, Lionel, Philippa, and Blaike. Honesty forced me to add Gemma to that list as well.

Did they all have secrets that could injure their reputations or businesses? The more important question was, would they kill to save themselves? Survival of the fittest and all that. The waterfront project meant money—big money. If Paul was indebted to unsavory types, it meant saving his life.

Tilda looked like she could resort to violence if the occasion demanded it, but she supported the project. I still believed, despite the existence of her alleged memoir, that Paul stumped up the cash to support her lifestyle. Maybe they were partners who had a falling out. Given her flamboyance, it was hard to believe there was any material left in her personal life with blackmail potential. Besides, sordid details would only enhance sales if she published the book.

If Mayor Zach and Lionel opposed the project, Paul had to turn either Philippa or Blaike his way. Despite my dislike for her, I doubted that Philippa harbored any deep secrets unless she had the shriveled corpse of a wayward student secreted in her basement. She was a woman of principle, known for her unshakable integrity. That made her dull and tedious but unlikely to murder.

"Did he mention Blaike at all?"

"Nope. But his mom had plenty to say about Paul Prentis. You know how quiet Mrs. Soto usually is. Wow! Mention Paul's name, and she went berserk. Didn't think she even knew some of those words!"

"Maybe she's taking a cue from Norman Mailer, or Erica Jong. After all, she spends her life in a bookstore."

Gemma's puzzled look reminded me that reading had never been one of her strong suits. She had plenty of practical intelligence, though, and keen instincts.

"Oops. I almost forgot." Gemma reached into her purse and scooped out a business card. "You'll never guess who showed up today?"

"I'm too tired to guess. Indulge me." I leaned back in my chair and closed my eyes.

"That giraffe guy. You know. The reporter. Crane."

That woke me up in a hurry. "Tell me everything. Blaike says the guy's nothing but trouble."

According to Gemma, Crane had said very little but listened a lot. Comments made in an unguarded moment were grist for the podcaster's mill. For all we knew, he might have recorded every word, including those vituperative comments from Mrs. Soto.

"He's kind of cute in a cartoon way," Gemma said.

"Ugh!" I urged my friend to think twice before getting entangled with him. Gemma had a good heart and could easily be hurt by a big city huckster.

"Pickings are pretty slim around here, Marky. We don't all have an ex-football hero mooning over us. Besides, things didn't end well for Crane. Something he said got Josephine riled up, and she threatened him with a broom." She snickered. "That guy made tracks so fast you could see his dust."

If only Gemma knew. My feelings for Blaike were confused and contradictory. In high school, he was every girl's dream, a prototype hero. That was a long time ago, and the Blaike I saw now seemed feckless, not a figure of romance.

"Has Blaike's dad been around much lately?" I asked.

"Nah. Since his wife passed, Mr. Harrington doesn't show up for stuff like he used to. He still looks pretty good for an old guy, though. I wanted my mom to put the moves on him, but she said he had other interests, whatever that means."

Gemma described him as elderly, but Mitchell Harrington was sixty at most. Not quite ready for the rubbish heap. Come to think of it, he might be a good prospect for Aunt Violet.

We'd agreed to join her at my parents' home for what Violet called an old French country dinner. I wasn't sure what that entailed, but any meal my aunt produced was bound to be good. Besides, knowing her, she might have snagged some useful information at the church service.

Tantalizing aromas wafted out from my mother's kitchen as Violet greeted us. She wore a pristine gold and scarlet apron festooned with roosters. A bandanna covered her hair. On most women, this would have suggested a peasant look, but on Violet, it was the height of chic. After we settled in the dining room with a glass of wine, I begged for any crumbs of information.

"Of course," Violet said, "But first, our menu. Vegetable soup, crusty bread, sole meunière, and for dessert, fresh baked meringues."

"Yum!" Gemma said. "How do you ever keep your figure?"

"The French have a secret that's worth emulating. They indulge but don't gorge themselves."

I thought back to meals I'd consumed in French restaurants, and of course, my aunt was right. Portion sizes were adequate but by no means generous, and the breadbasket was seldom refilled unless the customer requested it. There was no need for the dreaded "doggy bag" when dining à la Françoise.

We dove into our dinner with gusto, and it exceeded all expectations. As we enjoyed dessert, Violet described her morning with the Congregationalists. She was made welcome and quickly renewed acquaintanceship with those from her past. At the fellowship gathering, any number of congregants were eager to discuss the murder and air their pet theories about suspects. Paul was not a favorite, and more than a few suggested that he got what he deserved. "You reap what you sow" was a constant refrain. But Blaike—he was well-liked. If there was a jury trial, he would fare well in Harbor Bay.

"What about that waterfront project?" I asked. "Seems like the council was split on approving it."

"Hmm. Philippa Gordon goes to that church. Kind of a pillar of the institution. Not surprising I suppose. She heads their teen support group that's so popular. I don't recall the name. Something dreadful and Churchy I presume."

That didn't surprise me one bit. Philippa was the bossy type that volunteer organizations relied on. Lord help the teens who fell into her clutches.

"Anyway," Violet said, "Opinion was split on that development deal. Lots of chatter about that. Typical arguments. You know, preserving the essential character of Harbor Bay versus the need for commerce and jobs." Violet paused. "And there was talk that someone had bought up a lot of that rundown real estate on the waterfront. Probably Prentis properties, I suppose, although no one seemed to know for sure. I was surprised at the criticism of Zach Thanos. He was always such a beloved figure around here."

Mayor Zach? He was the stereotype of the nice guy. Always had been since I was a tot. Gemma didn't seem surprised.

"You know how wishy-washy Zach can be, Marky. Always was. Normally that's okay. Nobody wants a firebrand in Harbor Bay, but the guy has no balls."

Since I'd never considered that part of the mayor's anatomy, I was stunned into silence. Mayor of a small town was largely an honorific post except for the occasional squabble. Controversy was foreign to Zach's nature, and a bully like Paul Prentis could easily cow him. Then there was that rumor about his Honor's alleged gambling problems.

"I don't suppose the ladies had any opinions about Kim Stevens?" I was beginning to question whether there was any religious element to that Sunday gathering. Clearly, charity wasn't high on their agenda.

Violet read my mind. "Don't be too hard on them, Marky. That congregation does lots of good in the community. But to answer your question, Kim's name didn't come up. Thankfully neither did Tilda's. That might have stretched their capacity for good works to the breaking point."

I kept my thoughts about Blaike to myself. After all, he was a businessman, not a social activist. Harbor Bay needed visionaries as much as it needed traditionalists. I counted myself firmly in the middle of that debate. Surely preserving the past while forging toward the future was an attainable goal. I had no solutions to offer, only reservations about drastic change. I mulled over those thoughts later while preparing for bed. This time no late-night visits or phone calls disturbed my rest. More's the pity.

Chapter Ten

A new customer arrived at Poppet the next morning. Josephine Soto, mother of Benny, edged warily into the shop as if she feared for her life. She was a tall, sturdily built woman with pronounced features, a wealth of glossy black hair, and fierce dark eyes.

"I don't hold much with paint," she said, "but a woman alone must keep with the times. Facing the public isn't easy."

According to Gemma, Mr. Soto had vanished in the arms of a British tourist that past summer. A bitter divorce and recriminations subsequently followed.

"What did you have in mind?" I asked.

She looked around, confounded by the vast array of products on our shelves. Her one concession to beauty was a slash of red lipstick and a heavy hand with black brow pencil. The look aged her by about ten years.

"Why don't you describe your daily routine," I said. "Then we can go from there."

Mrs. Soto cruised down the aisles, selecting and discarding various samples until she came to a sudden halt. "That's what they found on him, isn't it?" She pointed to one of the violet extension cords that anchored a display. I'd intended to replace all of them, but in the confusion, it had slipped my mind.

I nodded but said nothing.

"My boy said it was around his neck. Like a bow tie." There was no sorrow in her words. In fact, the idea seemed to please her. "He was an awful man. Vile. Tried to bully me into breaking my lease. Said they wanted a different image for Harbor Bay. Upscale, he called it. Like I was something to be ashamed of."

"That must have hurt you," I said. "He was my landlord, but I didn't know him well."

Josephine folded her arms and grimaced. "I handled it. Benny wanted to fight him, but I said no. The good Lord has ways of dealing with evildoers."

"Surely you don't think…". Before I finished that ill-advised comment, Gemma appeared. She greeted Josephine and immediately took charge of her cosmetic quest. By the time she left Poppet, Mrs. Soto was equipped with an arsenal of products designed to moisturize her skin and lighten her appearance. Gemma conducted a brief tutorial, and the results spoke for themselves.

"What was that all about?" I asked. "Mrs. Soto can be rather intimidating. No wonder Benny is a touch weird."

Gemma waved me off. "Ah, she's okay. Not much of a sense of humor, but she's had a tough life." A mischievous grin lit her face. "I asked her who she suspected. For the murder, you know."

"And?"

"Her money is on Tilda Egan. She even used that British phrase you see in those old Christie books. You know, "no better than she should be.""

I wondered if Benny and Gideon Hall shared that suspicion or if it was based on Tilda's being firmly in the hussy category. "You did a nice job with her," I said. "Took at least ten years off her look. She's actually rather attractive in a dominatrix way."

Gemma took a bow and handed me a sealed envelope. It bore no stamp but was clearly addressed to me. "This came in with today's mail. Maybe it's a note from an admirer."

Highly unlikely.

Fantasia had given me more affection than any human since my return to Harbor Bay. I was more likely to draw a stalker in my hometown than an admirer. When I ripped open the envelope, I got a nasty shock. Someone had used cutouts from several newspapers and fashioned a threatening message. "Mind your own business, or you'll be next." It was succinct, if not very imaginative, and reminded me of something from another century.

"Hey. What's wrong?" Gemma rushed to my side and grabbed the message. "Unbelievable! Must be from the murderer. I'll call the cops right away!"

"Hold on. Let's think this through." The letter was most likely a prank by some local kid. Gideon Hall would think I was just some hysterical woman, or worse still, someone seeking publicity."

We argued back and forth until Aunt Violet joined us and ended the debate. "I insist that you contact Gideon," she said. "Someone targeted Prentis and chose your business to do it." The look on her face was implacable. I'd seen that same expression many times on my mother's face. No appeal to logic or common sense would sway her.

"No arguments, Marky. Call him now, or I will."

* * *

Gideon Hall arrived right away. His haste was probably attributable more to Violet's presence rather than a pressing concern for my welfare. As usual, his uniform was perfectly pressed, and his boots shined to a luster. Spit and polish was the expression. He moved gracefully for such a big man and appeared to be perfectly at ease in the midst of feminine frippery. After I handed him the letter, along with the crumpled envelope, he scrutinized both items.

"You don't seem worried, Ms. Davis. How come?"

I couldn't explain it. Despite the menacing words, the entire incident seemed contrived. Unreal. Sort of like amateur hour run amuck. The flinty look in Gideon Hall's eyes told me that he was troubled.

"I'm no detective. Never claimed to be."

"Glad to hear that. Murder is no place for amateurs, Marky. They tend to get hurt." He waved his arm in the air. "Looks like you have plenty here to keep you occupied." He pointed to the array of hair styling tools on the side aisle. "Still using that violet extension cord, I see." He frowned. "Why keep a reminder like that around? Customers can't miss it."

He was right, of course. Mrs. Soto had spotted it right away, and others were bound to. Perhaps they'd consider it some sort of bizarre souvenir, like the trophies kept by serial killers.

Aunt Violet interceded. "You can't blame us for being curious, Gideon. After all, Paul was our landlord, and he was found outside our store. Do you have any suspects yet?"

I detected a softening in his expression as he faced my aunt. "Suspects are plentiful, Violet. Prentis wasn't the most popular man in town, and old grudges die hard. But I need proof. Evidence. And frankly, that's in short supply." He tipped his hat as he left Poppet, giving us a final admonition. "Ladies, be careful. And remember what I said. Leave this to the professionals."

To resort to a cliché, Gideon's warning left me bloodied but unbowed. By sending that absurd note, someone had made the murder personal, and that angered me. I'm no weak vessel cowering under the bedclothes. On the other hand, my knowledge of self-defense was more theoretical than practical. I preferred to avoid physical confrontation if I could.

"Got a gun, Marky?" Gemma's question made me jump. "I can get you one and show you how to use it. My mom taught me everything about them." That was a shocker. I knew she was a sharpshooter but still couldn't envision petite Mandy Watts packing heat!

"Certainly not!" I'd survived the Windy City by carrying pepper spray and a confident attitude. Surely sleepy Harbor Bay would be less of a challenge. Besides, my weapon of choice, if I had one, was my rapier-sharp wit backed up by a dagger or perhaps a valiant dog. Fantasia immediately sprang to mind. She was gentle, but collies, like most herding dogs, had strong protective instincts. Would Blaike let me borrow her if I asked, or would he think it was a sympathy ploy on my part and come running to the rescue? Come to think of it, I'd always pictured Blaike as a sort of knight errant capable of slaying dragons. Based on his puny efforts to vindicate himself, it now seemed more likely that I might have to rescue him.

Violet sat on a stool and adjusted her makeup. "I own a gun, but I left it in Paris. A lovely little pearl-handled number. Small but mighty. Discreet, but it does the job." She swiveled around to face me. "Guns are a big responsibility.

If you don't feel comfortable, or won't use it, don't bother. Gideon will probably handle the paperwork if you want one, Marky, but I suggest you wait." She held up the latest edition of the *Harbor Bay Gazette*. "I see that there's a meeting of the town council this evening. Might be interesting. According to the agenda, they plan a final vote on that waterfront project."

"Can outsiders attend?" I was fuzzy on the workings of town government, especially when a contentious issue like this arose.

"OF course. Michigan open meeting laws apply. You know the drill. After all, we're citizens, or at least the two of you are. How about it?"

Gemma jumped at the idea, and after some hesitation, I agreed. Every one of my party guests and murder suspects would probably be present. It was the ideal opportunity to face them down and show that I was unafraid. On the other hand, my presence might well embolden the murderer to strike again—with me as his target.

Chapter Eleven

I decided to freshen up before the meeting. Nothing fancy, just a twin set in a particularly flattering cherry shade topping a pencil skirt. My hair badly needed a trim, so I tamed it in a French braid. I felt very grown up as befits a prominent business owner, or so I hoped. Gemma wore her goth attire, complete with huge gold hoops and Vamp nail varnish. I would have looked like a freak, but on her, it worked. Be true to yourself was her code, and she lived it every day. My aunt chose a camel-hued coat dress with matching court shoes and hose. Very sedate but stylish as always. I'd recently glimpsed a similar look on the pages of *British Vogue*. Apparently, the Royals chose court shoes over the more sensuous stilettos favored by celebrities.

We arrived at the City Hall auditorium well before the meeting, but I was surprised to find the viewing gallery almost full. Was it attributable to the topics du jour or a lack of activity in Harbor Bay? Boredom can incline one to all manner of odd pursuits.

The front row was filled with local notables, including Chief Hall, his deputy, and the imposing form of Josephine Soto. The cosmetic makeover improved her outward look, but the grim set of her lips told me that she was still seething inside. No need to ask if she had or would use a weapon. That woman was locked and loaded. With the demise of Paul Prentis, however, I was uncertain who her target was. Could she be the anonymous letter writer? I put a mental tick mark next to Mrs. Soto's name. A worthy adversary for sure and one who could pulverize me like a ripe melon.

Right before seven, Kim Stevens slipped into an aisle seat. An oversized

Burberry cloaked her, and her lovely face looked strained and troubled. I noticed that she had destroyed her manicure by picking at the polish and that her cheeks could have used a spot of blush. For some reason, that woman was a bundle of nerves. Behind her, obscured by an imposing pillar, a most unwelcome guest sat hunkered down. Despite his efforts to conceal himself, his size made it impossible for Jonathon Crane to hide. No doubt his phone would record every word and nuance of the evening proceedings. The citizens of Harbor Bay and their foibles would serve as fodder for the amusement of Crane's podcast audience.

Mayor Zach Thanos called the meeting to order and asked that we stand for the pledge of allegiance. I noted that Tilda Egan mouthed the words without much enthusiasm but that Philippa Gordon's voice rang out loud and clear. I recalled from days at the high school assembly that Principal Gordon was a strong advocate of patriotism. Some things never change. Tilda's eyes scanned the entire audience as the meeting convened. Did I detect a note of challenge when she fastened on me? Her expertly applied eye shadow gave her a winged look, much like a predatory hawk. If I were painting her, I would portray her that way in contrast to Kim Stevens, who would be a sparrow or a fledgling.

The rest of the council sat motionless on the stage, giving me plenty of time to observe them. Lionel Stevens, garbed in shades of grey, had that morose look I had come to recognize. It was debatable whether or not that man ever smiled. Gemma swore she had seen him grin one time, although no other witnesses could corroborate the event. Honestly, with a husband that grim, it was little wonder that Kim looked perpetually depressed. I'd never thought much about marriage, but the Stevens were certainly no endorsement for the sanctity of that state.

Mayor Zach, on the other hand, had adored his late wife, Helen. Everybody knew that. She had run his dental practice, and I recalled the camaraderie and quiet affection they had shared. Without her, he seemed lost and more than a little sad. Perhaps he was one of that species that mated for life and floundered without his partner.

On the far end of the dais sat Blaike. His face was an expressionless mask, his features etched in stone. He nodded our way when we arrived but otherwise sat statue still.

When Mayor Zach requested a moment of silence in tribute to former Councilman Prentis, Josephine Soto folded her arms and loudly snorted. Benny Soto put an arm around his mother to either comfort or restrain her. Respect was in short supply when it came to Paul Prentis, and affection was nonexistent. Although the audience complied, they did so with very little enthusiasm.

The first agenda items were mundane. Lionel droned on about tax issues, and Philippa discussed the upcoming tourist season. The council entertained a few desultory comments from the audience, but it was obvious that the evening's main event was the waterfront project. I noticed that the crowd included several fishermen, proprietors of the bait shops, and a trio of eccentrics representing the artists' colony. Zach described the proposal and invited a spokesman from Prentis Properties to address the group. He was a stranger to me, a small, rather squat individual in a beautifully tailored three-piece suit that tried mightily to camouflage his bulges. I fervently hoped that he wore Kevlar under that garment because some of the locals were itching for a fight.

At first, everyone listened attentively to him, aided by a very professional powerpoint presentation that stressed the commercial benefits of development to Harbor Bay. Increased tax base, influx of upscale customers for merchants—these wonders were cited as if the Holy Grail had at last been found. When public comments were encouraged, all hell broke loose. Members of the fishing alliance loudly questioned the impact on their livelihoods. Their supporters were both vocal and raucous, causing Mayor Zach to flail helplessly, pounding his gavel.

They were followed by a group of environmental activists who questioned the impact on Harbor Bay's natural resources. Although Tilda distributed a study commissioned by the Council, it was immediately denounced. In fact, the group's leader leapt to his feet and tore the document in two. All in all, the proceedings provided a lovely spot of theater that rivaled that of Chicago's famed Second City.

When Philippa urged Zach to table the proposal for further consideration, he jumped at the idea and hastily adjourned the meeting. Would the outcome have changed if Paul Prentis had been present? He was a domineering personality, a force of nature who was not above using intimidation or threats to win the day. Had his killer opposed the project or settled a personal score with Paul? Either way, the fate of the waterfront site was a casualty of Paul's death.

As the crowd exited, Jonathon Crane wedged himself between the podium and the speakers' table and thrust a microphone at the mayor. "Any comment, your honor? Is the waterfront project officially dead? You know about death, don't you?" As Zach sputtered helplessly, Crane continued his barrage. "How did the Prentis murder affect the council? I understand he had the votes for approval. Were you one of the supporters?"

Before Zach became apoplectic, the strong arm of Gideon Hall intervened. "Enough already, Mr. Crane. We won't tolerate harassment of public officials, even by the fourth estate." Soto grabbed Crane's elbow and escorted him rather forcefully out the door, ignoring the scribe's rant about first amendment freedoms and vows to exhaust his legal remedies. Jonathon Crane was a plague on humanity or at least a pestilence inflicted on peaceful Harbor Bay. I wondered if he were my anonymous letter writer, although his motive was unclear. Perhaps he did anything to stir the pot.

"What a creep!" Gemma said. "Someone should shut him down."

"Although you must admit he did enliven the proceedings." Violet was amused by the tempest in our very small teapot. "I wonder what his game really is. Perhaps I should beard the lion in his den. Let him interview me. It might be very instructive."

Podcasts only attracted an audience when murder or mayhem was involved. A local squabble about construction would elicit no more than a massive yawn. I suspected that Mr. Jonathon Crain fancied himself a detective who would confound the local yokels and solve Paul's murder. Gideon Hall would certainly have another view about that.

Violet suggested that we stop for a drink at our local bistro. "I understand that the council tends to patronize that spot. Probably need some reinforcement after that session."

* * *

As usual, she was right. We entered Bistro Bis just in time to capture the last available table. The spot adjoining ours was shielded from view and had a "reserved" sign prominently displayed. Not long after our drinks arrived, so did the members of the town council. I've heard that you can tell a good deal about a person by his drink preferences. In this instance, it proved to be true. The ladies went first. Philippa opted for Perrier, Kim ordered a cosmopolitan, but Tilda chose hard liquor—Scotch straight up. Their male counterparts settled for draft beer.

Zach guzzled his drink as if it were salvation itself. I'd always had a soft spot for the old dentist and knew that he eschewed controversy whenever possible. True to type, Lionel cautiously sipped his brew while Blaike merely stared at his. They spoke in hushed tones that were difficult to overhear, but the name Jonathon Crane figured prominently in their discussion. I fully expected that Crane would appear at the bar, playing his role of specter at the feast, but it was not to be. Violet was curious about the environmental impact study that Tilda had brandished, particularly who the author was.

"Not a problem," Gemma said. "My Mom's best friend is the mayor's secretary. We'll get it first thing tomorrow."

Typical Harbor Bay. Connections meant everything. Come to think of it, Chicago operated on a similar principle. Aldermen and other politicians-built alliances and used them whenever necessary. Influence greased the engine of progress or whatever passed for it.

* * *

I was wary when I entered my loft that night. The threatening note had spooked me more than I was willing to admit. I didn't check under the bed, but I did ensure that all the locks were fastened and the alarm set. Despite those precautions, my sleep was troubled. Every hour on the hour I awakened and stared at my alarm clock.

The absence of REM sleep left me groggy and out of sorts the next morning as I stumbled out of bed and fired up the espresso machine. When Gemma appeared full of vitality and cheer, it was a sharp rebuke to my own sorry state. Her day was filled with a full schedule of nail and massage appointments, including an early session with Kim Stevens.

"Wonder what Kim thinks about last night?" Gemma said. "Lionel probably clammed up. That man has the personality of a mollusk, anyway."

Her description was so accurate that it cured me of my bad temper. I slapped Gemma on the back, thanked her for putting things in perspective, and hustled off to the Grand Traverse Conference center to conduct a seminar on skin care. When the session concluded, I felt rather proud of myself. The audience stayed engaged and asked several intelligent questions about starting and maintaining a healthy routine. They were educators from around the state who valued their time and their pocketbooks. Samples and coupons for discounted services were eagerly gobbled up, and Poppet's customer base was enhanced by what I hoped would be loyal shoppers.

I was famished by the time I returned to Harbor Bay. My cupboard was bare so a stop at the local Boulanger was a necessity. Hang the calories. I yearned for the comfort of tomato soup and crusty baguettes. As I hunched over my meal, savoring each delicious morsel, and contemplating dessert, a lanky form loomed over me, pulled up a chair and plopped down.

"Mind if I join you?" Jonathon Crane asked, wrapping his long limbs around the chair legs.

I saw no need to indulge this uninvited cipher. "Frankly, I do. I'm almost finished, and I'd like to eat my lunch in peace. Alone."

A lock of ginger hair fell over his eyes, heightening his resemblance to a giraffe. Crane flashed what he no doubt supposed to be an ingratiating grin. "Big blowup last night. What'd you think of it?"

I managed a quizzical look that could freeze fire. They hadn't dubbed me the ice queen in high school for nothing. "Whatever do you mean?"

"Ah, come on now, Matty. I saw you there with your aunt."

"First of all, my name is Marketta. Marky, not Matty. Get it? Secondly, I have nothing to say to you now or ever." I rose, gathering up my plate and utensils.

Crane wasn't bothered one bit by my rebuke. No doubt, he was quite accustomed to rejection. "No need to get testy. Besides, I think you'll have plenty to say when you hear this. Bet you didn't know that your boyfriend and Paul Prentis were courting the same woman." He sneered. "Courting is such a refined term, isn't it? Love triangle—a great motive for murder, wouldn't you say? I wonder what the chief thinks about it?" He grabbed my arm and squeezed.

At first, I was too shaken to react. Blaike and Paul? The woman in question could only be one. *Tilda Egan.* I recovered quickly, elbowed him in the side and gave Crane my insect larvae stare. "I have no idea what you're talking about and could not care less. Leave me alone if you value your vital parts."

He wasn't deterred at all. In fact, Jonathon Crane laughed at me. A deep belly laugh that echoed throughout the restaurant. He couldn't resist one parting shot. "Your partner had some history with Paul Prentis. Pretty serious stuff. Men have been killed for less. Might have driven her to desperate measures."

My heart sank, but I summoned my remaining shreds of dignity and left the restaurant. His taunt about Gemma made my head spin and my stomach roil. I was still fuming when I reached Poppet. "Of all the nerve. That man is insufferable."

Violet swiveled her stool my way and laughed merrily. "They all are dear. Deal with it. By the way, who's the insufferable boor in question?"

I described the reporter's conduct, citing chapter and verse. For some reason, I kept his remarks about Gemma to myself. Was it fear, discretion, or loyalty that made me shield Gemma, even from Aunt Violet? I switched subjects and mentioned the supposed romantic rivalry between Blaike and Paul. Violet's eyebrows rose.

"Interesting. Very interesting. Too bad you let him distract you. Details might have proved helpful. But no matter. Our Mr. Crane will be only too glad for a sympathetic ear like mine. I'm meeting him tonight for cocktails." She checked her wristwatch. It was some impossibly pricey number with diamonds. "Whoops! I must dash. Just enough time to freshen up before my appointment." Violet winked. "Or should I say assignation?"

My aunt enjoyed teasing me, although she had once stated that French women were untroubled by age and chose suitors who were both younger and older than they were. When Gemma finished with her final customer and locked the front door, I was still puzzling over that cryptic remark.

"Hot news, Marky. We've got to talk." I'd seldom seen my friend so frazzled. Gemma paced about the room, muttering to herself.

"Kim Stevens was my first client today."

I nodded, not certain where the conversation was going. "So?"

"She wanted a full Swedish, you know, concentrating on her back and shoulders." Gemma hesitated. "She was full of bruises, Marky. Deep tissue ones. Kim made some feeble excuse about falling, but I think she was lying. I think Lionel beats her."

"Lionel? That pillar of rectitude? Get serious. He's twice her age and dry as dust."

Gemma pressed her lips together. "That explains her behavior, though. Wounded bird look. Face it. Lionel's got the bucks."

"She could leave him."

Gemma snorted. "And do what? Not much demand in upper Michigan for a thirty-something ex-model. You just don't get it, Marky. Things came easy for you. You're educated. Your family has bucks."

For the first time ever, I detected a note of envy in Gemma's voice. Before I responded, Mandy suddenly spoke up. She had slipped into the store unnoticed while we were having our little spat.

"Kim was a different person before the tragedy. Lionel too. They were considered a fun couple believes it or not. I guess you can't really blame them. That kind of shock would change anyone."

Since I had absolutely no idea what the tragedy was, I could only utter something intelligent like, "Huh?"

Mandy bowed her head. "Oops. Forgot you've been out of the loop for a while, hon." She lowered her voice. "Kim and Lionel lost their only child about five years ago."

"Oh no!" I felt guilty for all the mean things I'd said about Lionel. "What happened?"

Mandy's voice grew husky as she told the story. "Their son Patrick was a great kid. Handsome and very smart."

Gemma nodded. "I'll say. He looked exactly like Kim."

"He was saving his money for a car. Doing a paper route on his bike when someone ran him down. Didn't even stop." She looked away. "Patrick died on the spot, and they never caught the driver. Probably a drunk, they think."

No wonder the Stevens marriage was so unhappy. I'd heard that very few couples survived that kind of trauma. Most ended up in the divorce court.

"There's more," Mandy said. "Patrick had asked his dad for a car, but Lionel insisted that he earn the cash himself. I don't think Kim ever forgave him or that he ever forgave himself."

Sounded to me like Lionel Stevens held a gut load of guilt and took it out on Kim. Was that what Paul Prentis held over him? Unlikely. Most everyone in Harbor Bay, except me, knew the sad story. They might not be aware of the domestic violence angle, though, and a prominent attorney could ill afford that kind of reputation. Learning the inner workings of this town reminded me of peeling an onion. Always another layer to uncover. Suppose Lionel Stevens had discovered the identity of the hit-and-run driver. Paul Prentis was known to drink heavily and drive recklessly. If he was responsible for Patrick Stevens' death, his family would have moved heaven and earth to conceal his crime. The bereaved parents might have acted to avenge their son.

Once again, I had avoided quizzing Gemma about her relationship with Paul.

You're a coward, Marketta Davis. Face it!

Couldn't do it with Mandy there, I told myself, but that was basically an excuse. I was avoiding the issue, afraid of finding out something I'd regret. Gideon Hall was probably plugged into all the local scandals, and if he found out the truth, both Gemma and I were in trouble.

I yearned to hear about Violet's dalliance with the dreadful Jonathon Crain, but that would have to wait until the next day. To prepare for our discussion,

I forced myself to binge-watch five episodes of Craig's podcasts. As expected, they were built on the flimsiest of foundations and fortified with innuendo and outright falsehoods. He was cagey enough to cloak himself in the first amendment by posing his more outrageous charges as questions or quotes from unnamed reliable sources. After watching those charades, I cleansed myself in a soothing bubble bath.

Chapter Twelve

The birth of Poppet was the featured article in what passed for the business section of the *Harbor Bay Gazette.* I was surprised and a bit flustered to see my face alongside Aunt Violet's, grinning widely and pointing to the opening banner. The reporter mentioned Gemma and Mandy and quoted Mayor Zach on the superb quality of our services. Only the concluding paragraph struck a nerve. It referenced the murder of Paul Prentis, linking his death in the alley to our opening night party and the lethal violet extension cord.

"Don't focus on the negative, Poppet. All the public will recall is this big fat plug by our local rag." Violet sipped her latte and flashed a Cheshire Cat grin. "I suppose you're curious about my rendezvous with young Mr. Cain?"

I managed a yawn. "I suppose." Deception had never been my strong suit, and I didn't deceive my dear aunt for even a second. After finishing her drink, she finally took pity on me. "Okay. It was quite illuminating. Your Mr. Crane can be quite the charmer."

My face expressed disbelief and the utter disdain I felt for that cretinous scribe. Violet chuckled and put me out of my misery. "He seems quite focused on Blaike. Almost as if it's something personal. Furthermore, I think someone with deep pockets is bankrolling him."

That didn't surprise me. Someone had a keen interest in our little hamlet and was willing to stump up plenty of cash to defray Crane's expenses. After watching five of his investigative podcasts, I was more convinced than ever that he was a vicious thug willing to defame anyone to achieve his own ends.

Violet's experiences had left her with few illusions about her fellow men and women. Until recently, I had been naïve, inclined to believe the best about almost everyone. The crumpled corpse of Paul Prentis was a major reality check that changed things for me. I had now seen the seamy side of life up close and personal. When Violet observed that Crane might be a blackmailer, I was not surprised. Who knew what secrets he had unearthed about his potential victims?

"It wasn't anything he said directly. More like what he hinted around about." She laughed. "Believe it or not, he even dangled a few tidbits about me in the air and left them hanging."

"You?"

"Too bad my life is an open book. I told him that I was firmly in the "publish and be damned" camp. After all, I'm an artist and live in Paris. People expect a certain degree of unorthodox behavior. It titillates them. Enhances the image."

I'd never considered my aunt's personal life before, and frankly, I saw no need to do so now. Everyone deserved a zone of privacy. But Crane was playing a very dangerous game. Many so-called respectable people hoarded their secrets and would do almost anything, including murder, to safeguard them. "In books and movies, blackmailers come to some very bad ends," I said.

Violet nodded. "Exactly what I told him." She fixed herself another latte and cleared her throat. "You should know this. He included Gemma in his litany of potential suspects. Nothing specific, but I'd swear that boy knows something. Something you should find out from Gemma before it goes public."

When I was a child, I buried my head in a pillow to avoid hearing uncomfortable things. *Gemma is no killer.* That was a mantra I repeated to myself. Still, it was time to confront her about the history she shared with Paul Prentis.

I planned to do some investigating of my own. Jonathon Crane wasn't the only one capable of unearthing secrets.

* * *

Before I could get to Gemma, Blaike phoned me that evening asking for a favor. He'd planned a trip to Chicago and needed help with Fantasia. "She's really no trouble," he said. "It's just that she's never been in a kennel, and I worry about her."

I was thrilled with the chance for company, especially after that threatening note. Besides, that gave me a chance to quiz him about Tilda and his relationship with Jonathon Crane. He arrived bearing a beautiful bouquet of orchids and a duffel bag filled with doggy paraphernalia. Fantasia stepped daintily over the threshold like the well-bred patrician that she was. "I really appreciate this," Blaike said. "My regular pet sitter canceled at the last minute."

He soon realized that his only problem might be getting Fantasia back from me. I loved all animals, especially dogs, and she was a splendid ambassador of her breed.

"Have a seat," I said, pointing to a leather wing chair. "We need to talk."

Blaike got that uncomfortable look common to men in awkward situations. "Sure."

It wasn't easy to confront him, but with both Gideon Hall and that so-called journalist nosing around, the time had come. I told him everything I knew about slimy Jonathon Crane and his podcasts. Blaike crossed his legs and sat immobile as I cited chapter and verse. When the name Tilda Egan came up, he frowned.

"Tilda? What about her? She's a client and kind of a friend. Nothing more. My dad handles her investments."

When I quoted Crane about the alleged ménage a trios, his reaction shocked me. Blaike laughed—he guffawed. "How naïve are you, Marky? That's the craziest thing I've ever heard! Crane's off his rocker. Absolutely nuts!"

Blood rushed to my face. I felt ashamed and abashed. Good thing I hadn't landed a post during the Inquisition, or Torquemada would have sent me packing in a flash. My prosecutorial skills were virtually nonexistent.

"Forget Crane for a moment," I said. "We need to find a viable suspect in Paul's murder."

He held his hands up in protest. "Whoa. Wait just a minute. There is no we involved here. My attorney is handling everything. You stay out of it." With that, Blaike leapt up and bolted for the door. "Crane better hope he doesn't run into me, or I'll break his damn neck. That guy is nothing but a rumor monger."

After Blaike left, I consoled myself by cuddling Fantasia. What was it with that guy? I hadn't planned to fend him off, but for heaven's sake, he could have shown some interest in me as a woman, not just a pet sitter. Maybe he already had someone. The sultry image of Tilda Egan appeared unbidden. No way could I compete with that femme fatale, and I wouldn't even try. Better to hone my detective skills and solve the murder. I slipped off to sleep, counting the ways I could do just that.

Chapter Thirteen

An early morning visit from the police seldom brings good news, particularly when it involves murder. I was jolted out of a sound sleep by a persistent pounding on the front door, accompanied by the stentorian shouts of Benny Soto. His actions goaded Fantasia into a cacophony of growls and menacing barks that probably alerted the entire block. I glanced at my watch and grabbed my robe, surprised to see it was barely six o'clock. What in the name of holy hell would prompt Soto to invade my space at that hour? I don't believe in cursing. It's the refuge of the intellectually bereft and vulgar. Nevertheless, I uttered several rude oaths as I hustled down the stairs and flung open Poppet's main door.

"Where is he?" Soto barked, puffing out his rather scrawny chest for effect and barging into my store. "I know he's here." He pointed at Fantasia. "That's his dog."

I was now fully awake and filled with righteous anger. Soto's boorish conduct ticked me off. "What's going on? What gives you the right to barge in here? I presume you have a search warrant unless they've suspended the bill of rights in Harbor Bay."

Benny looked abashed, as if I had not followed the police playbook. "Exigent circumstances, Ms. Davis. Stand aside."

"I will not." I held Fantasia's collar to restrain her from lunging at this minor minion of the law. "Tell me right now what's going on, or you'll have to leave. Be advised that I'm also filing an official complaint."

He pulled out his handcuffs and brandished them. "You'll be talking from a jail cell if you don't cooperate, and that mutt will be in the pound. Stand aside."

Fortunately for both of us, at that moment, Gideon Hall's cruiser pulled to the curb. He glanced at his deputy and waved him back. "No need for a fuss. Mind if we sit down and discuss this calmly, Marky? I sure could use some of that great coffee you brew." As Benny and I exchanged glares, I waved the chief in. "Can you please tell me what in the world's going on?"

"Murder, Marky," he said. "Jonathon Crane was strangled last night."

I gulped and eased into one of the French armchairs that lined our waiting area. I've never fainted in my life, but I came awfully close this time. "Murdered? That's impossible. My Aunt saw him just last night."

Benny, having recovered his courage, gave me his version of a manly scowl. It was cheap theatrics, worthy of a grade-C police drama. "Yeah. That's why we're here. Your boyfriend had a fight with the victim. Threatened him. Just like he did Paul Prentis. Both murdered. Coincidence? I wonder."

Gideon motioned. "Enough. Now Marky, we're looking for Blaike Harrington. Is he here?"

"Certainly not! I'm just taking care of his dog while he's in Chicago. Why suspect Blaike, anyway? Crane was a cretin who collected enemies everywhere. Watch those podcasts of his if you don't believe me."

Gideon looked momentarily nonplussed. "I haven't seen them yet, but I intend to." He glared at Benny. "Deputy. Why don't you go rustle up those podcasts and send them to my computer?" After Benny stalked out the door, Chief Hall turned my way. "Mr. Crane left me a message last night. Must have been shortly before his death. He said he'd solved the murder—both, actually. Not exactly sure what he meant about that. Asked to meet me today. The guy sounded real cocky. Said the killer would surprise me and everyone else in Harbor Bay." The lawman grimaced. "Course, he never made it. A guy walking his dog found him in the alley behind the community center." He leaned toward me. "And Marky, one of those purple cords was around his neck."

I gasped. How could I ignore yet another link to Poppet? Fortunately, Gideon's manner was kindly, not accusatory, like his minion's. When I recovered my wits, I asked. "Why link this to Blaike? Do you have any witnesses?"

He shook his head. "Not to the murder per se, but Tilda Egan heard them mix it up right before then."

I recalled Blaike's rage and his words about taking care of Crane. He had threatened to break Crane's neck. Better to keep that thought to myself for the time being.

"Listen carefully," Gideon said. "Keep out of this. You were warned off by that note. Take it seriously. This killer won't hesitate if you provoke him."

"Him? You think it's a man?"

"Yeah. Crane was a big guy. Not many women could handle that."

His reasoning was sound, if somewhat sexist. Paul Prentis was a muscular former athlete known as a brawler. Crane was bony but tall. Neither man would be wary of a woman, and that would give any female a tactical advantage. I considered the women in my orbit. Years of tennis and other sports had made Philippa wiry and strong. Kim excelled in martial arts, and her addiction to yoga made her very flexible. Tilda seemed more likely to seduce than strangle, but I wouldn't rule her out. She wouldn't hesitate to eliminate any person or thing that posed a threat to her. Nor did I exclude Mandy, Gemma, or that formidable figure Josephine Soto. The list of possible suspects grew exponentially. Aunt Violet got a pass. I knew she would avoid physical violence or, at the very least, use a more refined method of murder.

"He had drinks with my aunt last night," I said. "Maybe he dropped some clues. She can be very persuasive."

Gideon chuckled. "Yep. Violet could worm information out of almost any man and leave him smiling. I'll call her today." He stooped over and ruffled Fantasia's thick coat. "Good thing you've got this little lady to watch your back. I think she scared Benny out of his socks when she charged at him." He held out his hand. "No more playing detective. Promise me?"

I agreed, although my heart wasn't in it. If Jonathon Crane had discovered the murderer, how hard could it be? He was no Sherlock Holmes or Poirot. If anything, Crane was a bumbling Inspector Clouseau more likely to stumble upon the answer than to deduce it.

Once I was alone, I sat at my easel for some art therapy. I believe that an artist may see into a subject's psyche, either consciously or unconsciously, and glean insights into his personality. My first choice was easy. Tilda Egan. Her outsized personality and aura dictated sketching stark lines and bold strokes. The result was a dark and unsettling glimpse of our town's resident author.

When Gemma looked it over, she grimaced. "Ugh! Not something I'd want in my boudoir, Marky. It'd give me nightmares."

I admit I got defensive and a tad uppity. How dare Gemma impugn my work. "Well, that's how I see Tilda. It's my artistic vision."

"Hmm. Do I detect some jealousy in that? All this talk about Blaike and Tilda. Not that I believe it for even one minute...."

I launched into an impassioned denial. Blaike was a free agent, and so was I. There was nothing romantic between us, and never would be. Besides. If he preferred a much older woman who was known as the town strumpet, so be it.

"Strumpet!" Gemma gave a deep belly laugh. "You sound like someone's grandma. Forget about Blaike and ask yourself. Why would she kill two men? Kind of out there, isn't it? I don't see Tilda as a skilled assassin any more than a great writer. Frankly, she's not that smart."

Motive. I had to admit that Gemma made a good point. What motive would Tilda possibly have? Her memoir—if it existed—would make her the target, not the assailant. I was sure she had all manner of sordid things to disclose, some of which might be fodder for the vice squad. In contrast, my dull and relatively blameless love life was scarcely even PG and would bore a middle school audience. Perhaps there was something more. Some indiscretion related to that other crowd pleaser...money.

Tilda had supported the waterfront project. According to Prentis, he had convinced at least one other council member to switch sides. Blaike, Zach, Lionel, and Philippa were the opposing forces. Had one of them been coerced or cooped into changing? Moreover, what had Jonathon Crane unearthed? He'd bragged that he knew the identity of the killer and that it was a real shocker. That may have been bravado, but such talk may also have spooked the murderer into silencing Crane.

I was stumped. In times like these, I had to turn to the one source I could always rely upon for sound advice.

* * *

When Aunt Violet strolled into Poppet, I immediately confronted her.

"Tell me again everything Crane said yesterday. Every word. If he uncovered the murderer, we should be able to do figure it out too."

She'd already heard about Crane's murder. News, particularly bad news, traveled fast in a small town. Although she was as perfectly put together as always, I noticed a change in my aunt. Her manner was more deliberative, and her features composed. She was clearly shaken. I recalled my manners and offered her a beverage before pressing her further.

"Forgive me, Marky. I'm no stranger to death but Jonathon was so full of life and high spirits," she paused to dab her eyes. "I grew to actually like the boy. Oh, I knew he was impetuous and full of hot air, but he also had what the French call, joie de vive. I hate thinking that someone expunged his life so callously. It's wrong and it must stop."

"He told Gideon that he found the murderer." I watched my aunt closely, trying to detect any reaction. "In fact, he said he'd solved two murders."

"Yes. He mentioned the same thing to me. No names of course. He planned to confront his source that evening and then spring it on the world through his podcast." She cautiously sipped her espresso. "Let me think. I warned him. Told him not to take any chances with a killer, but he laughed it off. He said something about being able to control things with one hand tied behind his back."

In my view that cleared Blaike.

After all, Crane was no superhero. He had about as much muscle mass as a toddler whereas Blaike's body was a testament to the value of constant workouts. Even if Crane didn't fear Blaike, he would at least be wary of confronting him. "Could he mean Lionel? Remember Paul ridiculed Lionel when they had that dust up at the party. Plus, he's old. Lionel, not Crane."

Violet shrugged. "Let's face it, Marky. We're being sexist. He might have been referring to a woman. Tilda, Philippa, and Kim look fit, and Mrs. Soto has a physique equal to a man's. Even Gemma would put up a good fight. Still, Crane like most men would never admit to fearing any woman. Not physically at least." She grinned. "Even I know the rudiments of karate. Take someone by surprise and you'd be amazed at the results. It's a new world out there, Poppet. Women aren't weak vessels anymore. They can fight back."

She was right. I knew that. My own skill at self-defense was pitiful but many of my peers took pride in kick boxing, martial arts, and the use of weaponry. I usually joked that I could fend off an opponent with my rapier sharp wit. My aptitude as a detective wasn't impressive either. I'd already evaluated a list of suspects and come up empty. "Why did he think we'd be shocked? That suggests that the killer is someone unlikely or at least well regarded. Did he give any other hints about his investigation?"

Violet closed her eyes and pursed her lips. She always did that when she was deep in thought. "Well, he was somewhat cryptic. He said old sins can come back to haunt even the mighty. Stuff like that. Oh, and he laughed when he said just because somebody seems so prim and proper doesn't mean it's true. Connections. He mentioned connections and said they wouldn't keep a murderer from a jail cell."

Old sins? I needed someone with insider knowledge of Harbor Bay to supply those pieces of the puzzle. "Any thoughts spring to mind about unsavory secrets from the past? Most people have something they'd like to hide or at least conceal from the public even if it wasn't illegal."

Violet shook her head. "What's your point?"

My approach was one that I'd given a good deal of thought to. "Maybe we should consider what each of our suspects values most. Zach is beloved, for example, but what if he had some heinous crime in his past? Philippa is a pillar of respectability. Suppose she fudged her academic credentials or took bribes to help students cheat? And Josephine Soto—who knows her full story?"

It made sense all right. I already suspected Lionel of being a wife beater and if that were public knowledge his stock would plummet. As for the others, I needed to chat with the best local source I could think of —Mandy Watts. If anyone swept dirt under the carpet, she was likely to know about it. Since she served as a local housekeeper, Mandy may have even swept up some of that dirt. Asking about Gemma would be tricky though. For that I needed to go directly to the source.

Violet got up and put her arms around me. "Listen, Marky. Maybe you should take Gideon's advice and back off. After all, none of this really involves you and the danger is very real."

I can be stubborn at times. My dad used to say I was like a terrier with a bone once I got my teeth into something. My body language said it all. Violet, that skilled practitioner of emotional intelligence read my reaction but didn't flinch. "Consider this too. You may find out some surprising things about people you care for. Things that may irreparably damage your relationship. You'd have to include Gemma, Mandy and Blaike in your investigation." She laughed. "And me too, of course. I was one of the last people to see Jonathon Crane alive. In fact, Gideon already made that very point to me."

I pondered what she said. Judging others by my own impossibly dull life wasn't a sound strategy. My entire existence had revolved around disgustingly wholesome activities. While others had embraced all aspects of the art scene in Chicago, I had doggedly stuck to my painting. No wild parties, illegal substances, or torrid affairs for little Marky Davis, the good girl of Harbor Bay. Gemma had hinted at her own escapades by saying that she had lived a "full life" whatever that meant. I'd never pursued the subject. How would I feel if Blaike owned up to something shocking or if Mayor Zach revealed a deadly secret? Perhaps it was time for me to grow up and view the world as an adult.

Violet moved back, her eyes never leaving me.

"You're probably right," I said. "Let me think things over. Meanwhile, I promised to join a panel at the library this evening. The topic is intriguing—fascinating womanhood at any age.

My aunt nodded her approval and promised to join the audience. We agreed to bring plenty of samples and discount coupons to attract potential customers. A flurry of customers from a Chicago tour bus kept us busy ringing up sales until closing time. My aunt attracted an enthusiastic group, as she illustrated some of the Parisian products we now stocked. *Clarins* and *Guerlain* were big crowd pleasers. One customer even conquered her fears and submitted to a full-face makeover. The results drew admiring comments from the rest and a clamor for similar products.

* * *

By six p.m., I closed the shop and scampered upstairs for a quick personal makeover. Although the librarian had assured me that she expected a large turnout, I knew that evening sessions were unpredictable especially with a murderer prowling the streets. I chose an ocelot print ensemble that accentuated my coloring and hopefully enhanced my quest for animal magnetism. No more girl next door looks for me. I was officially a temptress on the hunt. After feeding and walking Fantasia, I gave her a nose kiss and sped off toward the center of town. Time to meet my public.

Perhaps the scent of danger had aroused the good dowagers of Harbor Bay to reclaim the night. I noted that they arrived in pairs or more and guessed that was a concession to uncertain times. For whatever reason, the session had standing room only. Our panel was quite an eclectic group. In addition to me it included Kim Stevens, Philippa Gordon, and Josephine Soto. I waved to Mandy and Gemma who were wedged in between Aunt Violet and a fleshy matron who could have used a larger chair. Our moderator started by asking how many in the audience felt invisible once they reached fifty? Hands immediately shot up. One wag added, "Fifty? How about forty?" We then launched into a discussion of pathways to a fulfilling life.

Kim described her career as a model, admitting that as she edged toward thirty, assignments became scarce, and she'd had to look elsewhere.

Philippa focused on education, a field where longevity was valued and rewarded. She had never felt inadequate until she retired. Then she drifted, feeling somewhat rudderless until she joined the volunteer community.

Josephine Soto's views were much starker. She shared her devastation when her husband summarily discarded her for another woman. A much younger woman from England of all places.

After hearing their stories, my contribution felt inadequate. I admitted that success was something I had always achieved and expected. When I crashed and burned at the Art Institute, the pain was almost unendurable and for the first time I had faced reality. The conversation then switched to alternatives with the moderator asking each of us how we had transformed our life.

Kim hesitated, then spoke about the value of family support. No one mentioned the loss of her son. That area was too personal and devastating for a public forum. I was surprised when Kim broached the subject herself.

"Most of you know that I lost my son five years ago." Her voice quivered a bit, but Kim stayed the course. "I've tried to involve myself in constructive things—support groups, and the like, but frankly I'm still a work in progress. Losing a child…it's something to endure but never forget. They never caught the person who did that. Left him on the side of the road to die alone. I never believed in revenge until this happened, but I'd gladly kill the person who robbed me of Patrick.".

Several us teared up at Kim's story. Even Philippa, the original Sphinx, dabbed at her eyes. When it was her turn, she mentioned the youth groups she led, and her zeal for eliminating drugs and alcohol from their lives.

"I've seen too many lives ruined by substance abuse," she said. "It's such a waste. If I can save even one, my time is well spent."

Josephine had a different strategy. She suggested that each person decide what her dream was and be brave enough to pursue it. For her, the bookstore represented a lifelong love of reading. It meant everything to her and had resurrected her self-esteem. She had summoned the courage to move on to graduate studies, something her ex-husband had disparaged. "He always told me I wasn't smart enough to finish my education. Funny thing. I believed him for years."

Then it was my turn. "With the help of a friend and my aunt, I took a hard look at my life. Painting, at least being a renowned artist, was no longer an option, so I hoped to incorporate my love of color and beauty into something else. The result was Poppet, a place where every customer could feel valued. At least I hope you will. I know it's a gamble. Small businesses usually are, but life itself is a gamble too."

During the question period, the audience came to life. For the most part they asked intelligent things that tied in beautifully to our theme. They snapped up my samples, and pocketed the brochures offered by the other panelists. All in all, an evening well spent.

"You were terrific," Gemma said, slapping me on the back so heartily that I almost collapsed. "I bet we gained some customers tonight."

Aunt Violet nodded her approval and Mandy gave me a big thumbs up.

* * *

Afterwards, we went to Bistro Bis for a celebratory drink. "This doesn't seem too callous, does it?" I asked. "I mean with the murders and all."

"Hell no," Mandy said. "Both of those guys were losers anyway. Reap what you sow, isn't that the saying in the Good Book? I'm a survivor. Lord knows, I've had to do all kinds of things just to clothe and feed my child." She tossed her head defiantly. "I don't regret one thing and I'll be damned if I let some bully boy like Prentis or a big city snoop threaten me."

After toasting her and our collective futures, Violet asked Mandy about Mrs. Soto. "She's rather dour. No wonder her husband found other company."

"Her life has been all hard work," Mandy said. "You can hardly blame her. She pinned all her hopes on Benny getting a good education." I was surprised at the defensiveness in Mandy's voice. Perhaps she identified with the bookstore owner more than one would have expected.

That led to yet another thought. Paul Prentice had threatened to terminate Josephine's lease. Would she have killed to eliminate that possibility? And what about Benny? He was protective of his mother and might have reacted to any threat to her either real or perceived. I'd seen the aggressive side of Benny with my own eyes. He was no longer the pimply kid from the high school who was scared of his own shadow. That boy had gained muscle and confidence in the ensuing years.

"Philippa seems really invested in that youth group" I said. "She's quite the zealot."

Mandy laughed. "You know, believe it or not, Philippa used to be kind of fun."

I rolled my eyes. "Hard to believe. She's always seemed so prim and proper. We used to say that she probably slept with a rule book by her side and a ruler up her backside."

"I get it. Seriously, she joined us for happy hours, and she loved karaoke. Man, that girl could imitate all the big tunes." Mandy's smile said she was reliving good times. "Then she changed. Found religion. Became a teetotaler."

"People like that are no fun at all." Violet shook her head. "Remember the French mantra: everything in moderation. Makes for a much happier world."

Gemma stayed silent, quite unlike her normal lively self. She seemed distracted as if her thoughts were far away. When she finally spoke, there was a note of pathos in her voice. "I keep thinking of Kim. She acts so sad all the time. Like she lost her son only yesterday. Maybe that's why she sticks with Lionel. Self-imposed punishment."

We exchanged glances, knowing that some losses never fade away. I wondered if the bruises Kim wore were badges of honor, battle scars from a war that never ceased. Women, especially mothers, often felt guilt even in situations where they were guiltless. Had Paul Prentis unearthed some fact that made Kim's existence unendurable? Even Lionel might react violently if his wife's peace of mind was threatened or if his own spousal abuse was publicized. Leverage—Paul and even Jonathon Crane knew what that was and how to use it. Lionel had changed his vote on the expansion plan. Some said it made sound business sense, but I was unconvinced.

"Didn't see Blaike tonight," Mandy said. "Course he might still be with his dad. Those two were always tight especially after his mom passed. Something changed things and Mitch started spending time in Chicago. We heard he was leaving Blaike in charge of the business."

I owed Blaike nothing but still felt the need to defend him. "He takes good care of Fantasia. You should see the amount of gear that he brought over with her."

Violet laughed. "Fantasia is one roommate who pulls her own weight. I heard she gave Benny Soto quite a turn when she charged him."

"Serves him right," Gemma snorted. "Feeling his oats now that he has a badge. Kids used to call him little big man in high school. Always narking on anyone he could get in trouble."

No one broached the subject of Jonathon Crane's murder. It was the ultimate elephant in the room, and too sensitive a topic to explore at that late hour. We left together and piled into Mandy's old wagon for a safe journey home.

Chapter Fourteen

When Blaike phoned me early the next morning, he already knew about Crane's murder and the Chief's suspicions. There was a touch of arrogance in his voice as he responded. "I spoke with Gideon a moment ago. Explained that I went directly to Chicago and hadn't seen Crane. That seemed to satisfy him."

I couldn't help asking. "Did he believe you? The way Benny charged in here yesterday, I thought you were the prime suspect."

Blaike uttered something profane. "That Soto! I already complained to Gideon about him. Talk about harassment. I barely spoke to Crane, let alone killed him. Besides, Benny's mother makes a viable suspect if you're taking names. She went after him with a broom last time he was at her bookstore."

For some reason, just picturing that scene made me laugh. In a fair fight, I'd lay odds on Mrs. Soto every time. That woman had both heft, heat, and passion on her side.

"When are you coming back here?"

Blaike paused. "Soon. You and I need to have a serious conversation. I know you've been poking around these murders, trying to help out. Stop it. Leave things alone."

I said nothing. Why deny the obvious, especially when Blaike was acting so guilty? I also had Gemma to worry about. She was hiding something, something that might sabotage our business or land her in jail.

We ended our conversation on that very discordant note, and I readied myself for a new day. Fantasia made a great exercise companion, allowing me to jog along the deserted streets without fear. Most people, especially men, gave us a wide berth when we came into sight. Fantasia was an imposing guardian who never left my side. I hadn't mentioned her to Blaike, fearing that he might take her back. I'd grown very attached to the lovely Collie. She filled a space in my life that I hadn't known existed before. She was also a perfect adjunct to our shop.

Most customers of Poppet were women, and women tended to also be animal lovers. Fantasia stayed on her corner bed, allowing people to approach her if they so chose. Just seeing her seemed to relax customers, start conversations, and humanize our surroundings. I wasn't sure that I could ever let her go.

When Lionel Stevens burst into the store, I didn't know what to expect. As always, he was garbed in a sober three-piece suit and brusque to the point of rudeness.

"Where's Gemma," he barked. "She's the one Kim went to."

I blinked, trying to decipher what in the world he meant. As it happened, Gemma and Mandy were handling a wedding party, giving massages and pedicures to a bevy of giggling attendants and a manicure to the bride herself.

"She's away. May I help you, Mr. Stevens? Would you like to book an appointment?"

He spoke through gritted teeth. "No. And if you want to avoid a lawsuit, I suggest you mind your own business and stay out of your customers' lives."

Despite his anger, Lionel was rational enough to realize that I had no idea what he meant. "Just who does she think she is? A girl like that giving my wife ideas. Everyone in Harbor Bay knows her story. Advice from Gemma Watts! I tell you, I won't tolerate it!"

I am slow to anger, but in this instance, my self-control deserted me. "Perhaps you should take your complaint to the authorities, Lionel. The chief might be interested in the story."

His face contorted into a most unpleasant shape, and his cheeks became flushed. I'd forgotten that Lionel was elderly and a good candidate for a stroke. A medical emergency might be a legal conundrum that would sink Poppet.

"I told Prentis and that muckraker from Chicago," Lionel spat. "You better not tangle with me, or you'll be sorry."

Anger and the presence of Fantasia buoyed my courage. "Funny thing. Both of those guys ended up dead. Are you threatening me too?"

At that moment, the woman I recognized from the library event entered Poppet ending Lionel's tirade. He quickly collected himself, nodded to both of us, and exited.

I forced myself to power down and attend to my customer. She was a tad timid but eager to sample some of our more adventurous products. After our consultation, I suggested an Armani foundation, NARS blush, and loose powder by Chanel. Nothing overpowering, although we both giggled at the name of the NARS product: Orgasm. I assured her it was their most popular item and produced a very natural effect. All the while, thoughts of Lionel Stevens flooded my mind.

Why would this stodgy, buttoned-down lawyer fly into such a rage? Knowing that Gemma had glimpsed Kim's bruises probably panicked the old coot. I pictured a neon light blinking "Motive for Murder." Lionel treasured his reputation and position in the town. He might lash out if it was threatened. The theory appealed to me, but in fairness, I had to question whether he could disable two fit young men. Rage could fuel a surge in strength, but the odds were against it happening twice.

* * *

I slipped her harness on Fantasia and took that little lady for a comfort break. We left via the front door since I found it hard to brave the alley, even with her at my side. Mayor Zach, wearing his genial grin, crossed the street to greet us. "What a sight for sore eyes. Two lovely ladies. I didn't know you had a dog, Marky?"

I explained that, unfortunately, Fantasia was only a visitor. The mayor nodded and got a wistful expression on his face. "My wife loved animals. Her dog Disraeli was a Corgi mix. Such a comfort in her final days. That dog cuddled up and never left her side." Zach teared up. "Disraeli didn't last long after Helen passed. Almost as if he wanted to be with her in the next life."

I changed the subject to allow the mayor some time to regroup. Since neither murder victim was likely to elicit any emotion, I asked how the townspeople were reacting. Zach gave that some thought. "You know, after Paul's death, most people were shocked but not panicked. This second murder kind of changed things."

"How so?"

He lowered his voice even though there was no one else about. "That Crane fellow was a stranger, so normally, it wouldn't have affected people. But the idea that some crazed killer is roaming around Harbor Bay...that's a different kettle of fish."

The *Gazette* had soft-pedaled both deaths out of deference to our local economy, and that was fine with me. I was counting on busloads of well-heeled tourists to fatten the coffers of Poppet. On the other hand, the threatening letter loomed over me like a noxious cloud. "Any leads or suspects?" I asked.

Zach scrutinized me with the same skeptical look he'd given me years before. Then I had fudged the truth about flossing. Now I was nosing into police territory.

"Heard you got a scary note, Marky. Maybe you should back off." He wagged his finger my way. "Gideon thinks it was probably some big city criminal. From Chicago or Detroit, most likely. You don't want to tangle with that kind."

"Really? I think it's somebody local. Someone with secrets to hide."

Mayor Thanos gave a semi-smile. "Harbor Bay has good people for the most part. You're young, Marky. When you get a bit older, you'll see that everyone has something to hide. It's just part of living." He patted my shoulder, waved goodbye, and ambled down the street toward City Hall.

The phone rang just as I unlocked the door. To my chagrin, Benny Soto was on the line sounding more officious than ever. "Chief wants to see you, Marky. Right away."

My patience with this minion of the law was threadbare, and I felt fearless. "No problem. After the store closes, I'll be there."

He huffed through the phone line. "Not good enough, Ms. Davis."

I tried sweet reason. "Look. I'm here alone. Your mom knows all about running a small business. Ask her what it's like."

His temper flared to boiling. "Leave her out of this, or you'll regret it."

Since I had obviously annoyed him, it seemed wise to capitalize upon it. "I heard your mom mixed it up with both of the victims. Maybe you should question her. She's got quite a temper."

His response was vitriolic and quite unseemly for a law enforcement officer. Fortunately, Benny slammed down the phone without making any further threats. I laughed aloud.

"What's so funny?" Aunt Violet had slipped into the store so stealthily that I never even heard the door chimes. That gave me quite a start.

"Oh, just Soto playing tough guy. Very unconvincing." I stepped into the storeroom and switched on the kettle. A mug of Earl Grey would hit the spot and help clarify my thoughts.

"I had breakfast with Tilda Egan this morning." Aunt Violet lowered her eyes. "Quite enlightening, I must say."

"Oh?" I was sharpening my skill at one-word interrogatories. "Come on. Don't be coy. Give."

Violet had perfected the art of nonchalance. Who knew if it were natural or a skill she had learned in Paris? I loved my aunt, but some of her antics were extremely vexing. "I have something to trade. Three things, in fact."

The kettle whistled, and for once, I got the better of my wily relative. "You win. Tilda had plenty to say. No, that's not exactly right. She's cagey. Insinuates rather than saying something outright. Most of it was quite poisonous but interesting still."

I poured water through the strainer and filled two mugs with the fragrant brew. After I handed my aunt her share, she finally spoke.

"Was Gemma in your high school class? She's a year older than you, I believe."

"Yeah. So what? She got a bad case of mono or something like it. Lost a lot of time."

The look on Violet's face was both troubled and compassionate. "Tilda hinted that Gemma left school for the usual reason. If so, she might want to keep that quiet. It might constitute a motive for murder."

I wasn't born yesterday. No one was naïve enough to miss that subtext. "Gemma was pregnant? That's what you meant, wasn't it?"

Violet nodded. "According to Tilda, the likely father was none other than Paul Prentis. If true, that is a bombshell. It's also a motive for murder."

It took a while for me to collect my thoughts. Surely Gemma wouldn't hide something like that. Not from me. After all, I was her best friend. Besides, this was the twenty-first century. Unwanted pregnancy was nothing scandalous. It certainly didn't constitute a motive for two murders.

I leapt to my friend's defense. "Tilda probably fabricated the whole thing."

"She said she had it on good authority. From the horse's mouth, so to speak."

"Paul Prentis?" My voice rose by several octaves. "Was he the horse in question? What happened to the child?"

Violet sighed. "The situation was handled by the Prentis family. They paid to eliminate the problem. Gave Gemma and Mandy a stipend as well to pay for Gemma's massage training."

Now Paul's cruel comments and Mandy's reaction made sense. Small communities, even upscale ones like Harbor Bay, had long memories and unyielding prejudices. The Prentis family had probably insulated Paul from other scrapes and indiscretions during his teenage years. They had no intention of sullying the family name and used their bountiful checkbook like a magician's wand to make trouble vanish.

"Any other tidbits?" I asked. "I can't mention that last thing to Gemma. She's tried so hard to make a life for herself. It must be devastating."

Violet nodded her approval. "You saw Mandy respond. She might act aggressively to protect her daughter's reputation. Don't discount maternal instinct and all that."

When I returned to Harbor Bay, I envisioned it as a peaceful enclave with neighbor helping neighbor. I now realized that human nature was the same in a huge city like Chicago or an idyllic seaside hamlet. *Nature raw in tooth and claw.*

Violet hadn't finished her account. "Women like Tilda spew venom like a cobra. She laughed when I mentioned Philippa. Said it was amazing how sanctimonious some people get when they try to hide their sins. And no, she never specified what sins Philippa might be guilty of. I think she was just salting the conversation with possibilities to deflect suspicion from herself."

It was appealing to think of Principal Gordon being led away in handcuffs heading for the big house. Unfortunately, it was also difficult to believe. I repeated my encounters with Lionel and Mayor Zach, emphasizing Lionel's outrage and Zach's sadness. There were motives aplenty in Harbor Bay but very little proof.

Chapter Fifteen

Shortly before closing time, I left for my meeting with Gideon. I had no possible idea of the subject other than the murders, and I had nothing new to report. To avoid the clutches of Soto, I edged cautiously into the squat brick building that housed the seat of justice. Harbor Bay had a limited police presence during the winter. When Spring arrived and the population swelled, the force was augmented by several auxiliary deputies and traffic officers. The desk was staffed by a genial matron I recalled from my high school days. She pointed toward the office at the rear of the building and told me Chief Hall was expecting me.

Gideon sat behind an enormous oak desk, looking neat and unruffled. Come to think of it, I'd never seen that man with a wrinkled shirt or a hair out of place.

"Hey, Marky. Thanks for dropping by." He motioned toward a table with several straight-back oak chairs. "Have a seat. I'd say make yourself comfortable, but that's impossible with those monstrosities. No one wants to linger in this place, believe me."

For some reason, I felt nervous and vaguely guilty. Unpleasant memories of days in the principal's office resurfaced. Not that I had done too much of that. Marky Davis, professional good girl. I folded my hands in my lap and awaited his next move.

"Listen. I understand Benny was a bit overzealous today. That won't happen again."

"Good. Thanks. Being manhandled by the cops sort of hurts my image."

Gideon planted his hands on the desk and stared me down. His hands were enormous, large enough to squeeze the life out of any miscreant. "Enough of this small talk. Tell me the truth. What do you know about Gemma's involvement in these crimes?"

"Nothing. She couldn't possibly be involved." I ignored Gideon's massive frown and soldiered on. "I'll bet you don't have one iota of proof either. Everyone hated Prentis, and the reporter was no prize either."

"Was Gemma alone in that alley with Prentis? You're concealing something, Marky, I can sense it."

"Make up your mind. Benny said that Blaike was your main suspect. Not that you have any evidence against him either."

Gideon reached into his folder and produced a sheaf of papers. "See these. I found them in Jonathon Crane's effects. I really shouldn't share them with you, but I want your help. I need your help, Marky."

Something was terribly wrong. I visualized a noose tightening around Gemma's neck with me as the hangman. "I'm no lawyer. Why ask me?"

This time he pounded his desk with one of those massive fists. "Because I want you to understand. This is no time to shield some high school pals. These documents prove that the Harringtons were hand in glove with Prentice on that land deal. No doubt about it."

I'd always thought that expression "my heart sank" was merely hyperbole. Now I realize just how accurate it was. Two people I considered my friends had misled me. Gemma, through omission and Blaike with an outright lie. He had stared into my eyes and sworn that he had no interest in that development project. I focused on the documents in front of me and saw that was not true. Harrington incorporated had a signed contract with Prentis properties to manage the Harbor Bay improvement project. It bore the signature of Blaike's father and was notarized by their corporate attorney. In consideration for their "support," Prentis properties paid a fee of one hundred thousand dollars due when the town's approval had been secured. Maybe it was just a routine business deal. Perhaps it was nothing illegal, but it seemed awfully like the formalized offer and acceptance of a bribe.

"Blaike opposed that resolution," I said, "or at least he stayed neutral. Why would he do that if Prentis already had his vote?" I suddenly recalled Blaike's cold indifference to the fate of those businesses displaced by the Harbor project. That was a side of him I hadn't seen before. Maybe I'd deliberately chosen to ignore it.

"Bought his vote, you mean. Sounds like his so-called opposition was a charade." For the first time, Gideon Hall frightened me. No longer the genial cop, he had morphed into a fierce lawman. "I've known Blaike Harrington since he was a boy. Watched him grow into a fine man. At least, I thought so." He pursed his lips. "Just shows how wrong even a cop can be."

"Have you spoken to him?" I asked. "After all, those papers don't prove anything. Why would he murder not one but two men to suppress something that was bound to be public record? It doesn't make any sense."

Gideon gave me that tough cop look popularized in television dramas. "Maybe he reconsidered, or maybe he was trying to protect his father. Mitchell hasn't been the same since his wife passed. They were together for a lot of years. That kind of loss can change a man."

I'd always liked and respected Chief Hall, but his current behavior bordered on the irrational. Pressure, either political or social, must be coming down from above. He obviously didn't have enough evidence to charge either Blaike or Gemma. Otherwise, he would have done so.

"I'm not going to be your mole. Forget that." I slowly rose and faced him. "Seems to me more than one person in Harbor Bay had reason to hate Paul Prentis. As for Crane—muckrakers make plenty of enemies too. Maybe you should do some old-fashioned police work instead of persecuting my friends. If Crane said he had solved two murders, I'm wondering who the other victim was. Something to consider, wouldn't you say?" I squared my shoulders and strode out of his office without saying another word.

* * *

"It was maddening," I muttered as I buried my face in Fantasia's soft coat. "They're trying to frame someone. I'm worried for Gemma and Blaike."

Aunt Violet was the voice of sweet reason. "Odd. That doesn't sound like him at all. Gideon is usually so cautious. And fair." She remained stoic, even after I explained about the contract with Prentis Properties. "Face it, Marky. That sounds suspicious."

"Huh!" My response wasn't eloquent, but it did the job. "You should have been there."

When Gemma entered the store, her manner was subdued. She kept her head down as she folded clean towels and said very little. Silence was very unlike her. She would normally leap into the fray and take a stand. That made me wonder what kind of trouble was brewing inside her tangle of russet curls. Meanwhile, Mandy busied herself running in and out of the stockroom with new products. The Watts women were noticeably mum on the subject of guilt.

"Okay," I said. "Out with it. Tell me what you know or heard."

After exchanging glances with Gemma, Mandy spoke first. "I hate to gossip but I suppose it's a good cause."

I glowered at her as she destroyed a box containing Oribe shampoo. It was one of my favorite brands, both pricey and elegant. Customers might shrink from paying premium prices for the mangled mess she now held. Mandy looked down at her hands and panicked.

"Oh, I'm so sorry, Marky. I'll pay to replace this."

"Nonsense," Aunt Violet said, rescuing the shampoo. "We'll use it as a display item. Now, what got you so upset. Come on."

Mandy was normally a tough cookie, but now she looked almost teary-eyed. "It's just that a couple of times while I was taking my walk, I saw something. Maybe it meant nothing."

Even Gemma lost patience with her mother. "Stop stalling, Mom."

"Well. I saw Mr. Harrington leaving Tilda Egan's house."

"Big deal," I said, forcing myself to remain calm. "He could have been there for any number of reasons."

Mandy shook her head. "Both times, it was early in the morning. And he had lipstick on his face. Besides, he acted guilty. You know what I mean. When he saw me, he turned the other way and almost ran. Didn't say a thing."

I thought of several scenarios that would explain Blaike's behavior, but they all ended in one word: sex. No wonder he had changed his vote. Getting cozy with the town vixen was apparently one of the fringe benefits that sealed the deal.

Gideon Hall was building his case, and I couldn't blame him.

"Just a minute, Mandy." Violet put her arm around me. "You said Mr. Harrington. Did you mean Blaike?"

Mandy looked puzzled. "Blaike? Oh no. I saw his father, Mitchell."

My relief was palpable. That explained it. Tilda had probably manipulated his dad. Blackmailed him even. Any son would defend his family. That didn't mean he murdered anyone. It was the honorable thing to do. A tidal wave of relief engulfed me. Mr. Harrington had always been stodgy but very kind. Like many men with long, happy marriages, he was relatively innocent about women. Tilda Egan could have easily snared him in her web. Still, a dalliance between two single adults, however tawdry, was an unlikely motive for murder. That signed agreement was another matter entirely. Blaike and I needed to have a conversation, an intense, no holds barred exchange. The next day was the annual founders' day picnic. What better time to face him? All the town luminaries would be in attendance and I was keen to speak with Kim about her husband's behavior. The subject was sensitive, especially if it related to their son's death. I knew that most couples didn't survive that kind of trauma. Somehow, the Stevens' marriage had limped along for five years since the tragedy. Something, whether grief, guilt, or inertia, had kept them together. I wondered if Paul Prentis or Jonathon Crane had learned the answer.

After Violet and Mandy left, I confronted Gemma. "We've got to talk."

She blanched, and the freckles on her skin stood out. "What's the problem?" She lowered her head as if she expected a beating.

"You and Paul Prentis. Normally I wouldn't intrude, but this is serious. Gideon practically accused you of his murder. Why would he think that? If he knew you were alone in that alley, we'd both be in deep trouble."

Gemma closed her eyes and sighed. "Nothing spectacular. Pathetic, really. When a guy like Prentis starts buzzing around the poor kid in town, it feels good. I believed his lies, but my mom warned me. Never occurred to me that we stayed under the radar. You know, cheap motels outside town, and dark bars. Anyway, oldest story in the book. When I told him I was pregnant, he laughed. Laughed! Said that no one would believe the town slut." Tears were streaming down her face. "I wasn't like that, Marky. It broke my heart."

I felt like a monster for even broaching the subject. "Don't say anything more," I said.

Gemma shook her head. "Nope. I should have told you right away. My mom went ballistic and marched right up to that big Prentis house. Of course, Paul denied everything, but his parents knew. Mom and I went to Chicago until it was over and stayed there on the Prentis dime until I finished massage studies." She grimaced. "My higher education came with a big price tag. I hated Paul Prentis and still do."

I put my arms around her and squeezed.

"Ouch! What are you, a python?" Gemma spun me around and looked me in the eye. "I didn't kill him, Marky, but I'm glad someone did."

Chapter Sixteen

Most businesses in Harbor Bay rented booths to support local charities and showcase their brand. Gemma and I gladly joined the others with our proceeds earmarked for the local animal shelter. Even Fantasia joined in by sporting a festive bandanna. As an extra incentive, Aunt Violet sat at her easel and sketched portraits for a modest fee. A long line of excited townspeople soon awaited her and including my quarry, Kim Stevens.

"Kim! I'm so excited about painting your portrait. Come, have some tea. No sense waiting outside." Kim's eyes widened, and she dove for her cell phone. "Let me call Lionel first. He worries about me."

Kim's double-breasted blazer and crisp navy slacks were a perfect choice for the occasion. I felt a pang of envy comparing my nondescript duds with hers. She really was quite lovely, sophisticated but subtle. Tilda, on the other hand, tried too hard. Admittedly she was garbed in a pricey outfit, but it screamed for attention. She had rejected the axiom that less is more and sported designer initials on most of her visible body parts. I scolded myself for being unkind even though, in contrast, my own choice of garb now seemed virtuous.

"Check out our former principal," Gemma hissed. Philippa made no concession to the festive occasion. She wore the same tired tennis togs she always wore. In fairness, I reminded myself that Philippa was competing in a charity doubles tourney and needed practical clothes. Still, good grooming was never out of style. Philippa frowned when she approached our booth and saw me. "Working hard, Ms. Davis," she said without much warmth.

"Good for you." She leaned in. "I was hoping to speak with Mandy."

I explained that Mandy would staff the booth after lunch. When I selected several samples she might enjoy, Philippa glared at me as if I had proffered poison. "No, thank you. I'll swing by later." *Please let her be the killer. She deserves to live in the big house even though Michigan abolished the death penalty.*

I'd forgotten all about Kim. She approached me, looking bewildered until I motioned toward the side of our booth. "I don't want to spoil your day, Kim, but what's wrong with Lionel? He confronted me yesterday at Poppet and frightened me."

Her face grew pale beneath that exquisitely applied foundation. "In public? Lionel made a scene. Oh, Marky, I'm so sorry."

I tried a sympathy ploy even though direct action was more in my wheelhouse. "I know these murders have everyone on edge…."

Kim dabbed at her eyes. "That's not it. Yesterday was the anniversary…" she gulped, "We lost our son five years ago, and Lionel has never been the same."

Guilt nearly overwhelmed me, but I stayed strong. "Oh, forgive me. Did they ever find who was responsible?"

She shook her head and wiped away a big tear. "It keeps eating away at us. They think it was someone local. A drunk driver. That's why when Mr. Crane said he knew who it was, Lionel went crazy. He offered him money, anything he wanted, but that Crane just laughed. Said to wait for his podcast when he'd unveil "the secret sins of Harbor Bay." Can you believe it? He actually planned to call it that."

I plucked a tissue from a pack on the table and offered it to Kim. How like that cretin Jonathon Crane to taunt grieving parents for his own advantage. Was that what led to his murder? I wondered what other secrets he planned to unveil. No doubt he also knew or thought he knew the identity of Paul's killer. Had Lionel Stevens killed him in a frenzied attempt to learn that name, or had another victim acted?

Kim must have read my mind. She gasped in horror and clutched my arm. "He wouldn't hurt anyone. Please believe me. Lionel isn't violent."

I immediately took the coward's way out by nodding weakly and assuring her that all was well. "Tell your husband to think before he acts and stand up for yourself."

Her response aroused my guilt and compassion. "I haven't cared about anything since my son died. I only wish I'd gone with him." She walked away with the grace and movement of the model she had once been.

"What was that all about?" Gemma breezed in, ready to take over her shift.

I simply shrugged and snapped Fantasia's leash on her harness. "Never mind. I'm taking this good girl for a walk." I took a leisurely stroll around the town square visiting the various booths and sampling some of the local wares. Most of the shopkeepers offered plenty of treats for canine visitors, too, so Fantasia managed to cadge more than her share of them. So absorbed was I in lollygagging that I ran right into the very person I had sought to avoid.

"We need to talk," Blaike Harrington said, clutching my elbow.

"You've got that right, buster. If Soto sees you, look out. They think you're a double murderer."

"What!" Blaike's normally tanned complexion grew pale. He was either acting or genuinely shocked. "You've got it wrong, Marky. I didn't hurt anyone."

"Oh yeah? Don't pretend with me. I saw that document you signed with Prentis Properties. Quite a lot of cash changed hands. By the way, Gideon Hall has it too."

He shook his head. "My dad arranged that. Prentis had some kind of hold on him and blackmailed him. That's why I went to Chicago, to try to straighten things out."

Fantasia reacted to our raised voices by nudging Blaike's arm. He suddenly relaxed and gave the collie a nose kiss. "She always knows how to settle things, don't you, girl?"

A few pedestrians were eyeing our little tableau, so I lowered my voice to a hoarse whisper. The sins of Harbor Bay? Does that ring any bells?"

"What? Sounds like the title of a low-end romance."

I explained the title and urged Blaike to contact Gideon right away. "Sounds like motive with a capital M to me, big guy." I looked across the square and panicked. "Oh no. There's the chief coming straight at us."

Blaike seemed curiously untroubled. "Fine. I'll clear this right up. But listen, Marky. I finally changed my vote because it made economic sense. For the town, not me personally. My Dad's situation involved Tilda, so you can guess what that was all about." He dropped my elbow, but before he left, Blaike asked one more thing. "Can you keep my girl a bit longer?"

That was an easy ask. "I'll keep her forever. Just try to take her away."

I watched Blaike saunter up to Gideon, shake hands, and accompany him back toward city hall. There was no drama, no fracas. I held my breath, expecting that at any minute, Benny Soto would charge out, waving his gun. He didn't appear, and the entire exchange was very civilized.

"Guess they've got their murderer," a fierce voice behind me hissed. I had inadvertently stopped at Novel Exchange and fallen into the clutches of Josephine Soto.

"You're wrong, Josephine. Blaike had nothing to do with either murder."

She snorted something quite unprintable and stepped aside. "Think you're something special, don't you, princess? Your family always acted like they were royalty. Putting on airs."

That comment was so inaccurate and unfair that I was rendered temporarily speechless. My parents and aunt were civic-minded but certainly not snobbish. I knew for a fact that they had supported the Soto bookstore in every way possible. I wondered if guilt, not envy, was swirling about in Josephine's febrile mind. After all, her husband's sudden disappearance had never been questioned. Perhaps there was more to it than *an affaire de Coeur*.

"You had words with both victims. What do you have to hide, Mrs. Soto?"

Her indignant squawk could be heard around the square. "You're crazy. My son was right about you."

Fantasia whirled about and immediately went on guard, emitting a low growl.

"Get that beast away from me!" Josephine jumped back, her eyes wide with fear. I realized, to my surprise, that she was genuinely terrified. To avoid trouble, I grasped my dog's harness and walked away. Hard to think of that formidable female Josephine Soto fearing anything, let alone a gentle creature like Fantasia. My questions were innocuous, but her response was surprising. Maybe that explained Benny's fierce reaction as well.

* * *

By the time I returned to our booth, Mandy was there to staff it. I recalled that Philippa was looking for her. "I didn't know you two were buddies," I said.

Mandy grinned. "Not exactly. Drinking buddies at one time. Like a told you before, a bunch of us girls used to hit the casinos on weekends." She bit her lip. "I say girls, but we were grown women without husbands pretending to have fun. It gets lonely around here especially during the off season. Sometimes things go too far."

"What changed?" I asked.

Mandy sighed. "Life, I guess. Philippa went on this kick, you know, no smoking or drinking. Kind of dropped out of our crowd. Now she just works with those kids. At risk teens, she calls them."

I couldn't picture former Principal Gordon ever having a girls' night out, even though her good works with young people were well documented. Aunt Violet beckoned to me before I could ask anything else. "Zach's about to start his speech. Let's give him some support."

Few people excel at public speaking and Mayor Zachery Thanos was not among them. His genial manner and genuine good cheer led citizens to make allowances for his deficiencies as an orator even as they silently encouraged brief remarks. Zach's stump speech hadn't changed much since I was a kid sitting in his dental chair. He extolled the beauty of Harbor Bay, praised the good citizens of the town, and predicted prosperity for all. There was one addition this time. Zach announced that the Harbor Bay development project had been temporarily shelved for more study. The reaction of the crowd varied from puzzled, pleased, or perturbed. I studied one person whose face resembled an approaching storm. Tilda Egan's grim visage stood out among the bland expressions of her fellow citizens. It was obvious that the announcement came as a most unpleasant shock to her. I scanned the crowd for the other council members. Philippa stayed impassive, and Lionel crossed his arms and nodded with more animation than usual. Blaike was nowhere to be found. I wondered if he was decorating one of Gideon Hall's cells now or getting the third degree from Soto.

Violet nudged me. "Very interesting. Looks like that controversy has finally been laid to rest—for now at least. I wonder why Tilda looks so upset. Perhaps she'd like to chat." She ambled over to the councilwoman and immediately started a conversation. Leave it to my aunt to confront Tilda directly. I had no doubt that she could squeeze blood from that stone called Tilda Egan if anyone could. That reminded me. Blaike had been delegated to search property records in the town. I was curious about the results of that little venture, especially if any of our prominent citizens had recently invested in land.

The entire imbroglio could be laid to rest if only those pesky murders were solved. I for one would be unable to sleep peacefully while a double killer roamed free, and I doubted very much if Chief Hall would either. There were other questions unanswered as well. Would Harrington Inc. have to return that hefty retainer or was there a proviso protecting the firm? Jonathon Crane had discovered some scandal during his visit to our town. He had ruffled the feathers of at least five prominent citizens and probably more with his threat to podcast the sins of Harbor Bay. Crane was a big fellow, the cocky type full of hubris who might have taunted the murderer. This time, he had woefully underestimated his opponent and paid the ultimate price.

"Perk up, Marky. Looks like you're dreaming." Mayor Zach's cheery voice brought me back to reality. It was hard to resist his infectious grin try as I might. "Don't you just love this event? Helen and I never missed it. Not once in the thirty years we spent here." His voice broke when he said her name.

"Good thing that podcast died with Jonathon Crane," I said. "The sins of Harbor Bay. Quite a catchy title."

Zach blanched as he responded. "Someone mentioned it, but I didn't pay it much mind. Scandal doesn't go with this town. I know my friends and neighbors, Marky, and they're an honorable group if ever there was one."

He had a gift for viewing people in the most positive light. Even at my age I knew that in any group of humans, one could find corruption and evil as well as good. The mayor couldn't sugar coat the fact that someone—probably one of our friends or neighbors—had taken two lives.

"It frightens me, Mayor Zach. How do we know who to trust?" Fantasia edged closer, hoping for a treat. To my surprise, Zach ignored her and stepped aside. How could anyone resist such a beautiful soul? I was offended on her behalf. "I thought you liked dogs," I said.

He laughed. "My wife was the animal lover. I stick to kissing babies. But you listen here, Ms. Davis. I have faith in Gideon Hall and so should you. Stop playing detective and let the man do his job. He'll find the culprit and I'll bet you a cream soda that its someone from out of town. Chicago or Detroit. Mark my words. All kinds of criminals in those places."

Out of respect I didn't contradict him. I knew, however, from living in Chicago that I'd never felt as uneasy there as I did in sleepy Harbor Bay.

Chapter Seventeen

Blaike was leaning against the door to Poppet when I returned from the festival. His arms were folded, and he looked curiously untroubled—no signs of trauma or the third degree. Fantasia wagged her plummy tail and gave him a toothy grin. I restrained myself from doing likewise.

"So. How did it go?" I asked. "Gideon didn't clap you in irons, I see."

His show of indifference was maddening. Was this a display of machismo or a galloping case of denial. "Don't suppose you have some of that espresso on hand," he asked. "I could use a shot of caffeine."

I unlocked the door and waved Blaike in. No time like the present to confront him and resolve outstanding issues. "What did Gideon say?" I asked, taking care to appear calm and unemotional. No sense in playing the shrew or harridan.

"Gideon and I understand each other. I explained my dad's situation and my own assessment of the business case. As for Jonathon Crane, I wasn't even in Harbor Bay when he got killed."

I handed him the espresso, using silence as a weapon. "Funny thing, though. He asked if I'd tagged anyone as the killer and could it have been a woman. I hadn't considered that. I mean, they were both big guys. But Gideon sounded serious."

I'd had this discussion before. Paul Prentis was intoxicated when he died, probably unsteady on his feet. A woman could have easily subdued him. Crane was another matter entirely. I wondered what the autopsy report would find. If someone clobbered him on the head, he, too, could have been strangled by almost anyone. I made a mental note to ask Gemma or Mandy if they could use their contacts at the coroner's office once more.

Blaike finally mentioned the property search he'd made. He checked his phone for notes that listed the transactions. It seemed that more than a few of our townspeople had a hankering for land. Lionel owned several tracts in the general vicinity of the proposed development site. Not surprising. He was known as a shrewd speculator and investor with an uncanny sense of timing. No wonder Kim stuck with him. By all accounts, the old curmudgeon was loaded! The next two items surprised me. Tilda Egan had splurged on a choice parcel of waterfront land that currently housed one of the ramshackle hotels! The sum recorded was truly eye-popping. That explained her strong reaction to the project's shelving.

"How could she afford that kind of purchase?" I asked Blaike. "Surely the advance from her so-called memoir wasn't that generous?" My doubts sounded petty and a tad jealous, but they were still worth considering.

"Maybe she's a good saver," Blaike teased, "or got a legacy from some relative."

The only relative able to cough up those kinds of bucks was a sugar daddy. I had to ask, even though it was a most intrusive question. "Tell me this. Did your dad pay her anything?"

He stiffened, and I expected him to refuse to answer. "Dad didn't give her that kind of money. Just small things. You know, gifts and such. Besides, they're both single. He'd be embarrassed if it came out, but so what. He agreed to partner with Prentis Properties, but that was a good deal for both parties. No reason to kill that sleaze, Paul, and certainly no reason to eliminate Crain."

I scanned the rest of the list but found no other items worth noting. Philippa and Zach hadn't purchased anything. In fact, Philippa had sold her only holding several years before. If Council members had compromised their positions, it was hard to prove it from these transactions.

"Where does that leave us, Ms. Marple? Might be time to back off and leave things to the police."

He had a point. Playing detective had been a diversion for me, a tonic for the boredom I'd felt after leaving Chicago. I'd always devoured mystery books and usually solved the crime. The fictional crime. Unfortunately, I had done little to distinguish myself in real-time. Two men had died, and I was no closer to finding a suspect than I was to painting like Mary Cassatt. Better to sit down at my easel and exercise the only real talent I had. Before grabbing a brush, a thought suddenly occurred to me. "What do you know about Josephine Soto? That woman is plenty hostile about something, and I'll bet she could throttle most men."

Blaike wrinkled his brow. "You're kidding, right? Mrs. Soto as a double murderer? I just can't picture it. Do you have any evidence?"

I explained my theory about the sudden disappearance of Mr. Soto. "Who knows the real story? He might be buried in her front garden or in her basement. That would explain Benny's vendetta toward you. He's rabid about it."

"Now I know you've gone round the bend. I met that British tourist he ran off with. Actually, "ran off" sounds rather melodramatic. They fell in love and left Harbor Bay. It happens all the time, Marky."

"Oh yeah. Tell me more. Describe her."

"Whoa. She was a very refined librarian who worked at Oxford University. At the Bodleian, I believe. Graduate of Balliol, just like your detective hero Lord Peter Wimsey."

He was goading me, but I refused to concede. "Okay. What about her appearance? Was she another Josephine Soto or something more alluring?"

Blaike laughed. "Not a temptress, for sure. Certainly not glamorous, but pleasant. Yes. Very pleasant looking. Wore twin sets, pearls, and the occasional tweed. Charming accent. A real lady."

I was crestfallen. In other words, the British librarian existed and was as unlike Mrs. Soto as any two women could be. The idea of Josephine wearing tweeds, let alone pearls was unthinkable! No wonder Mr. Soto had fled the scene. Burial in the garden now seemed more like fantasy than fact. Blaike probably thought I was delusional.

"Hey! Cheer up," Blaike said. "You're not the one with a noose around your neck. Hall is still eyeing me as a viable suspect. Although I've got to say he seems interested in someone else as well. Our company hasn't suffered yet, but my dad has gotten some calls. Kind of feeling him out about my involvement."

Despite his brave words, I could tell that Blaike was worried. Whatever happened, even if the real killer was found, people would still associate murder with the Harrington name. That was the downside of life in a small town—intolerance and long memories. No wonder Gemma and Mandy were so prickly about their past, and Kim tolerated Lionel's abuse. Neither forget nor forgive was the Harbor Bay mantra, and it cut offenders or suspected offenders to the core. Before Blaike left, I confronted him with the question I'd been summoning up my courage to ask.

"Tell me this. Who do you think did it, and why? I think we can exclude thrill killers and the occasional stranger. This is a local crime unless I'm mistaken."

He gave me a look that almost frightened me. His face had the cold, hard expression of a stranger. An unfriendly, ruthless stranger. This was not the high school boy whose ring I had proudly worn, or the football hero whose exploits thrilled the entire stadium. I pinched myself, recalling that high school and my memories of it had faded long ago. Blaike was no longer a callow youth, and I was a grown woman with a business to support and a life of my own. I backed up a few steps, using the display counter as a barrier between us.

"You asked me a question, Marky, but I have no answer. Folks in this town have been good to me for the most part. I can't name anyone who would take another's life. On the other hand, anyone—including me and even you—is capable of violence if the stakes are high enough." His tone was brusque and dismissive. "I said it before, and I mean it. Stay out of this and mind your own business.

* * *

His abrupt departure left me in a quandary. On the one hand, I was angry at his treatment, but on the other, I was more determined than ever to pursue the matter and find the killer. It was ego talking, even I realized that. All my life, I had strived to be the best and achieve my goals even when I'd trampled innocent bystanders like Blaike. Some call that selfishness others say it's resilience and a need to excel. Most successful men had it in spades. Women weren't immune to the lure of achievement either. My Aunt Violet defied all the conventions of Harbor Bay life by fleeing to Paris, burnishing her immense talent for painting, and establishing a cosmetics empire. I knew—because she told me—that she had rejected any number of suitors, enjoyed the company of some exciting men, and broken more than a few hearts. Some people called that selfish. I thought it was splendid.

My efforts seemed puny and inconsequential in comparison, but I was just getting started. Blaike Harrington could just go peddle his papers elsewhere! I was so absorbed in this internal pep talk that I missed the arrival of a new customer.

My mistake.

Tilda Egan was not a woman to be ignored. She stepped in close to my face and hissed a warning. Fantasia moved silently to my side, keeping watch and buoying my confidence.

"You've been asking questions about me all over town. I don't like that."

"Do you have something to hide?"

That reaction puzzled her and gave me another opening. "You and Paul were working overtime to sway the City Council. Your land purchase is a matter of public record."

Tilda was a worthy adversary. My accusation didn't frighten her one bit. Instead of folding, she laughed. "When is a perfectly legal sale anything to hide? And furthermore, missy, that land is proof positive that I didn't kill Paul. No motive. Dead he was of absolutely no use to me. Think again, genius."

I was down but not totally out. "What about Jonathon Crane? He knew about your memoir scam. That podcast could have made trouble for you if you were extorting people."

"Crane? Didn't know him and never even spoke to him. As for my memoir, I can prove everything in there. Truth is an affirmative defense, according to my publisher. Try again, Marky. Maybe you should chat with your business associates. Mandy has quite a temper, and Gemma…let's just say that Gemma had her own reasons to eliminate Paul. Or better yet, stick to painting. You may have some aptitude for it."

After Tilda stalked out the door, I took deep breaths to calm myself. My questions had obviously annoyed her, but somehow, I no longer considered her a potential murderer. She was ruthless enough to eliminate any obstacle in her path, but as she so rightly pointed out, neither Paul nor Jonathon posed much of a threat to her. The bottom line was one that I couldn't cross. Which one of my party guests had a secret so devastating that it generated two murders and threatened anyone who interfered?

Chapter Eighteen

Few things rejuvenated me like a brisk morning walk. With Fantasia at my side, I felt optimistic and perfectly safe traversing the deserted paths of our local park. I sat down on a bench when a pesky pebble in my shoe temporarily halted our progress, and was surprised to see that we were not alone. A sprightly senior accompanied by her dog was also taking a break. Her pooch, a Cardigan Corgi, stayed by her side, watching our every move. He and Fantasia acknowledged each other but remained aloof.

"Your pal keeps his eyes on you," I said. "Corgis are tough little guys. He's a Cardigan, right? The kind with a tail."

She nodded and extended her hand. "I'm Virginia Lanter, and I know who you are." She saw my expression and laughed. "I was at the library for your talk. Very enjoyable."

"May I pet him? What's his name?" I bent down and allowed the Corgi to inspect my hand.

"Disraeli. I can't take credit for that, though. I adopted him from the shelter. He used to be the mayor's dog, or, I should say, his wife's. Helen adored this good boy, but when she passed, Zach didn't want him. Too many memories, I suppose."

I bit my tongue before I voiced my opinion about anyone who would discard a beloved pet. Nevertheless, Zach dropped several notches, in my estimation. He certainly gave me the impression that his wife's dog had died. Then I recalled how he had ignored Fantasia when she approached him. *Calm down, Marky. That doesn't make the mayor a killer. Just a lesser being.*

After a few more comments, I excused myself and continued our walk. Okay. Not everyone was an animal lover. At least Blaike earned points for taking exquisite care of Fantasia. Her gentle nature convinced me that she had been raised with care and affection by people who loved her. That didn't exonerate Blaike, but his explanation about the waterfront deal rang true. Still, I couldn't help wondering how many of my fellow citizens I'd misjudged. Perhaps Lionel embezzled funds from his clients, or Philippa ran a human trafficking ring. Despite what Blaike said, I still pictured the mountainous form of Josephine Soto, shoveling dirt upon her errant spouse or Tilda, blackmailing men with compromising photos or sex tapes. It felt disloyal, but I also had to wonder how far Mandy would go to shield her daughter from ruin. Paul Prentis, with his cavalier treatment of Gemma, was a vile creature who considered pregnancy a mere inconvenience. Would Jonathon Crane have exploited that information in his podcasts? How many sins of Harbor Bay would he have unveiled?

Another thing troubled me. The killer had taken pains to implicate Poppet in the crimes by including those violet extension cords. Did someone have a grudge against me personally, or was it an attempt at misdirection? I remained vigilant but somehow unafraid. Before I realized it, Fantasia and I had trekked all the way back to Poppet. Gemma had just arrived and was in the process of unlocking the door.

"What's this," she said, waving a package at me. "Kind of early for a delivery."

Something stopped me. Call it a premonition or merely dumb luck. I grabbed Gemma's arm and cautioned her. "Hold on. Something's wrong."

"What?"

"There's no postmark on this. No return address either. Maybe we should call the police." I was ashamed of myself for such a cowardly reaction but that old saw, "better safe than sorry," came to mind.

"You chicken." Gemma chuckled at my sudden turnabout. "Imagine Benny's reaction. Don't be silly."

"What's up?" Aunt Violet swept into the store and stopped short. I explained the issue, expecting her to laugh at my cowardice, but she surprised me. Violet dipped into her purse and plucked out her cell phone. "Let's get Gideon's take on this. It can't hurt."

She explained the situation when Gideon answered. "He's sending Benny over. Just to be safe. After all, you did get that threatening note."

Soto was Mr. Rapid Response. He strutted into the store, listened to our story, and viewed the package warily. "Probably nothing, but the Sheriff wants to be careful. I'll check this thing out and let you know." Was I mistaken, or did he exchange meaningful glances with Gemma as he exited the store? Apparently, love was in the air for everyone but me.

Aunt Violet unveiled a new slate of European skin care products designed to cleanse and exfoliate the skin. "American women tend to avoid this, but they shouldn't. Daily exfoliation and a weekly hydrating masque are the keys to a youthful complexion."

"Gosh," Gemma said. "My grandma thought good old soap and water was enough for any woman. And cold cream. She did put cold cream on her face at night."

Violet reminded us that at one point, women were told that by age thirty, they should cut their hair, lengthen their skirts, and think only of their children. "Not that there's anything wrong with any of those things, but if the hidden message equates cosmetics with frivolity, I really object to that."

We acknowledged that today's consumer had a vast array of products to choose from as opposed to a limited selection in prior years. My father's mother, Grandma Tess, had maintained a career in clothing sales all her adult life and was a fervent disciple of a cosmetic line called "Dorothy Gray." She was roundly criticized for such unwomanly pursuits, and in truth, Grandma Tess was mean as a snake and twice as deadly. On the plus side, she lived to be 104, still had beautiful skin, a thick head of hair, and a sharp tongue. Go figure.

Our chat fest was interrupted by the wail of sirens. Gemma stepped outside to see what all the fuss was about and soon came streaking back in. "Something's going on at the Chief's office. Ambulance and fire truck on site."

I glanced at my aunt, wondering if this had anything to do with our mysterious package. Violet agreed to remain at the store with Fantasia while Gemma and I checked things out. We jogged the three blocks to Gideon Hall's office, dreading what we might find. We joined a throng that had gathered around the outside of the building just as the imposing figure of Josephine Soto plowed past the barriers.

"My son. He's in there." Her stentorian tones quelled the chatter of the crowd, and a hush descended upon us. There was no stopping her, and the deputy on duty was wise enough to recognize that. I edged up to a familiar face and asked what was going on.

"Some kind of explosion," mayor Thanos said. "A package filled with cayenne pepper spray. You know, that strong stuff the police use. Benny opened it and got blasted right in the face. Nothing fatal, fortunately, but the poor guy's in plenty of pain. Hope his vision clears up. Eye damage and all." Just then, the EMTs rolled a heavily bandaged Soto out on a stretcher and loaded him into the ambulance. His mother followed close behind, creating a formidable barrier to any interference. I felt an odd combination of relief and guilt, knowing that he had suffered for my sake and that I was the intended target. Gemma's face had turned deathly pale, revealing freckles I had never seen before. She swayed and clutched my arm for support. "Oh Lord, Marky, I almost opened that thing…."

I tried my best to comfort her, although my heart wasn't in it. "We're not sure about that. Let's check in with the Chief and see what really happened." At that moment, a grim-faced Gideon Hall emerged from his office and waved us inside. His manner was brusque, and his words were tinged with menace. "Sit down and tell me everything about that package."

There wasn't much to tell. I explained that it awaited us when we opened Poppet that morning. Before he responded, Gemma chimed in. "Is he okay?"

Gideon shrugged. "As of now. We don't know for sure, but the EMTs were optimistic. No postmark or return address on the thing. He tore it open, and it blew up. Poor guy. Right in the face."

For the next hour, we reviewed every event, however trivial, that had transpired since Paul's murder. When I shared my list of suspects and motives, Gideon snorted some scatological term and bared his teeth. "I don't believe it. Bad enough, you put yourself and others in danger, now you think you're a detective. This isn't fiction, Marky. These people are your friends and neighbors. Do you really think Josephine Soto would put her own son in danger? She adores the boy."

Gemma finally summoned up her courage and jumped in. "Yeah, but she didn't know who would open that package, did she? I nearly did. Besides, she's got a mean streak a mile wide. She already threatened Marky. What makes you think she'd stop there? Everyone knows her temper, Sheriff. Maybe she did knock off her husband and his girlfriend. I wouldn't put it past her."

Gideon pursed his lips together to regain control. "So, according to you, Tilda might be running a blackmail ring and extorting money from her victims. Have I got that right?" He narrowed his eyes into mean little slits. "And Lionel. Siphoning money from his clients' accounts. Just because he bought waterfront property doesn't mean he cheated someone. Let's see. Our mayor doesn't like dogs, meaning he has the killer instinct and is automatically a suspect."

"He lied about that," I said. "At the very least, he misled me. Gemma found out that Zach likes to gamble too. How's that for motive? Maybe he's taking bribes and got caught."

I kept my suspicions about Philippa to myself. Using her youth group as a front for a human trafficking ring was probably a stretch, but she was smart enough and tough enough to do it. My dislike for the woman probably blinded me to the truth, and I was honest enough to admit it. Besides, Gideon might combust if I shared that theory with him.

His attitude annoyed me, so I threw discretion and caution to the wind and soldiered on. "Friends or not, somebody murdered two people, and that someone probably lives right here in your sleepy little town."

This time, Gideon sneered. "I notice your boyfriend isn't a suspect or your friend here. Why is that?"

I had no satisfactory answer to offer him. High school memories and kindness towards animals were a poor defense against a murder charge. Even famed attorney Perry Mason might have trouble with that one. Gemma tried to help, but she only made things worse. "Blaike wouldn't hurt a fly," she said. "Besides, he was trying to protect his dad. That's what anyone would do."

Gideon's reaction said it all. "And what about you, Ms. Watts? You had motive, means, and opportunity to kill Paul. Not that I'd blame you much. I've never quite bought that story in the alley. I believe you were first on the scene, no matter what you and Marky cooked up. For most policemen, that makes you the prime suspect or one of them. Frankly, assurances by Marky or your mom don't cut any ice with me."

"Why not arrest her if you're so certain," I said, going for broke. "And tell me this. Why would she send explosives to her own store?"

Very little flustered Gideon Hall. "Maybe she knew she wouldn't be the one to open it," he said. "After all, it was addressed to you."

Gemma's face grew so pale that I expected her to faint. Still, I was on a roll and had to continue. "Try convincing a jury that she could subdue two men all by herself. They'd laugh you out of the courtroom."

Twenty years in law enforcement coupled with a sizable intellect made Gideon Hall cagey. He wouldn't allow himself to be drawn into my trap. Instead, he simply grinned, an action that enraged me beyond measure. "Believe it or not, Marky, I thought of that. One woman might have had a hard time, but with help from a relative—or friend—she could do it. Mandy is one tough lady who loves her daughter."

Gideon had put me firmly in my place, and I had nothing much to contribute about Jonathon Crane. We'd met only casually, although that was enough to convince me that he was a major creep, or a bounder, as my aunt would say. Gideon raised his eyebrows when I mentioned that Aunt Violet had shared a meal with that shady journalist. He knew from experience that tackling her would be no easy task. Tempers cooled as the three of us discussed "the sins of Harbor Bay" without reaching any meaningful conclusion.

According to the chief, nothing helpful had been found in Crane's personal effects. His killer had apparently stolen any notes as well as the personal computer that always accompanied Crane. I asked if his Chicago editor had additional information.

"Nope. Everything in the podcasts was top secret, and Crane only divulged it right before his broadcasts. He did say it contained bombshells that would shake Harbor Bay to the core, but that sounded like the usual hype these guys use to sell stories."

Someone took that "hype" seriously enough to eliminate the author and any evidence. Had Crane really discovered the identity of Paul's killer? I wracked my brain for any clues that I had overlooked. And who was the second victim he'd mentioned to Gideon? Probably just a tease for attention.

"Did you hear me, Ms. Davis?" Gideon asked, pounding the desk with his fist. His voice was gruff, the no-nonsense version of a tough lawman. "Apparently, someone thinks you're a threat. Whoever it was sent you a warning today. Next time it could be a bomb or another one of those violet nooses around your pretty neck. Stop snooping." He turned to Gemma and pointed. "That goes for you and your mom too. I don't have to tell you that right now, your position is precarious at best."

"What about Aunt Violet?"

Gideon shook his head in despair. "Even I know my limitations. Your aunt is a force of nature. Besides, she can take care of herself. Heaven help the criminal who tangles with Violet Davis."

Chapter Nineteen

After Gideon dismissed us, Gemma went haring off to the hospital to check on Benny. We didn't discuss Gideon's accusations or what had prompted them. For Gemma's sake, I fervently hoped that Mrs. Soto had left the scene. Her attitude was fierce toward anything or anyone, particularly any female, who got close to her son. Call it mother love. I called it unhealthy obsession. Gemma was tough, but Josephine could slap the spirit out of her with one blow.

I trudged back to Poppet, lost in thought. The sunny day had inspired a number of citizens, including Blaike Harrington, to stroll the streets. He tugged my arm just before I entered my store.

"Hey, Marky. I heard about that package. How are you doing?" Clear blue eyes and sandy hair accentuated his claim to the all-American boy label. The terms "clean cut" and wholesome were coined to describe Blaike Harrington. Why couldn't Gideon see that? On the other hand, good looks and pleasing ways might have blinded me to his flaws. Killers with social graces were not unusual. Their superficial charm often helped them disarm potential victims and stalk their prey.

I examined my conscience. Once I had been in love with Blaike. Maybe not love exactly, but something very much like it. That was several lifetimes ago. Would lightning strike again for us? I really couldn't say. Little quirks that were once endearing seemed suspicious and cringe-worthy since Paul's murder. I'd always heard that violence affected those who were touched by it, making them wary of everyone around them. Now I was living proof of that.

"I guess I'm okay for having an enemy who wants me dead. I'm not used to having enemies. People always like me." I managed a self-deprecating smile.

He cocked his head and grinned. "A bit melodramatic, wouldn't you say? Welcome to the real world, Marky Davis. You got a warning today. If I were you, I'd take it seriously and back off."

Words of wisdom, no doubt, but somehow, I found them patronizing and offensive coming from a prime suspect in two murders. "What would you do in my place? You seem to have all the answers."

Blaike flushed. "I'd be mad as hell. Nothing would stop me from finding the culprit, and when I did...."

I put my hands on my hips and stared him down. "So?"

"Yeah, but you're a girl. A woman, I mean. I'm good at using my fists, but I bet you've never had a physical fight in your life."

"I've won my share of battles," I said airily. That shaded the truth, but no one could prove anything.

Blaike snickered. "Girl stuff. Words. We're talking gruesome murders here. Real violence. Whoever did this has killed twice and won't be shy about doing it again. Take some advice, Marky. Stick to painting." He read my reaction and hastened to repair the damage. "Look. I care about you. Always have. I don't want to see you get hurt. Give me some credit here."

I told myself that he was well-intentioned. Blaike was gallant and protective, two qualities I no longer had a need for. In high school, I'd called him my Lancelot, my knight errant. With those memories in mind, I controlled my temper and thanked him for caring. Then I strolled into Poppet and got down to business. Violet had just closed a rather impressive sale to a well-preserved matron from Petoskey. Once again, I was amazed at my aunt's ability to connect with customers without using pressure tactics. Before the woman left, I scooped a few samples into her bag along with our business card. "Call if you can't make it in next time," I said. "Or check our website. No charge for shipping."

"Phew," my aunt said when we were alone. "She was demanding but very knowledgeable and willing to shell out the big bucks to get what she wanted. By the way, that customer had some interesting observations about one of our suspects."

"Who?" Dare I hope it was something scandalous about Philippa or Tilda?

"Lionel. Her husband invested in some stock scheme or other that Lionel touted and almost lost his shirt. I guess there were bad feelings all around after things went south."

An interesting tidbit but nothing spectacular unless Lionel cheated his investors and Paul blackmailed him. Violet reached behind the counter and produced a Manila envelope. "Here. Read this, Marky."

I wasn't a lawyer, but the language seemed simple enough. It stipulated that Violet Davis, the purchaser, was now the sole owner of the parcel at 401 Main Street, Harbor Bay. It took a moment before I realized what it meant. "Hey. That's Poppet's address. You mean you bought the property? You're my new landlord?"

She bowed her head. "Exactly. I hoped that the Prentis family wanted to unload a property with some very unpleasant memories attached to it. As it so happens, I was correct. Lionel handled the whole thing very nicely."

For once, I was speechless. Ever since Paul died, I feared that his family would raise the rent and drive me out of business. Just out of spite. Now by the grace of my aunt, that fear was gone. "I don't know what to say. Except thank you. I promise to be the perfect tenant."

Violet waved away my gratitude. "Hey. This is a great investment. Property on Main Street always is." She enveloped me in a tight hug. "I have faith in you and Gemma. Poppet will be a huge success."

Fantasia joined in the festivities by placing her beautiful head in my hands. I suddenly recalled what Gideon had said and repeated everything to my aunt.

"He's probably right. Usually is. Still, I don't want to do his job for him, but a little nudge wouldn't hurt. By the way. We should send flowers or something nice to Benny. I know he was doing his job, but it would be a kind gesture." She reached for the phone and dialed our local florist. "They'll have it ready in thirty minutes, Marky. Why don't you swing over, pick them up and take them to the bookstore? Who knows what Josephine might have to say?"

I blanched at the thought. "She scares me, and more to the point, she hates me. Especially now with her son being injured." Violet ignored my excuses. That's why I soon found myself walking toward Novel Concept clutching a manly arrangement of carnations. I hoped against hope that the store was closed, but Josephine Soto was there, bigger than life, doing her inventory. As my survival instincts kicked in, I banished all thoughts of Mr. Soto nestled in a garden grave and proceeded to make nice with her.

* * *

My first attempt fell flat. Josephine looked up and growled, "What do you want?" Then she saw the flowers and relented. "Carnations are his favorite flower. Always had one in his lapel for school dances." She dabbed at her eyes with a tissue.

Even though her son was an officious twit, my concern for his well-being was genuine. The prognosis for a full recovery was positive, and his vision had almost fully returned. "Always had good eyesight," his mother mumbled. "20/20 every time. Got that from his father." She spent a few more minutes reminiscing about her son before returning to her stiff matriarch pose. "Guess you've had enough detecting. Smart girl like you should figure that out by now. Someone wants you dead."

Something emboldened me, and I faced her head-on. "I didn't ask to be involved, but Paul Prentis was murdered practically at my front door. Then someone sent me a threatening message. Now this package bomb thing. I don't like being intimidated."

Her expression turned grim. "Maybe you should go back to Chicago. You're a stranger here, no matter what you think. Thomas Wolfe said it best. 'You can't go home again.'"

I was startled by the literary illusion, and it showed. Even though she owned a bookstore, I had relegated Mrs. Soto to the ranks of the undereducated. My mistake for judging a book by its unimpressive cover.

"Bet you thought I'd never read the classics," she said. "It just so happens that I majored in English at the University of Michigan some years back.

158

Wrote my senior thesis on Thomas Wolfe." She glared at me. "He was right, you know. You can't go home again."

I had the uneasy feeling that Mrs. Soto was either warning or threatening me. I made some very forgettable remarks and, feeling suitably chastened, fled the scene as soon as possible. Obviously, I had misjudged Josephine. There was considerably more to the woman than her gruff exterior suggested. A woman smart enough to quote Thomas Wolfe also had the intelligence to plan and execute two, perhaps three murders if one counted her former spouse.

The woman wasn't decorative, but she could be a devious and dangerous adversary.

* * *

I scurried back to Poppet, where the soaring ceiling and bright open space provided sanctuary. Quite a refreshing change from the dark, dank confines of Novel Idea and its dour proprietor. Both Mandy and Gemma were there assisting clients, although Aunt Violet had left for an appointment. Fantasia let me know in her own inimitable way that she would very much appreciate some attention. After giving her a resounding nose kiss, I fastened her harness and headed for the town square. Several hours of daylight remained, subduing any fear I might have of an assailant. Even as a child, I had always feared the darkness. Many times, I had crawled into my parents' bed seeking protection from some unseen malignant force. As an adult, I substituted wariness, a canine companion, and a night light for that protection.

Kim Stevens was also enjoying the mild Spring weather. She bent down and cradled Fantasia's lovely face in her hands. I watched her make cooing sounds to the Collie and the response it evoked from Fantasia. "You have a way with dogs, Kim. Do you have any pets?"

She shook her head sadly. "No. Lionel is a major germaphobe." She gulped. "When our son was alive, he begged his dad for a dog. How I wish I had shown some backbone. Patrick would have loved having someone like Fantasia around, and so would I."

"It's not too late," I said. "Shelters are overflowing."

Her reaction touched my heart. "I'm afraid my time has passed for a lot of things." She gave Fantasia a final hug and walked away.

Was eternal sadness and guilt the price parents paid when they lost a child? I pondered that, wondering if finding the driver who killed their son would have freed Kim and Lionel from their prison of despair.

"Deep in thought, eh, Marky?" Mayor Thanos had a bemused expression on his face, and I noticed fine lines around his eyes that had not been evident before the recent trouble. Had Zachery Thanos, the genial dentist and affable politician, been engulfed by the blemishes on his beloved town? He patted the bench and said, "Sit down and join me."

"Okay." I sat down, keeping Fantasia well away from him. "You look tired, Mayor."

He laughed. "Guess I'm just getting old, my girl. Harbor Bay means a lot to me. I hate seeing folks lose faith in it."

"Surely Chief Hall will sort things out."

"Perhaps. Ever since that damned Harbor development project started, things changed. And not for the better, either."

I squeezed his hand. "Change can do that."

"Not change, Marky. I accept that. Everything evolves sooner or later. I'm talking greed. Wave a slug of money in some folks' faces, and they go wild."

I had no answer for that. Money, filthy lucre, had corrupted many otherwise sterling characters over the ages. Harbor Bay and its denizens were no different.

"Haven't you any clue? You know most everyone here. Know their families for generations back. Surely if someone was homicidal, you would have seen some indication before now."

He shrugged. "You'd think so, wouldn't you? Sometimes little things sort of pass you by. An action or comment doesn't mean much at the time, but later, you wonder."

It touched my heart, seeing the genial dentist I'd known all my life laid so low. He had always been the town cheerleader, lifting our spirits and touting the virtues of Harbor Bay and its denizens. I changed the subject.

"Kim Stevens just left. She always seems so sad, Mayor Zach. I wish I could do something to help her."

He shook his head. "That's a sad case. Nothing much to be done, I'm afraid. Maybe if they'd found the driver. That might have given them some sense of justice served. People always talk about closure, but in cases like this, I don't think it exists."

"Didn't the police have any clues? I always thought they used paint chips or dented fenders to track down the culprits."

Zach laughed. "You never change, Marky. Still reading those detective stories and confusing fiction with real life. Gideon Hall did everything by the book. Pursued every lead like a bloodhound, but nothing worked. Only thing they found out was that it was a sports car of some kind. Probably some young fool with too much money and no sense."

I detected something in his voice that alerted me. "Did you have any suspects in mind?"

This time, Mayor Zach's response was testy, almost rude. "Do you believe in redemption, young lady? Giving someone a chance to make amends and change their life? No one could bring back that fine young man, no matter how stiff a jail sentence was imposed. Why ruin two lives when it made no difference?"

His rebuke left me suitably chastened. I thanked him, called to Fantasia, and wended my way back to the store deep in thought. Discounting Zach's hokum about salvation and redemption, a careless person had taken Patrick Stevens' life and never confessed. Would that same culprit kill twice to remain free?

Chapter Twenty

My mind was jumbled, so much so that I barreled straight into Mandy as she opened the door. Fortunately, neither one of us took a tumble, although we got tangled up in Fantasia's lead and almost fell.

"Wow! You're in a fog today," Mandy laughed. "It must be love."

"Hardly. I just had a conversation with the mayor about Kim and Lionel's son. It's so sad."

Mandy closed her eyes. "I almost cry every time I think of it. Such a loss."

"Who found him? Patrick, I mean."

Mandy blanched. "Don't you know? Mr. Harrington, Blaike's dad, found him. He was a wreck afterwards not that I blame him. For a while, people even wondered whether he was the driver. Just gossip, of course, and not true. The police said it was a sports car that probably headed straight for Chicago or Detroit. But it scarred him like it was a betrayal. That, plus his wife's death, changed that man. Blaike left for graduate school about then, so Mitchell was lonely. Spends most of his time in Chicago now."

I wondered why Blaike never told me that when we'd discussed Kim and Lionel. A queer sensation crept down my spine. Perhaps Tilda Egan found out something. She lived awfully well for an unpublished writer and was certainly capable of extorting money to feather her very plush nest. I recalled Zach's words about redemption. So much bilge water unless Zach himself was the driver. According to Mandy, his good works and public service started around the time Kim's son was killed. Was there a connection?

I consoled myself with a cup of tea while Gemma finished her last appointment. Harbor Bay was not the idyllic refuge I had sought. It was no better or worse than Chicago or any other place on the planet that was ruled by humans. Evil could flourish anywhere, even behind the genial grins and soft words of one's so-called friends. Blaike and I had both traveled a long way since the Senior prom. I knew Blaike the youth but really had no knowledge of him as an adult. Even Gemma, my putative bestie, harbored a dark secret that she chose not to share with me. If Prentis told the world about her pregnancy, it would hurt but not destroy her. Bloodied but unbowed, she would survive, as the saying goes. He would fare far worse in the court of public opinion. But Mandy might feel otherwise. How far would she go to protect her daughter's reputation?

My mind reeled, and my head ached with all the possibilities. Kim Stevens was the only person who had nothing to gain from Paul's death. If he knew some horrifying secret about her, it wouldn't matter. The woman was already a shell, impervious to those slings and arrows of outrageous fortune that Shakespeare spoke of. Her husband still made my list. Lionel's business dealings might be shady enough to attract a soulless blackmailer. Plus, he had a temper.

Naturally, my preferred suspect was Philippa Gordon, with Josephine Soto a close second. I had no reason for that other than a healthy dislike for both women, and that would scarcely withstand a legal test. When Aunt Violet had returned, I summed up my conclusions. They sounded inadequate and pitifully weak, and she had no problem telling me that.

"Sounds like you suspect everyone, Marky. Lots of people have secrets, but they aren't murderers. Gideon once told me that during a murder investigation, everyone lies. Most of them haven't done anything criminal, but they value their privacy. They may be ashamed of something you and I wouldn't turn a hair at." She folded her arms and stared at me. "Think about it, Poppet, before you start accusing others."

Her words left me chastened. I valued my aunt's opinion, and quite frankly, I had hoped to dazzle her with my investigative skills. Fat chance. As she rightfully pointed out, I had no substantive theory, no proof, and little reason to play detective. Poppet had not been tainted by Paul's murder. Not really. Despite those purple extension cords, most townspeople ignored the connection. If anything, we had gained an air of mystery that many customers found alluring. Business had been good thus far. Not spectacular, but certainly encouraging. All the experts warned that most new ventures failed within two years. Poppet would not become one of those statistics. That was a vow I had made and intended to fulfill. The key was to keep things fresh and exciting. I wracked my brain for marketing schemes that would capitalize on the spring influx of affluent tourists into town. Brainstorming was far more effective with four brains contributing ideas, and when Gemma and Mandy marched in, they joined in. I knew the key to success was identifying Poppet's unique qualities and capitalizing upon them.

Customers could order products over the internet without entering any establishment. What did we have to offer that set us apart from the madding crowd and would lure them to our store? Initially, there was a stunned silence. Then Mandy raised her hand. She reminded me of a schoolgirl, timid, tentative, and fearful of offending.

"This probably sounds silly," she said, scanning our faces for a reaction.

"Ah, for crying out loud, Mom, spit it out." Gemma had little patience for delay.

"Painting. You and Violet are artists, and nobody else has that. Her voice trailed off. "It might be fun. Maybe a contest or something."

A thundering silence filled the room, causing Mandy to shrink into her chair. Finally, I spoke. "You're a genius, Mandy. I've heard of paint-and-sip parties, but ours would be unique. We'd feature art on canvas and complexions! Go whole hog. Plenty of door prizes and free samples."

Once we started, ideas came tumbling out. We decided that our initial offering would be a "paint your pet" party, guaranteed to tug at the consumer's most vulnerable heartstrings—her furry friend. Gemma agreed to feature massage tips, and Mandy, flushed with excitement, volunteered to serve drinks and snacks. At Aunt Violet's suggestion, we agreed to partner with the local pet spa and offer premium shampoos and other pet products as well.

"One more thing," I said. "Let's donate any profits to the local animal shelter. They need all the help they can get."

"We'll banish the blahs all right," Gemma said. Her cheeks were flushed with excitement. "Let's sketch out some ideas for posters. Maybe we can start next Friday night."

The evening concluded with all of us in high spirits and even higher hopes. No one even hinted at murder or mayhem, and that was fine with me.

* * *

Several days later, I stood outside admiring our posters and congratulating myself on our progress.

"Hear you're having a party," Benny Soto said. He crept up behind me so silently that I screamed. Apparently, his injuries had healed, although his manners certainly hadn't improved. Accompanied by Fantasia, my own special girl, I was focused on posting notices in store windows about the Paint your Pet gathering. Thus far, other business owners had been very cooperative.

"Kind of risky," he said. "Can't afford another murder in this town."

With great effort, I stifled the tart response on the tip of my tongue and managed a pleasant smile. It was more of a smirk with a touch of snarl, but he never noticed. I bent down and ruffled Fantasia's fur. "We think Harbor Bay is ready for some fun. Don't we, girl?"

He faced me, hands on hips, touching his weapon. His gun, to be precise. I wasn't sure he had any other hardware to flaunt. "The chief may not like that," he huffed. "You're still on the suspect list, you know."

Benny's puny attempt at intimidation had the opposite effect. It enraged me. I whirled around and gave him my own version of toughness. "Last time I checked, this was still a free country. As a business owner, I'm well within my rights. Bug off, unless you intend to arrest me."

He stepped back, clearly astonished by my response. That emboldened me to throw another log into the fire. "Furthermore, if you continue to call me a suspect, I plan to consult my attorney. That's libel, mister, and it could cost you your badge." I wasn't certain if it was libel or slander, but neither was he. My counterattack had the intended effect of stunning him into silence. On that triumphant note, I called to Fantasia and sallied forth with all flags flying.

"Quite a performance," Blaike said. He was standing outside the art supply store waiting for me. "Benny better watch his back." After he patted Fantasia, we spent a few minutes discussing my painting party and its possible effect on business. "Seems like a sound strategy to me," Blaike said. "I'm glad to see you took my advice seriously."

A second overbearing male was one man too many. I lashed out without considering the damage. "Are you my advisor now or my keeper? Poppet will do just fine without you, thank you very much, and so will I." I turned to leave, but he blocked my path.

"Whoa, Marky. No need to be that way. You know I worry about you."

"Don't bother. I can take care of myself."

He heaved a gigantic sigh and squeezed my hand. "We've had this discussion before. Need I remind you that a double murderer is still at large? Probably in Harbor Bay. More than that, I care about you and don't want to see you get hurt. I haven't forgotten what you meant to me. How things might have turned out for us."

I could feel my resistance lowering, a danger sign for an independent woman. My feelings for Blaike were complicated. While I liked and admired all that he had achieved, his behavior and inconsistency were unsettling. Upon reflection, my best course of action was to remain firmly in the neutral column. At least for the foreseeable future.

"Is that painting thing a hen party, or can guys muscle in too?"

"Everyone with a checkbook and a pulse is welcome. Naturally, we can share Fantasia if you want." I waved a few posters his way. "Make yourself useful. See if you can post a few of these around town."

He grinned and accepted the task. "Wow! Henpecked already. Marky, you've captivated me. I live to serve."

"Smart aleck." I stifled a laugh and made my way toward Novel Approach. Was I bold enough to beard Josephine Soto in her den? I stiffened my spine and entered the bookstore. The proprietor was busily ringing up a sale at the cash register and chatting with a customer. At first, she didn't see me. Either that, or she just ignored me. I realized that I had yet to purchase anything in here since I returned to Harbor Bay, and that was bad business. After all, reciprocity cuts both ways, and Josephine had visited Poppet. I ambled over to the mystery section, selected two classics from Dorothy Sayers, and took my place in line. Josephine looked up, either surprised at seeing me or astonished that I was indeed a paying customer. She totaled up the sale and accepted my credit card after staring at it with obvious suspicion. I seized my opportunity to ask about posting the notice. Frankly, I wasn't certain what reaction to expect. Benny might have been poisoning his mother's mind and feeding her conspiracy theories.

"I guess you can post it," she grunted with a sour look. "What kind of pets are people bringing?"

"All kinds. Some want to bring just a photo. I have room for ten easels, so it's first come, first served. It should be fun."

"Hmm," she said. "Had a parrot once, but my husband couldn't stand him. He hated most everything I did."

"Come along if you're free," I said, avoiding the husband issue. "We've got door prizes and free samples too." As I exited her store, I left Josephine glaring at me with a most unfriendly look. She probably wasn't the murderer. I told myself that even though I wasn't entirely sure. Losing a spouse was heart-wrenching but survivable. Any threat to Benny might be a very different kettle of fish entirely. Josephine, the devoted mother, might easily avenge her son by striking out. I wondered what Paul Prentis's relationship with him had been. Probably like most of his fellow townspeople, he dismissed Deputy Soto as a minor player of little importance. No one likes to be discounted, and Josephine had a temper. So did her son. It was easy to envision either of them striking out in anger. Using the purple extension cords seemed less likely. That little touch of malice required imagination and planning, limited qualities in the Soto household.

I had only one more stop to make before returning home. The local community center had a gigantic billboard that was a magnet for the town. Everyone posted activities, advertisements, and items of interest on it. I scurried to the door, praying that it had not yet been locked. Most activities in Harbor Bay ended at or around six pm. I checked my watch and saw that, with a pinch of luck, I might squeeze in. I headed for the main corridor and ran smack dab into my nemesis, Philippa Gordon. She was garbed in her normal dun-colored clothes, garnished with that signature scowl for which she was famous. I forced myself not to falter.

"Hi," I said with forced cheer. "Glad I just made it."

"We're closing. As the sign indicates, we close early on Mondays." Her tone was frosty. The clear implication was that I was either too stupid or entitled to read their sign and abide by the rules. I gave her the "kill with kindness response."

"Oh, thanks. I'll just slip over to the billboard and be gone in a jiffy." This was perky Marky Davis at her best. Unfortunately, it didn't deceive former Principal Gordon at all. She scanned the poster and curled her lip. "Paint party?"

More hypocrisy at work. I was beginning to get the knack of fakery. "Sounds like fun, doesn't it? I hope you'll join us. Mandy said you used to enjoy impromptu gatherings."

Philippa stiffened. "That was a long time ago. What else did Mandy tell you?"

She took a step toward me. For some reason, her unpleasant manner now seemed menacing. Fantasia sensed that and stepped in between us. That gave me a shot of courage. Too bad Fantasia hadn't been around when I was in high school. I could have used the backup.

I deliberately kept my words light and relaxed my body. Not one sign of a stress reaction. "Oh, she didn't say much. Just that you were a lot of fun. Good at Karaoke too. I know how those girls' nights out can get when everyone lets her hair down. After a few drinks, we all think we're superstars."

Philippa's complexion grew ghostly pale. "I have no time for that frivolity now. The teens keep me busy."

I pitied those poor at-risk adolescents. As if their lives weren't stressful enough, they had the missionary zeal of Principal Gordon to contend with.

"Too bad. Well, you're welcome to join us if your plans change." I tacked the notice down, pivoted toward the door, and made my escape. At last glance, Philippa was staring at the poster with an intensity that bordered on mania.

* * *

Poppet was deserted when I returned. After attending to Fantasia's needs, I suddenly realized that I was ravenous. Famished enough to treat myself to a pricy calorie-laden meal at my favorite French bistro. All my errands that day had left little time for lunch or a snack. Even breakfast was a distant memory. Fortunately, Bistro Bis opened on the dot of six pm, and I was able to snag a cozy table in a darkened area adjacent to the bar. At one time, I would have been reluctant to dine by myself, but those inhibitions had vanished long ago. The menu was filled with tempting choices, and soon I was savoring morel mushroom soup and a delicious sole èremeuni. Alcohol normally didn't interest me, but this evening I splurged on a flute of champagne. Why not toast to the success of Poppet and the upturn in my life? Having blown my budget, there was no reason to refuse dessert, especially when Crème Brûlée was in the mix. I hunched over my meal guarding it like a jealous dog with a bone so focused that I was oblivious to the couple huddled together in the booth behind me—until I heard my name.

"She hasn't a clue," said a gleeful woman's voice. "Miss Marky. Little goody two shoes." Her voice was laced with venom. There was a familiar ring to that voice, but I just couldn't place it. Her companion muttered something, but his voice was too low for me to hear. I dared not turn around. That would alert them and end the conversation. I hunched down even further into the booth, straining to catch even a few words.

"Don't worry, sweetie. Things will work out. Wait 'til the next council meeting and bring it up again. I guarantee it will pass this time." Her laughter was malevolent. I felt a chill snake down my spine. "I've been counting votes, and it's three to two."

Council meeting? Are they discussing the waterfront project?

It had to be. I paid my check and made a decision. Like it or not, I had to confront them. I craned my neck but could only see one person. Tilda Egan! No surprise there. Like it or I had to identify her male companion. I slipped silently from my seat and whirled around. Tilda Egan was shocked when she saw me. She masked her contempt but not her discomfort. I pasted a faux smile on my face and approached their table. Unfortunately, Tilda sat alone. Her male companion was nowhere in sight.

Who was he? I greeted Tilda and tried my luck. "My ears were ringing when you mentioned my name. What did I miss?"

She was far too wily to fall into that trap. "Why darlin', you must be hearing things. I'm afraid no one thought of you at all. This was strictly a business meeting."

My cheeks burned, although I tried to brazen things out by mentioning the town council meeting. Once again, Tilda was two moves ahead of me. She gave me a pitying look and said nothing. She didn't ask me to join her either. Undeterred, I bent over and gave her a specious smile. "How's that memoir of yours going? I'll bet you have half the men in town nervous as cats. No one likes his secrets exposed."

This time my comments hit the mark. Tilda narrowed her eyes and hissed a warning. "Think you're smart, don't you, little girl. Well, you're way out of your league. If I were you, I'd run back to my little store and talk to Auntie."

I nodded merrily and quickly exited the restaurant. No doubt about it, that woman frightened me. Who knew the depths of her depravity? She'd already demonstrated that blackmail, adultery, and character assassination were child's play to her. Was double murder a step too far for a woman like Tilda?

Calm down, girl. You're getting hysterical. Think.

Three men remained on the town council, and one of them was plotting with the succubus at that table. If only I could be sure. Lionel, Zach, and Blaike were the only possibilities. Each of them had financial interests at stake, although Zach's was minimal. I firmly believed that the murders were directly linked to that land deal. Prentis was guilty of all kinds of skullduggery. He'd threatened the lives and livelihoods of Josephine Soto and even Gemma and fought with Lionel Stevens. Someone ended his reign of terror in a most brutal fashion and had implicated Poppet in the bargain. It hadn't stopped there. Through either blackmail or fraud, the members of the board had been compromised. Some of them, at least. Jonathon Crane had threatened to expose the killer and had paid the ultimate price. What had Crane learned?

* * *

My head was spinning by the time I got home. Thankfully, Fantasia met me at the door and drowned me in doggy kisses. No wonder so many people valued their pets over humans. Where else could one get unqualified love and limitless comfort? I sank my face into her thick fur and meditated. Maybe I should heed the warnings of Gideon and Blaike. After all, I neither knew nor liked Paul and Jonathon. In fact, I was willing to admit that the world was a far better place without them. I was no busybody. Maybe it was time to turn in the deerstalker and focus on the beauty business. When the cell phone rang, it jolted me out of my reverie.

"Hey, stranger." Blaike Harrington said. "Where've you been?" His voice sounded genuine enough. Warm and intimate. Maybe he wasn't Tilda's elusive dinner partner after all. The male voice had been a low mumble. Nothing I could identify. I decided to test him.

"I just had a fabulous meal at Bistro Bis. You should have been there."

He hesitated. "No kidding. I wish I had. Did you see anyone interesting?"

I took a deep breath, then plunged into troubled waters. "Yeah. Believe it or not, I saw Tilda with some guy from the council. They were plotting something about the land deal."

Blaike's voice was gruff. "Stay out of it, Marky. I told you that. There's no room for amateurs with this. Besides, the proposal will pass. Guaranteed. It's got the votes. Three to two."

His smugness annoyed me.

"You don't care even if some members had their arms twisted?"

"Not at all. That's the way the game is played in the big leagues. Like that old song says, only the strong survive."

I was not yet down for the count. "What made someone like Philippa cave in? Integrity was always her calling card, or so I thought."

"We all have our price, Ms. Davis. Even those closest to you. Think about that before you blunder into something that you'll regret."

Blunder! Now I was thoroughly aroused, but not in a good way. Blaike Harrington had crossed a line. How dare he show me such disrespect! "Good advice, as usual, Blaike. I'll have to think about that." I ended our conversation and possibly our relationship with the click of a phone. My sleep was restless that evening. I tossed and turned, checking the clock at hourly intervals. Despite everything, I had avoided calling Aunt Violet or Gemma. This was something I had to sort out for myself with a little help from a professional.

Chapter Twenty-One

Gideon Hall never changed. He was at his desk, uniform freshly pressed and his eyes alight. It didn't matter that it was barely eight a.m. or that it was Saturday. Fortunately, he was alone. His sidekick Soto must have slept in or had a hot date. Knowing Benny, I voted for door number one.

"Do you have a minute?" I asked. "I need your advice."

Gideon blinked. "Advice? Do my ears deceive me? Marky Davis asking for my help."

I let him savor his moment of triumph and enjoy my discomfort. After all, I probably deserved it. When I described the scene at Bistro Bis and my other suspicions, he listened carefully, taking notes as he did so. Perhaps Gideon was humoring me, but I didn't feel patronized. Not that he considered me a colleague or anything but an interfering amateur who read too many detective novels. He made that point very clear.

"Your aunt dropped by last evening," he said. Gideon kept his expression blank, impossible to read. The guy must be a heck of a poker player with that skill under his belt. Two could play that game, I decided.

"Oh?" If he was waiting for me to beg, he'd have a very long wait.

"Yep." This monosyllabic routine was getting old, but I could play along. "My aunt Violet?"

He couldn't hide the grin that split his face. "Didn't know you had any other, Marky. Look. Let's cut to the chase. She's worried about you, and so am I. Someone around here—someone ruthless—has a secret worth killing for and isn't shy about striking again. You and Gemma but particularly you, are in his crosshairs. Cut it out. Stop snooping and theorizing. Despite everything, I kind of like you." He lowered his head when he said that, as if he were confessing to a major felony. "More than that, I really like Violet. She's quite a woman."

I couldn't argue with that, so I didn't try. That didn't mean I was conceding defeat, just that a more subtle touch was in order. "Let me ask you something, Chief."

He sighed. It was a loud, discontented sigh that signaled he was losing patience.

"What if this whole thing had nothing to do with the land deal? Suppose it concerned the death of Lionel's son or the disappearance of Josephine Soto's husband? Anyone might kill to avoid a murder charge." I gave him my big-eyed look. "Well. What do you think?"

Then it happened. The normally composed, genial officer of the law exploded. "Enough! I won't play these games with you, Missy. Do you have a hearing problem? Stop snooping. Run your business and mind your own business. Do you hear me?"

At that moment, Soto sauntered into the office. He went on alert when he saw me, as if I posed a clear and present danger to his boss. I saw his hand twitch as he patted his gun holster. "Any problem here, chief?"

Gideon recovered his composure and shook his head. "No problem. Ms. Davis was just leaving."

I gathered my tattered shreds of dignity around me like a cloak, rose from the chair, and marched out the door. My options were narrowing every day. Gemma was too volatile to discuss things with, and Blaike was no longer on the agenda. Time to see Aunt Violet.

* * *

Gideon must have alerted her. As soon as I entered Poppet, Aunt Violet motioned me toward the stock room and handed me an espresso. "I understand you had quite a donnybrook this morning," she said. "At least you're not in manacles. Yet."

With great effort, I restrained myself. Instead of launching into an impassioned defense of my conduct, I merely sipped my drink waiting for it and my temper to cool down. "Gideon can be a real jerk at times," I said. "All I wanted was his assessment of the case. He overreacted. Badly."

Violet was smiling now. "He can be territorial at times, but his motives are good. I assume you shared your own thoughts about the murders."

"True. But I also gave him information he didn't have." I described the scene at Bistro Bis and the conclusions I had drawn. "Maybe we're looking at this the wrong way. I tried to explain my theories, but he totally shut me down. Will you at least listen?"

She nodded. "Fire away but make it fast. Gemma and Mandy will be here soon. I think we should keep this between the two of us."

I pride myself on being concise when the occasion warrants it. After I listed my theories point by point, Aunt Violet stayed silent for a moment. She was mulling over things in that quiet, methodical way she had. I could tell that. "Blaike and you—-that's over now, is it? As I recall, you were pretty rough on him when you left for the Art Institute. Brutal even. Your Mom said he wandered around like a lost soul for a long time, drinking and carousing." She shook a finger at me. "Men! Oh well, he obviously pulled himself together and moved on. Unless, of course, the spark flares up once more."

I wasn't sure that there was ever anything that serious between us except adolescent passion, but things had deteriorated. The guy had never even kissed me since my return or plied me with gifts and sweet words. Maybe it was my fault, but he seemed more interested in warning me off than warming me up. Besides, who wants to cuddle with a potential killer? Not this girl!

"He's way too pushy, and for all I know, he's the one who was dining à deux with the town strumpet. That woman gives me the willies. Trust me, she's number one on my hit parade. Wouldn't she enjoy planting that violet contraption on the bodies just to implicate me. She'd love to see Poppet bite the dust."

Violet lifted an eyebrow. "Rather extreme, wouldn't you say? I'll concede that Tilda is none too ethical. Perhaps even willing to commit some criminal acts. But I can't see her killing those men. Too risky. She might incite someone else to do the dirty work, though. Men can be quite credulous, you know. Easily led."

That cynical view was a real eye-opener. My aunt knew the ways of the world far better than I did. She finished her drink, dabbed daintily at the corners of her mouth with a napkin, and left me with her final observation. "You may be on the right trail, Marky. These murders may be totally unrelated to that waterfront nonsense. I admit, there's probably all kinds of shady doings involved in that, but I wonder if the killer has a more personal motive. Both Paul and Jonathon were the kind of men who enjoyed hurting others to gain power or just for the fun of it. Sometimes that can be their undoing."

The arrival of Gemma and Mandy ended our discussion. Mandy chattered merrily but Gemma wasn't easy to fool. She immediately sensed that something important had happened, and she wanted in on it.

"Okay, you two," she said. "Stop stalling. Something happened, and I want to know what it was." She stalked around our store, hands on hips like a predatory bird.

"Gideon read me the riot act," I said. "And your boy-toy piled on. He's truly obnoxious, you know. Benny, not Gideon, although Gideon has his moments too. I shudder thinking of Soto toting a gun and wearing a badge." As expected, the mention of Soto sparked outrage and stifled Gemma's curiosity.

Mandy folded her arms and laughed heartily. "You girls! Always kidding around. I'll bet Blaike has his hands full with you, Marky."

My reaction told the tale. "Mr. Harrington no longer has to worry," I said. "As far as I'm concerned, his hands are empty and can stay that way."

Mandy patted my shoulder. "Ah. You had a spat. Lover's quarrel. Don't worry, I'm sure you'll kiss and make up soon."

Before things worsened, a customer ambled into the store seeking advice on moisturizers for mature women. Aunt Violet turned on the charm while I fastened Fantasia's harness and bolted out the door. Fresh air would do me some good. Gemma would have pursued me to continue the inquisition, but fortunately, she was booked up with massage clients all day. Mandy took the hint and busied herself with tidying up.

* * *

We trotted briskly toward the park, stopping only briefly to exchange greetings with my dog's many admirers.

My dog.

I now thought of her as that and vowed that Blaike would have a battle on his hands if he tried to claim her. He'd never had a mean streak before, but I did recall that on occasion, when things went awry in his life, he had a dark side. Then again, most people did. Fortunately, the trails, even the more remote ones, had plenty of weekend joggers and dog walkers on them today. I wasn't worried with Fantasia in tow, but I was wary. A boisterous group of youngsters in front of me hogged both sides of the path, filling the air with typical teen chatter. That didn't bother me. I wasn't that many years away from those same high spirits, even though, after recent events, I sometimes felt ancient. When they branched off into a clearing near the tennis court, I recognized their leader. Philippa Gordon waved them on and planted herself directly in my path.

"Out for some exercise, Ms. Davis. Hope the teens didn't annoy you." Her sneer told me that she very much hoped that they had.

She didn't intimidate me any longer. After all, what could she do? Send me to the principal's office? "Heavens no. Youthful high spirits are invigorating.
"

Philippa narrowed her eyes and stared. With her stick-straight hair and cosmetically challenged features, she was exceedingly plain. That was my charitable description of Ms. Gordon. Homely was closer to the mark, and hideous wasn't out of the question.

"I understand you're curious about me," she said. "Asking around."

"Really? I can't imagine what you mean. I know all there is to know about you."

Philippa never had much patience, especially with obtuse pupils. "My vote. On the redevelopment project. It's no concern of yours, so stay out of it."

I remained calm because I knew that would infuriate her. "Oh, that. I did find it curious when you changed sides. Someone must have been very persuasive. Seems like a lot about you changed in the past few years."

Her pale complexion grew even more ghostly. Obviously, my words had hit their mark. Unfortunately. I had no idea what that was.

Her voice grew menacing. "Stay out of my business if you know what's good for you. Even in high school, you thought you ran the world. What an odious little twit you were." She glared at me. "And apparently still are."

At one time, I would have cowered. The gospel, according to St. Philippa, meant something to me then, even though I had never been one of her favorites. I knew that. But the venom she spewed truly confounded me. There was another element mixed in with the animosity.

Fear.

Philippa Gordon was afraid of something or someone. Was I that person? Hard to believe I posed any kind of threat to her, especially now. Instead of warning me off, she would have been wiser to ignore me. After this, I wasn't deterred at all. Only curious.

Fantasia strained at her leash, causing Philippa to back up. I recalled that dogs frightened her and used that to my advantage.

"Funny. Fantasia doesn't seem to like you very much. She usually vies for attention from anyone she meets."

Philippa squared her shoulders and sailed away to join her group, leaving me with this parting shot. "That newsman poked his nose where it didn't belong, too. See where it got him."

As we walked back to Poppet, I gave myself some tough love while Fantasia trotted smartly at my side, keeping alert. In the short time I had been back in Harbor Bay, I had managed to alienate most of the bigwigs in town. Not good! Mayor Zach, Chief Gideon, and Kim were still on my side, but that could change at any moment. Business owners who hoped to prosper needed allies, not enemies, a lesson that Aunt Violet had tried to impart. In my defense, someone had deliberately tried to pollute the atmosphere by leaving those violet extension cords at the murder scenes. They constituted a direct connection with Poppet that someone tried to exploit. I wasn't being fanciful or self-indulgent. I had a very real enemy. Add in a nasty note and the exploding parcel, and that spelled danger. If only I knew whom to trust and what to fear. It was a conundrum that I had to solve or risk losing everything.

* * *

Activity at the store was bustling when I returned. A busload of mostly female tourists had landed, cash in hand, ready to sample our products and beautify themselves. Mandy sashayed through the store with a tray of petit fours while Violet and I displayed products. Fantasia drew her share of praise and pats, proving once again that a lovely canine creature was a plus in the eyes of most customers. The next hour was exhausting except for the sound of the world's most beautiful music, product sales. I rather missed the zing of the old-style cash registers as they toted up receipts. That was terribly old school. Come to think of it, even the casinos used automated machines rather than the coin slots and levers of bygone years. Perhaps it was a case of progress outpacing charm.

Thinking about casinos made me wonder. Was Zach Thanos still a regular at our local hot spots, or had he merely enjoyed the occasional flutter at the tables. Unless he routinely beat the odds, which was unlikely, he might need a cash infusion. Had it come at the expense of the town treasury or made him susceptible to bribes? I loathed this suspicious side of me. Harboring doubts about a kindly soul like the mayor activated every scintilla of guilt within me. Had I morphed from the girl next door into Mata Hari?

Aunt Violet nudged me when a distinguished-looking older gentleman approached us. "This charming man is interested in buying your painting. He's an art dealer from Detroit."

I was flabbergasted, of course, and only too thrilled to discuss my work and consummate the sale. The size of his check elated me, and I glanced at it several times throughout the afternoon. When we finally closed the shop,

I felt like celebrating.

"Who's up for a night at the casino," I asked. "Feeling lucky?"

"Count me in," Mandy said. "I could use some excitement."

Gemma surprised me by opting out. She had a hot date with an unnamed fellow from Harbor Bay. By the way, she bobbed and weaved, I knew it was someone unexpected. Benny Soto was my guess. Everyone to her own taste, although personally, I would prefer to be bound, gagged, and thrust into Lake Superior before ever allowing that ungainly man to touch me.

"I'll join you, too," Aunt Violet said. "Maybe one of us will hit the jackpot. Besides, you need to celebrate your first professional sale. That man knew talent, and he loved your painting."

Naturally, I was elated. After freshening up, we set our sights on the Grand Traverse Resort and Casino.

* * *

On most Saturdays, it was crowded, and this was no exception. Violet suggested that we have dinner first before trying our luck.

"Aerie is supposed to be a wonderful restaurant," Violet said, "but without reservations, we probably can't get in."

Mandy's face lit up. "Oh, that's no problem at all. I know the main chef. He's a real sweetie." She blushed after saying that and sped off to find her friend.

Once again, connections triumphed. The three of us snagged a choice booth with a breathtaking view of Grand Traverse Bay and were cosseted with free drinks and treats galore.

"This was wonderful," Violet said after we finished our meal. "I'd like to compliment the chef."

Mandy scurried toward the kitchen and soon emerged with a hirsute man wearing a chef's toque. "This is Emile," she said, blushing furiously once more.

It wasn't hard to praise Emile's food or the venue. His accent had a hint of French charm in it, and soon, he and Violet were chattering away ala

Francais. Mandy and I were stumped, so we shrugged and left them to it. When Emile left, my aunt had plenty to report.

"Quite a charmer, your Emile. He made some interesting observations about our mayor too."

"Oh?" I held my breath, hoping to stave off the inevitable.

Violet laughed. "Nothing too incriminating. Just...well, Zach is well known here. Maybe too well-known. Emile says he visits the tables and spreads the wealth."

Mandy's eyes popped. Apparently, this was news to her. I had no idea about Zach's financial situation, but surely it was limited. Unless...was he subsidizing his habits through graft and corruption? Zach loved Harbor Bay. Would he despoil it by unethical means? I recalled how testy he became when I had probed into the murders, how vociferously he had defended his town. Still, he had opposed the harbor development deal and rebuffed the intrusive tactics of Jonathon Crane. Could this kindly man who had told me about the tooth fairy and fitted my braces be a ruthless killer? More to the point, would he threaten to eliminate me?

"Let's not overreact," my aunt said. "Let me make some discreet inquiries about Zach. I'm meeting with my attorney on Monday."

We said no more about it and spent the next two hours enjoying the casino's offerings. I stuck to the quarter slots and managed to eke out a small profit. Aunt Violet favored baccarat, a game popular in Europe. Her results were mixed, but her strategy was sound. She knew when to cut her losses and back off. To my surprise, it was Mandy who proved to be an accomplished gambler. She immediately headed for the blackjack tables, where she won several hundred dollars in short order. All in all, except for my nagging doubts about our beloved mayor, our trio left the resort in high spirits.

On the drive back, while Mandy dozed in the rear seat, I quizzed my aunt. "Do you really expect Lionel to tell you anything about Mayor Zach's finances? He's such a stick in the mud. Lionel, not the mayor."

Violet flashed a saucy grin. "Oh, I have my ways. You'd be surprised. I can inveigle information from most anyone, but I also have Kim as backup. I'm starting some preliminary sketches of her next week. Artists and models communicate more than you'd think."

I left it at that, trusting that once again, I could learn much from Aunt Violet.

Chapter Twenty-Two

Our big night out left me listless the next day. After giving poor Fantasia a very perfunctory walk, I crept up to bed and returned to slumber land. We'd decided to close the store on Sundays until the tourist season arrived, and I was thankful for the respite. Unfortunately, Gemma hadn't gotten the memo. Right before ten o'clock, she pounded on my door and demanded entry. Nothing deterred my partner when she was on a tear. I donned a robe and groped my way toward the coffee machine, muttering all sorts of imprecations at her.

"Were you sleeping?" she asked. Her face was the picture of innocence, but those green eyes twinkled with mischief. "I had some news and couldn't wait to share."

She ignored my sullen response and plowed ahead. "I did some detective work of my own last night. Guess what I found out?"

I snarled something quite impolite at her and said, "I'm not up for guessing games. Spit it out or leave."

"Touchy, touchy. Okay. Gideon Hall is closing in on the murderer. He's positive that someone wanted to hide a secret. Something big enough to kill for."

"Big whoop. We already knew that. Did your source indicate what it was? Maybe he was trying to trap you into incriminating yourself. Remember, Gideon put you high up on his suspect list."

That bit of cynicism deflated her. "Well, not really. Fact is, they aren't certain themselves yet." She brightened. "But they're getting there, and when they do, we'll be the first to know."

My head pounded, and that made me cranky. "He was just leading you on. I hope you didn't have to give up much for that non-information."

Gemma responded before thinking. "He was serious....." She shook her head and sighed. "You got me there. Yes, my date was with Benny, but he was actually very nice. Quite the gentleman."

She missed the eye roll I gave her and waxed on about her date with the deputy. "One thing he did tell me. I asked if the murderer could also be the hit-and-run driver, and he said that Gideon is mulling that over. His words, not mine."

Mulling versus arresting were too very different actions. "What about his mother? Did he mention Josephine at all?"

"Nothing new except that his mom despises Philippa Gordon almost as much as you do. Mutton dressed as lamb. I think that was the expression she used."

That was curious. I had assumed that Josephine and Philippa inhabited very different universes. "What sparked the feud?"

Gemma gave me a triumphant smile. "I asked the same thing. Apparently, Josephine suggested starting a teen book club at her store, and Philippa put her foot down. Something about creating the right atmosphere for those precious at-risk kids. Things got rather nasty, according to Benny."

Despite her use of questionable methods, I had to commend Gemma. Now we had an inside source at the chief's office, and that was valuable.

"I don't suppose he mentioned Blaike at all."

Naturally, that didn't fool her. "Aha! Not quite over our Mr. Harrington yet, are you? As a matter of fact, he did say a few things. For one, he can't stand Blaike. Entitled and sneaky, according to him. And get this. He hinted that Blaike and Paul Prentis were closer than you'd think. Business stuff, I didn't get any particulars. Oh, and one more thing. Kim Stevens got nabbed for shoplifting in Grand Rapids last year. Everything was hushed up, and Lionel paid for them to drop charges, so she didn't get a record."

Gemma took a little bow as if expecting applause. After that, my casino scoop about the mayor seemed puny in comparison, but it confirmed what we had heard previously.

"Benny didn't mention the mayor at all, and I forgot to ask about that hussy Tilda. We have a movie date on Wednesday, so I'll slip it in then."

When she saw my face, Gemma shrieked with laughter. "Hey. I didn't mean anything by that. Nothing dirty, anyway. I'm going to cook dinner for him, that's all. Chicken Alfredo. It's my specialty, you know."

I'd never envisioned Gemma having any culinary specialties. Cooking was a skill that had always eluded me. Truthfully, I had avoided learning for fear that it was too stereotypical. Now I wondered if my attempts to forge an identity as an independent woman were misguided. Would I end my days as a wizened spinster like Philippa Gordon?

I shrugged aside that issue and focused on our pets and paint event. Gemma reported that the response had been overwhelming. Twenty women and several men had signed the paint schedule listing an array of pets. Most preferred to bring a photo of a beloved companion, although a few insisted on showcasing the real things. In addition, Gemma had booked several pedicures and massages, and we had scheduled a "skin seminar" for later in the evening. I was elated by the response and already vowed to schedule at least one "fun" event each month. Perhaps a partnership with other local businesses would boost attendance too. My mind buzzed with ideas.

* * *

My nerves got the better of me on the evening of the event. Too much caffeine and too little sleep took possession of my imagination. What if more violence marred the day? As a precaution and an act of defiance, I replaced all the violet extension cords with ordinary, pedestrian white ones. No use in inviting trouble, especially if our killer intended to target Poppet in any dastardly deeds. Our guests should be focused on beauty and serenity rather than the scene of mayhem and murder.

All four of us made a special effort to look glamorous that night. Violet didn't need an inducement since she always radiated elegance and Gallic charm. Mandy appeared in a green velvet cocktail dress that accentuated every curve, and Gemma abandoned her usual goth look by wearing a slinky black sequined affair. I hadn't given much thought to fashion since I returned to Harbor Bay, but Aunt Violet urged me to consider changing my attitude.

"Remember Poppet, you have youth and beauty on your side. Why not capitalize on it and enhance your image?" She handed me a gold silk pantsuit that she had unearthed from her closet. "This should fit the bill. Every woman needs a touch of mystery in her life."

I was captivated once I tried it on. The palomino silk transformed me from humdrum Marky Davis into an elegant chanteuse who could grace any movie premiere. I envisioned myself as a combination of Katherine Hepburn and Carole Lombard, with a dash of Marilyn Monroe thrown into the mix.

"I love those old movies from the forties," my aunt said. "Women knew the value of artistry in those days. None of this unisex nonsense. What woman wants to look like a man if she has other weapons at her disposal?"

Once again, I deferred to the superior wisdom of my mentor and landlady. When we reopened at 7:30 pm, I embraced every aspect of our program. There were familiar faces among the group and several new ones. My park pal, Virginia Lanter, brought her Corgi Disraeli, who behaved with all the gentility one would expect from his breed. When Mayor Zach dropped in, he acted surprised and a bit discombobulated at seeing his wife's beloved pet. Virginia brought the Corgi right up to Zach and confronted him. "Recognize this good boy, Mayor? He's doing fine. You did me a big favor when you left him at the shelter."

Zach gave her a sickly grin and quickly moved on. Before long, he was shaking hands, slapping backs, and sharing jokes with constituents. Typical politician. Still, I couldn't shake the notion that the genial mask had slipped and the mayor's true nature had emerged. It was a disturbing coda to my relationship with him.

The appearance of Kim Stevens, toting a cat carrier and cradling a long-haired grey kitten, was another shock.

"I took your advice and visited the animal shelter," she said. "This is Petruchio."

It was none of my business, but I had to comment. "He's gorgeous. But I thought Lionel forbid you to get a pet."

Kim thrust her chin into the air. "I asserted myself for once. Lionel was shocked, but he calmed down eventually. Yesterday I even saw him patting this little fellow." Her voice quivered as she said, "I know that Patrick would approve and be proud of me."

I marveled anew at the miracle of the human/animal bond and sent a silent prayer that Kim would continue her journey. After greeting each guest, I ushered the participants to their easels and made a few opening remarks. Naturally, we also took some time to introduce each artist and her furry guest. With Fantasia serving as my model, I illustrated how easily one could create a viable image of her beloved pet. Between their efforts, Mandy's petit fours with punch, and Violet's tutorials, a good time was had by all. We also gained several new customers and rang up an impressive number of sales. After the evening ended, we did a light clean-up and a brief perusal of the artwork.

"Not so bad," Violet observed. "A couple of these are actually pretty good. Best of all, everyone had fun. Mark my words, they'll be back for your next event."

Gemma swept the floor and added this observation. "I noticed Tilda and Philippa were among the missing. Like a certain Mr. Blaike Harrington."

No one missed any of that trio. Their presence would have only dampened the group's high spirits. I made a mental note that Josephine Soto had also skipped our little gathering. Perhaps she was unhappy about her son's relationship with Gemma. More than likely, she was just unhappy.

The artists had left their paintings on their easels to dry overnight, and at Gemma's suggestion, they readily agreed to offer their work at an auction to benefit the animal shelter. Win/win, as they say.

I trudged up to bed feeling exhausted but euphoric about the future. That optimism was abruptly shattered during the night when I awakened to Fantasia's frantic cries, the wail of sirens, and the clang of fire engines.

Poppet was on fire.

Chapter Twenty-Three

It could have been worse. That's what Gemma said, at least.

Poppet itself had been spared, but some monster had stolen all our pet paintings and set them ablaze in the alley. The grisly scene was not far from where Paul Prentis's corpse had lain. Gideon Hall, his deputy, and half the town of Harbor Bay gathered around our store, standing in shocked silence as the fire crews did their job. So much for my spate of optimism. I hugged Fantasia until she winced. When Aunt Violet arrived, I abandoned my tough gal act, fell into her arms, and dissolved into tears. Fire terrified me. Like many other apartment dwellers when I lived in Chicago, I had purchased a makeshift escape ladder in case of disaster. I'd never had to use it, but it supplied me with a modicum of comfort. Perhaps I needed another one in Harbor Bay.

Gideon Hall beckoned to me, Gemma, and my aunt. His terse, "Let's talk," seared through me like an arrow. We entered Poppet and, by some act of legerdemain known only to the French and my aunt, were soon sipping hot chocolate and munching Madeleines.

I marveled at Gideon Hall's discipline. Despite the hour, his attire was still impeccable—perfectly laundered and creased uniform and neatly combed hair. My aunt was no slouch either. She wore a red caftan in some incredibly soft material—probably cashmere—with subtle makeup artfully applied.

In contrast, I was a mess. My hair was a mare's nest, and the robe I had hastily donned should have been discarded years ago. Gemma didn't fare much better.

"Look around you," said the Chief. "No one broke in here. The thief entered with a key. Either that or through an unlocked door." He gave me a hard stare. "Don't suppose you set the alarm, Ms. Davis, or locked everything up?"

I couldn't swear to it, but if life habits were evidence, I was a stickler for security. Surely, I had fastened the locks and set the alarm. Gideon's frown told me that he wasn't convinced. At his direction, we hastily surveyed our stock and found nothing else missing. That told me that the thief was either male or a particularly plain woman. No right-thinking female would leave without pocketing some of our fantastic products. I kept those observations to myself since I knew they would evoke scorn and derision from the male contingent.

"Someone's sending you a message, Ms. Davis." Gideon seldom addressed me that way, so it signaled just how seriously he regarded the incident. He held up a sheet of paper that contained a chilling warning. "Next time, you'll be on fire."

"This was pinned to your door. You have an enemy, someone who may well be a double murderer as well. I'm not trying to frighten you, but this is serious."

I blanched at that and leaned back in my chair. Had I not already been seated, I might have fainted. I'm not the fragile type. Fainting is a trope perpetuated by shady novels and wily women. Nevertheless, I admit to feeling lightheaded after reading that message. Violet pressed another cup of chocolate to my lips. I felt renewed and able to respond as the warm liquid slowly slid down my throat.

"I don't understand. Why would someone target us?"

"Not us, Ms. Davis," Gideon growled. "You. It's obvious that you pose a threat, either real or perceived, to the murderer. Thus far, he's sent warnings. Next time, you could face something much more deadly."

I'd forgotten that Soto was in the room until he asserted himself. "Yeah. You could end up with a purple cord around your neck like the other two." There was a degree of glee in his voice that he didn't try to hide. With great difficulty, I suppressed the urge to slap him silly. Gideon silenced his deputy with a frown, but Gemma leapt into the fray.

"Nice talk. Remind me to tell your mother about it unless she already knows more than you think. By the way, where was she tonight?"

The mention of Josephine Soto's name enraged her son. He forgot his role as neutral lawman and unleashed a string of expletives directed at both me and Gemma. From his reaction, I surmised that yet another Harbor Bay romance had gone awry.

Aunt Violet played peacemaker. "Let's take a step back. This type of discussion isn't helpful at all. Gideon, I'm concerned about my niece's safety. If that fire had spread, she might have been trapped in her loft. Tomorrow we'll have all the locks changed and enhance the burglar alarm system."

Those seemed like sensible precautions, but I wasn't satisfied. "Do you really think that the murderer did this? I swear I haven't done any more snooping. Not since you warned me off."

Gemma patted me on the back, but Gideon wasn't satisfied. "I can't help thinking this is something personal, Marky. Think hard. Who would have any animosity toward you?"

I reviewed some possibilities. Tilda, Josephine, and Philippa immediately came to mind, as well as Lionel Stevens. I excluded Mayor Zach and Blaike on principle. Both were upstanding guys who had bigger fish to fry than me. Besides, burning those portraits was a childish gesture unworthy of them. Tilda and especially Philippa were venal enough to engineer that kind of scheme, and Josephine Soto was unhinged. None of them had attended our party, but that wouldn't exclude them. I'd plastered posters that described the events all over the town.

I closed my eyes, trying to construct a coherent thought. "I'm sorry, Chief, but my mind is so muddled that I just can't think. Maybe after a few hours' sleep, everything will be clearer."

He nodded, then gave me the tough cop look. "I have to ask you this. Wouldn't be doing my job if I didn't." Gideon avoided my aunt's eyes. "Some people have suggested that you might have done this yourself. You know. Kind of a publicity stunt, a prank to gin up interest in your business."

I was too gobsmacked to respond, but Gemma retaliated immediately. "How dare you, Gideon Hall. You have some nerve. Do you seriously believe that we'd commit a crime just to get attention?" She swung around and faced Soto. "I'll just bet I know who put that idea in your head."

To avert a crisis, Gideon waved her off and apologized. "Forget I even asked."

He warily eyed the delicate chairs and chaise that surrounded him. No way could they support his muscular frame or even the spindly form of his deputy. "Why don't I stay down here while you go rest. Then you won't have to worry."

Aunt Violet intervened. "Thanks for the offer, Gideon, but this girl and her protector are coming home with me. I doubt that our antagonist will strike again, at least not immediately, and if he or she does, we'll be ready."

My protest was feeble. Even I realized that. This was no time for faux bravery or claims of independence. I gathered a few things, and before long, Fantasia and I were snuggled in my mother's feather bed, guarded by a first-rate security system and the vigilance of my aunt. Exhaustion claimed me quickly, and I slept like the dead.

Our local newspaper heralded the fire at Poppet with a breathless account of our "narrow escape" from perdition. There were pictures too. Some enterprising scribe had snapped a particularly unflattering photo of me in that tatty robe, clutching Fantasia. Naturally, Fantasia looked gorgeous while I resembled a ravaged Orphan Annie. The article included interviews with several participants at the Paint Your Pet party, all of whom expressed their horror at the crime. Chief Hall gave a terse "no comment," but Mayor Zach waxed eloquently about the need for a speedy resolution. No one linked the arson to the prior murders, although the reporter hinted that there was a link with other recent atrocities in Harbor Bay. Fears of a crime wave were mentioned.

"You're famous, Poppet," laughed my aunt. "Bet this gets picked up by the Detroit and Chicago papers too."

My spirits plummeted to new lows. "Really? No one will ever visit Poppet again."

She reminded me then of the old adage that all publicity was good if they spelled your name correctly. Small consolation.

When Blaike phoned, I wasn't surprised. Last evening's incident merely confirmed the dire predictions he had previously made. Still, I forced myself to conduct a brief though civil conversation with him. I told myself that he wasn't an enemy, even though it sometimes felt that way. When he offered to take me to dinner, I declined. Too much work to do sprucing up Poppet and contacting last evening's artists. At least, that was my excuse. If Blaike expected me to play the frail female, he was very much mistaken.

* * *

Promptly at ten a.m., we opened our store. Both Gemma and I plastered big smiles on our faces as if nothing was amiss. In an act of defiance, we mounted a sign on our front door with bright red letters announcing, "Fire Sale." Inside we placed a basket of discounted items and free samples with the same heading.

I wasn't certain what reaction we would get, but to my surprise, customers crowded in, applauding our spirit and commiserating about the fire. When Mandy arrived bearing lemon tarts and herbal tea for all, it felt more like a celebration than a wake. Afterwards Gemma slapped me on the back and hooted. "Nothing will defeat us, Marky. We're tougher than the bastard who did this. Just wait and see."

There was only one fly in the ointment. Philippa Gordon joined our group toward the end of the celebration. Wearing her typical scowl, she inched up to the front of the line and confronted me. "Someone doesn't like you very much, Ms. Davis. Not surprising."

I'm normally not a violent person, but in this instance, I longed for a weapon. Nothing lethal. Just something that would wipe the smirk off her face. I was weary of being the good little girl who played by all the rules and respected my elders. Philippa had aroused my fighting spirit.

"Maybe you know something about that fire," I said. "You seem more guilt-ridden than unpleasant to me. What caused your sudden reformation, Ms. Gordon? What were you atoning for?"

She didn't answer, but as she backed away, I noticed that Philippa's hands were shaking with either rage or fear. "Stay away from me," she hissed. "You'll regret it if you don't."

"Really? Mandy said you used to be fun, but everything changed rather suddenly. I wonder why." For the first time in all my dealings with Principal Gordon, I didn't flinch. It felt good.

Philippa uttered one vulgar epithet, turned on her heel, and left my store.

"What was that all about?" Gemma asked. "She looked like a thundercloud which, considering everything, may have been an improvement."

Gemma could always make me laugh. I giggled as I shared my exchange with Philippa. "Funny thing, though. The woman is hiding something. I know it. All these good works with her teens are highly suspicious. What caused the sudden reformation?"

"Ask my mom," Gemma said. "I never paid much attention to Philippa. Too boring."

I scanned the remaining customers and saw trouble looming. "Uh-oh. Look sharp. Josephine Soto heading our way."

Mrs. Soto sailed toward us much like a battleship with full regalia. The woman was a force of nature, too formidable to avoid. She ignored me but confronted Gemma head on

"You hurt my boy."

Gemma never backed down from a fight. She'd lived a hardscrabble life and was well prepared for combat. "Really? Does he send you to fight his battles for him?"

Josephine grunted. "Benny told me how you treated him. In front of his boss, too."

Gemma said nothing. She merely folded her arms in front of her and glared.

"God punishes women like you. Next time I hope this whole store burns down."

That sounded like a direct threat, one that had to be addressed. Before I responded, Aunt Violet stepped up and put her hand on Josephine's shoulder. "I'm sure you don't mean that. You're as attached to your bookstore as we are to Poppet. No harm will come to either of them. We'll see to that, won't we?"

Either her words or soothing tone calmed the situation. To my surprise, Josephine teared up. "He's all I have left," she said. "Never had much luck with girls, but he really liked her." She stared pointedly at Gemma. "Now he's alone again."

Violet nodded. "These young people and their lovers' spats. Drive you crazy sometimes. I think it's best to let them sort things out themselves, don't you?"

Josephine nodded and allowed my aunt to guide her toward the refreshment stand.

I hoped her beverage of choice would be herbal tea and nothing caffeinated. That woman certainly didn't need more adrenaline coursing through her system. Neither did I, for that matter. I'd experienced enough excitement over the past twenty-four hours to last me all week. By the time we closed our doors, both Gemma and I were exhausted, but Violet, who thrived on drama, was fresh as a daisy.

We did a quick postmortem of our day, focusing on the unpleasant encounters with Philippa and Josephine. Although we agreed that either was capable of mischief, we couldn't picture them stealing into our store and seizing the portraits.

"Can you imagine Josephine Soto lumbering in here and carrying out those canvases?" Gemma scoffed. "She'd make such a ruckus that anyone could hear her a mile off. Besides, that caper required subtlety, and Mrs. S. lacks that gene entirely."

I had to agree. Philippa was a far more likely suspect. She was whip-thin and very agile, not to mention crafty. Besides, she had no affection for pets of any kind. Destroying their portraits wouldn't bother her at all.

Aunt Violet was unconvinced. "Both of these women bear some ill will against you, but I doubt that they harbor the type of serious grudge we've seen here. Remember, we're dealing with a killer. A double murderer. Someone who's hiding a very dark secret."

For once, I was happy to leave those issues in the capable hands of the police. Despite my aunt's pleas, I decided to return to my loft for the evening.

New locks and an enhanced alarm system made me feel reasonably safe there, not to mention the services of my very own protector, Fantasia. The strategy was sound but horribly flawed. I would find that out when the killer struck again.

Chapter Twenty-Four

Mundane things can bring comfort. That next day I busied myself with the mind-numbing routine common to all small business owners. Computing taxes, taking inventory, and stocking display shelves were necessary tasks that someone had to take responsibility for. In a better world, an accountant and an assistant would handle petty details. Until that day, I was tagged with doing them. Mandy helped. She couldn't tackle our business taxes, but she was a whiz at handling accounts payable. Several bridal parties used our services and then conveniently forgot to pay the freight. I marveled at Mandy's technique for extracting payment from customers without alienating them. Firm but fair, she called it. Miraculous I called it.

As a reward, I treated both of us to lunch from the Boulanger. Nothing too imaginative, just tomato bisque with grilled cheese sandwiches. As we enjoyed our meal, I mentioned Philippa and her transformation.

"She really loathes me," I said, "and I can't figure out why. I never did anything to cause that. It mystifies me."

Mandy frowned. "Don't you get it, Marky? You're everything Philippa hates and wishes she was."

Now I was really puzzled. "Explain."

"It's simple. Five years ago or so, Philippa fell in love. Crazy in love with the new principal at the grade school. Timothy O'Shay. Oh, he wasn't my idea of a dreamboat, but she adored him. Everything was "Timmy this" and "Timmy that." It got kind of boring, but we were glad for her too. Philippa never dated much before."

I wondered how long this saga would last before we reached the main event. Mandy was absorbed in her narrative and nattered on.

"Anyhow, Philippa misread the signals or something. She was just about to buy her trousseau when Timothy lowered the boom. It seemed that he already had someone else in mind. A curvy little cutie who looked remarkably like you. Before you could say boo, he up and married her and moved to Grand Rapids. Got a promotion and a wife in the bargain. I heard that they have two kids already. Twins."

"She must have been devastated," I said, feeling a twinge of compassion for my old nemesis. "And humiliated too."

Mandy shook her head. "Never said one word about it. Not even to her best pals. But ever since then, she stopped drinking and going out and got involved with this teen stuff. Obsessed, I call it."

No wonder she hated me. It was irrational but almost understandable. Still, that was hardly a motive for double murder, especially since Philippa's disgrace was widely known in Harbor Bay. I had to believe there was something more to it.

"What about that accident that killed Patrick Stevens? Could Philippa have been the driver? Maybe she was drowning her sorrows and lost control of the car."

Mandy's eyes widened. "I never thought of that. Not for one minute. But now that you mention it, Philippa had kind of a snappy little convertible at that time. One of those Saabs that they stopped making. After Timothy left, she sold it and bought that ugly minivan. Still has it."

Quite a lifestyle change. Minivans had their uses, but they screamed suburban soccer mom rather than sophisticated single. Perhaps Philippa was telegraphing to the world that she had a new direction. Perhaps she was hiding an unspeakable crime.

"I asked her why she did that," Mandy said, "but she said it was to haul those teens and all their stuff around. Makes sense, I suppose."

We collected our trash and returned to our respective tasks. Mandy was hot on the trail of a corporation that had "misplaced" our invoices while I pondered the mystery of Philippa Gordon, scorned lover and uber bitch.

Tuesdays were relatively slow, so handling the few customers who wandered in was no big task.

Towards the end of the day, Aunt Violet strolled in, carrying my sketchbook and supplies. Her jaunty look told me that something good had happened. Despite my misgivings, I had shared preliminary sketches of Kim with my aunt As I awaited her assessment, my anxiety increased.

Violet's expression said it all. "You've done it, my dear. These are remarkable portraits of a beautiful woman in conflict. Like all great artists, you've managed to capture the essence of your subject. I am so proud of you."

I breathed a sigh of relief. Sorrow marked but did not mar Kim's lovely face, and I had recognized a strain of resilience in her that had eluded me before. The inclusion of little Petruchio added an additional element to the sketches. He was a symbol of Kim's blossoming independence.

"Well," I asked my aunt, "what's the verdict? Of course, we have a long way to go, but I really felt inspired today. Lionel poked his head in, and even he seemed pleased."

Violet never fished for compliments. She didn't have to. I envied the air of self-confidence that permeated her work. She was a gifted artist and knew it. I'd never managed to achieve that and probably never would.

"All in all, a most profitable day," Violet said. "Kim was most forthcoming about her life and her husband as well. It seems that Lionel had recently suffered some financial reverses, nothing catastrophic but worrisome. When Prentis pressured him, he resisted even though it meant losing more capital."

If I were a dog, my ears would have perked right up. "Oh?"

She nodded. "Kim was worried because our friend Jonathon Crane accused Lionel of malfeasance. Falsifying paperwork for a loan. That's a federal crime, of course. Could mean disbarment or even jail time."

I gasped. "Was it true?" Visions of Lionel being led away in handcuffs appeared unbidden. At his age, he might not withstand the strain.

"She said not. Just a misunderstanding between Lionel and some of his clients. I guess for a while after their son died, both Kim and Lionel were in a fog. Quite reasonable. Still, it's not the kind of charge that any lawyer wants to fend off."

Poor Kim. In addition to losing her son, she risked losing her lifestyle as well. Lionel had a compelling motive to eliminate both Prentis and Crane. The question was, could he do it? More to the point, did he do it?

I shared Mandy's scoop about Philippa, adding my own special spin about a connection with Patrick's death. Violet's reaction was subdued. She didn't exactly agree but she gave it due consideration.

"You may have something there," she said. "Philippa is a more complex woman than she appears to be. Those repressed types can have real depth of feeling, especially when it involves rejection. What intrigues me is this sudden transformation from party animal to teetotaler."

I suggested that Chief Hall might have some insights about that—ones that he'd confide to her more readily than he would me. Come to think of it, he barely spoke to me these days, let alone shared secrets. Too bad Gemma had severed contact with Soto. He was a poor excuse for a lawman, but he was privy to Gideon's game plan. Maybe my partner would have to take one for the team and reconcile with Benny. He'd be very easy to manipulate.

"Any word about Mayor Zach's gambling habits or how he's financing them?"

My Aunt got that cat with the cream look on her face. "I just happened to mention our little excursion to Grand Traverse Resort. We discussed the restaurant and the great food. That gave me an opening to casually inquire about Zach's spending habits. Kim had no information about that at all. She simply didn't bite. On the other hand, I got the impression that although she was telling the truth, Lionel is Zach's attorney, so he probably knows the story. Of course, attorney-client privilege comes into play, so that looks like a dead end."

I shivered at her words—dead end. Something had put Paul Prentis and Jonathon Kane on that lonely road, and I didn't plan to join them. Would the she-devil Tilda Egan be more forthcoming? I hadn't fared well in any encounters with her so far, but optimism always triumphed. Tilda was a greedy soul who loved free stuff. Perhaps I could leverage that to my advantage and get some information in return.

"Suppose Tilda won our spa day raffle?"

"What raffle?" Gemma asked as she entered the fray. "I don't remember sponsoring that, and of all the undeserving winners—Tilda Egan. Ugh!"

Aunt Violet caught on immediately. She flashed a big grin as she put her arm around Gemma. "Think about this. It wouldn't cost us much, and we might get some surprising results."

My partner was unconvinced. "Couldn't we just throw a scare into her? Beat her up a little? I know some guys who enjoy that kind of thing."

I was horrified, but Aunt Violet took it in stride. "Absolutely not. Finesse, Gemma. That's how you maneuver someone like Tilda. She's tough as an army boot. Probably responds to flattery, not force. So, we pour it on with a spoon. A ladle, actually."

"Who's gonna handle this," Gemma grumbled. "Count me out."

Gemma could make stubborn mules look reasonable. I was ready to abandon the scheme but persisted. "Come to think of it, a monthly drawing might be just the thing to try, especially before the tourist season gets started. Stir up the base, as they say in politics. Leave it to me."

I was ready to curl up with Fantasia and a good book until Gemma reminded me that the library was sponsoring a mystery book evening. Tonight was the first session, and our friend Virginia Lanter had begged us to attend.

"Come on," Gemma said. "Don't be such a stick in the mud." She brandished a circular containing all the particulars. Tonight's topic was the female sleuth, and attendees were invited to discuss their favorites. That appealed to me, especially since I hadn't left the store in a few days, and my social calendar was woefully empty. Gemma slapped me on the shoulder and gave me an "atta girl."

"By the way, the library is dog friendly," she said. "Bring your princess along for protection."

Including Fantasia in our excursion sealed the deal for me. Besides, enough people lately had accused me of snooping, so the topic was indeed timely. I grabbed a quick snack, fed my dog, and changed into a fresh outfit. Something mysterious would suit the occasion. I considered several choices and finally settled on an all-black ensemble that hinted at hidden secrets. To ease the chill, I added the red cashmere cape given to me by my aunt. I twirled around in front of the mirror, pleased by my slick new image. I envisioned myself as a heroine, Little Red Riding Hood with attitude. Glamour was something foreign to me, although I aspired to at least a modest aura of intrigue. The influence of Aunt Violet, my mother would say. The effect of growing up, I maintained. Lately, the wholesome midwestern girl next door thing bored me silly. My personal image needed a makeover as much as some of my clients did. Maybe that would inspire someone like Blaike to see me differently. For all I knew, a mysterious stranger might swoop down from the big city and lay his heart out for me. *Fat chance!*

Gemma knocked on my door so loudly that Fantasia barked.

"For heaven's sake," I grumbled. "Why didn't you just call me?"

"Bad connection on my cell," Gemma said. "This thing is a piece of junk. Remind me to get something that actually works."

* * *

We walked the few blocks to the library despite the lengthening shadows. Harbor Bay was still clinging stubbornly to the vestiges of winter despite what the calendar said. With Fantasia at my side, I had few worries. That herding instinct kept her alert to any possible danger to her flock which, in this case, meant me. I was pleasantly surprised to see at least two dozen mystery enthusiasts, mostly female, milling about the sign-in desk. When Virginia spied us, she gave both me and Fantasia a big hug. Disraeli stayed glued to her giving us the Corgi side-eye. "Oh, don't worry about him," Virginia said. "He's used to being the big noise around here. He'll get over it."

I motioned to Gemma and grabbed a seat just as Josephine Soto made her entrance. Despite her brave words, Gemma scrunched down in her chair, trying to look invisible. Fortunately, Josephine ignored her. The ninety-minute program was a delight and seemed to go at lightning speed. Many of my contemporary favorites, such as Sue Grafton's Kinsey Millhone, and Sara

Paretsky's VI Warshawski, shared pride of place with those classic heroines Harriet Vane, Tuppence Beresford, and of course, Miss Jane Marple. There was plenty of spirited discussion, even a rather contentious debate about contributions by less recognized sleuths like Nora Charles, Mrs. North, and Della Street. Audience members had been urged to submit written questions. Most were innocuous enough, but one stood out to me. When the librarian read it aloud, she hesitated.

"It seems like someone has a different view of female sleuths. This questioner asks if someone risks her life pursuing a killer, shouldn't she pay the ultimate price?" Virginia gulped. "I'm not quite sure what the point is here. Perhaps we'll discuss it after the program ends."

Afterward, I thanked Gemma for nudging me out of my comfort zone back into the real world. We enjoyed the modest array of snacks provided by the Friends of the library, including some special treats for canine attendees.

"Who do you think wrote that nasty question?" Gemma asked. "My money is on Josephine Soto. Just the kind of sneaky trick she'd pull."

I wasn't sure, especially since the question box had been openly displayed in the library for several days. Anyone could have stuffed that message into it. Still, it was worrisome. I clutched Fantasia and held her close, deriving comfort from the collie's presence.

"Glad to see you out and about, girls." Mayor Zach sometimes forgot the century he was in or the appropriate terms for his constituents. I gave him a pass, though. He had known us all our lives since we were girls, so I forgave him that breach of decorum. "Sorry about that mishap with your paintings." Trust Zach to call arson a mishap.

I noticed that he looked particularly dapper that evening and seemed quite keen on my librarian friend, Virginia. For her part, she appeared very receptive to his attention. Her cheeks showed a faint, very becoming blush, and a dab of lip gloss took a decade off her.

"We met a friend of yours at the Aerie restaurant," I said, trying to keep my remark low-key. "The French chef. Gave you high marks as a generous tipper, Mayor."

Zach's reaction was troubling. He flushed in a way that told me he preferred to forget the casino, and the chef. "I used to go there quite a bit," he said reluctantly. "But now I have other things to occupy my time." He glanced fondly at Virginia.

"What about Disraeli?" I asked. "Does he approve of your friendship?"

Zach bit his lip. "That dog never did like me. Almost as if he blamed me when Helen got sick." He reached into his pocket and produced a treat. Unfortunately, when Disraeli saw it, he sniffed disdainfully, gave the mayor a baleful look, and turned aside.

"Seems I just can't win," Zach said. "You see why I put him up for adoption. He hates me."

Virginia took his arm. "Disraeli's a work in progress. He'll come around." They wandered off, lost in their own special world, oblivious to the rest of us. Even though I felt a pang of envy for the elderly duo, I hoped in my heart of hearts that Mayor Zach wasn't the killer. He had motive, means, and opportunity, the big three for any murderer, but I was reluctant to blame him. Still, he was defensive about his connection with the casino and gambling in general. Everyone needs a hobby. I heartily endorse that, but when that hobby involves large cash expenditures that come from illicit sources, I draw the line. My thoughts were interrupted by Gemma clawing desperately at my arm.

"She saw me," she gasped. "Do something."

The she in question was none other than Josephine Soto, and that formidable matron clutching a plate of treats was heading our way.

I gave Gemma my most repressive frown. After all, she had to confront her nemesis sooner or later, and it was unlikely that Mrs. Soto would cause a ruckus at a library function. As a business owner, she also had a reputation to protect.

"Saw you chatting up the mayor," Josephine grunted. Her manner was gruff but not hostile. Since she was awkward in social situations, this may have been her feeble attempt to start a civilized discussion. Either that, or it was a particularly clever prelude to a blitz attack.

Both Gemma and I nodded and smiled as if we were dual puppets on a tight string. Anything to preserve tranquility and escape without internal injuries.

"You must know Mayor Thanos well," I said. "Such a kind man."

She scoffed. "Maybe now. When his wife was alive, he wasn't so nice."

I looked around in case anyone was lurking. Gossiping about our town's leader was certainly not in my best interest as a businessperson. "Illness affects everyone differently, I guess. Some people are just not equipped to handle it."

The look Josephine gave me could have melted steel. "Maybe. He was equipped to handle the money he inherited, though. Never turned a hair at that. Helen left him a fortune. I know because I witnessed her will. She was loaded."

Gemma gasped, and I gaped. Mayor Zach didn't look or act wealthy. No wonder he trotted off to the casino and spent so freely. An ugly shiver of doubt ran down my spine. Had the genial dentist helped usher his wife from this world to the next? If Paul Prentis learned about that or even suspected it, he had real leverage to use against the mayor. That was one secret worth killing for. Twice over.

While Josephine stuffed cheese wedges into her mouth, we seized our chance to escape. I needed time to mull over this new information and try to reconcile it with the other facts in the case. Gemma needed the opportunity to flee from her tormentor.

* * *

"Phew," Gemma said after we got outside. "Talk about your awkward conversations! Well, at least we know where Zach got his money. Sort of lets him out of being the killer."

"Does it? I shared my theory about his wife's death. "Just a possibility of course, and no way to prove it. But it does make you wonder."

"Not me," Gemma said. "It makes me want to jump in bed and pull the covers over my head. Harbor Bay isn't like Chicago or Detroit. We have good neighbors who take care of each other."

We exchanged looks, and Gemma finally admitted defeat. "Okay. I give up.

I'm living in a dream world. After two murders, you'd think that it would sink in. We're no better than any big city. Maybe worse."

One thing still puzzled me. The murderer had taken pains to implicate Poppet and especially me in his or her crimes. Not enough to make me a suspect, just enough to sully our image. That malice didn't fit with Zachery Thanos. We'd never exchanged a cross word or had any kind of disagreement.

I kept returning to Tilda and Philippa. Both had the temperament and animus against me to use those violet cords. Their venom may even have been directed toward my aunt. After all, Violet Davis was legendary, the kind of person that lesser women could easily envy. My achievements such as they were certainly couldn't compare with my dazzling relative's. I made a mental note to discuss this with my aunt. After all, she'd been in and out of Harbor Bay for years and could easily have wounded someone's vanity or punctured their pride. Someone might believe that Violet had abandoned the town for greener pastures or that her actions reflected negatively on their own life choices. Paris, the world's glamor capital, certainly fit the bill. "Uppity" was a word Michiganders used to describe those who felt they were better than others. That wasn't true of Violet, but perceptions could vary widely. Was someone we knew secretly nursing a grudge so lethal it had led to murder? I shivered at the very thought.

As we neared the town park, Fantasia went on alert. Her ears pricked forward, and a low growl emanated from her throat. Neither Gemma nor I saw anything suspicious but canine senses were far keener than ours. We quickened our pace to a brisk trot and reached Poppet in record time.

"Let me drive you home," I said. "Why take a chance?"

Gemma's response was emphatic. "Absolutely not. I've walked that route for twenty-five years, give or take. A nasty note won't scare me away. I could use a coat, though. It got chilly suddenly."

I rolled my eyes and handed her my red cape. "Be careful with this. Aunt Violet gave it to me. Loro Piana baby—Italian artistry at its best. No one would dare to mess with you. On the other hand, what about Mrs. Soto? You might run into her in the dark."

"Now that's a different story! You know how fast I can move." Gemma took a bow. "Track star in high school, if you recall." She pulled up the hood, winked at me, and sallied forth.

I should have insisted. Should have ignored Gemma's bravado and insisted on driving. As it turned out, our decision was a costly one that I would regret for the rest of my life.

Chapter Twenty-Five

J ust before midnight, Mandy called looking for her daughter. I was half asleep, and she was distraught and so incoherent that, at first, I couldn't understand her.

"Is something wrong?" I mumbled, not the smartest remark I'd ever made.

"Where is she?" Mandy cried. "Gemma would never stay out without telling me. She knows I worry."

I switched on the light and considered all the possibilities. "Maybe she met somebody and stopped for a drink. We left the library at about 10 o'clock. Gemma insisted on walking home even though it was dark."

"She probably took that shortcut through the park," Mandy wailed. "I warned her. Told her you're not safe anywhere these days. But you know how headstrong she is."

My synapses finally started to fire. "Have you called the police?"

Mandy kept blubbering meaningless phrases that made no sense. If Gemma had somehow hooked up with someone, she wouldn't thank us for causing a scene. On the other hand, better to face her wrath than risk her life.

"You contact Gideon. Meanwhile, I'll go pick up my aunt and meet you at the entrance to the park. Okay, Mandy? Don't worry. We'll handle this."

Try telling any frantic mother not to worry about her daughter. I knew it was futile, but Mandy responded to those worthless platitudes.

"Okay," she said. Her voice sounded numb, nothing like the vivacious woman I'd always known. I hastily donned my jeans and a sweater, grabbed my cell phone and purse, and summoned Fantasia. Having her there emboldened me. I didn't own a gun. Never wanted one before. Now I was thankful for the police-style torch I'd somehow acquired over the past few months. It emitted an incredible blast of light and was solid enough to deliver a convincing blow to anyone who menaced me. For just a moment, I considered calling Blaike. Feminism aside, having a partner with significant muscles appealed to me. I resisted the impulse even though I knew that he would gladly ride to the rescue. Three determined women plus one fearsome collie were enough of a search party. Besides, I expected Gideon and even the dreadful Soto to join the hunt. If there was one. Gemma might already be streaming toward her home.

Luckily Violet was still awake. Her reaction was measured and incredibly calm under the circumstances. "Pick me up," she said. "I'll be waiting at the door. And Marky, drive carefully. We can't help Gemma if we have an accident."

I took several deep breaths and scrambled out the door, stopping to activate the burglar alarm. No sense in inviting more trouble. I reached my parents' home in record time, despite Violet's warning. As promised, she was waiting at the door, an oasis of calm in a roiling sea. I noticed that she carried a large satchel, Italian leather, of course. "I grabbed a few supplies just in case we need them," she said. "Gemma may have fallen. Easy enough to do in the dark. Always be prepared—that's my motto. Comes from being a Girl Scout, I guess."

I forced myself to drive carefully, warring with the impulse to speed.

* * *

When we reached the entrance to the park, Mandy was there, shivering from either cold or anguish.

"I called Gideon," she said. "He's on his way. Gemma…." Tears streamed down her cheeks as she said her daughter's name. "It's been just the two of us for so long. I don't know what I'd do without her."

Violet gave Mandy a hug. "Let's get going. Remember, Gemma is a strong, resourceful young woman, and you made her that way."

208

Flashing lights alerted us to Gideon's presence. His face showed no emotion, but I felt reassured just by his presence. Even his sidekick, Soto, gave me some degree of comfort. We would find Gemma, and she would be fine. That was my mantra, and I recited it as we formed a posse.

"This isn't a huge area," Gideon said. "If Gemma's here, we'll find her." He handed each of us a whistle. We broke into two groups and began combing the area for clues. Gideon and Benny used thick branches to penetrate the bushes and brush while Mandy, Violet, and I searched the walking trail. Mother Nature cooperated by throwing a full moon into the mix. We called Gemma's name, straining, hoping for some response. I kept Fantasia on a very loose lead to allow her the maximum amount of freedom. Canine senses were far more acute than ours. I knew that and placed my trust in her.

After what seemed like an eternity, we heard a faint cry. Fantasia broke free and sped straight toward a thicket directly off the path. Thick grass impeded our progress, but Mandy flew through the brush with a speed born of desperation. When her whistle alerted us to the good news, I swear I had never heard a more beautiful sound.

"She's here! My baby's alive!"

We found Gemma at the base of a sturdy oak, mouth gagged and her hands bound by a violet extension cord. She was unconscious, bleeding from a head wound but breathing. My cashmere cape made the scene appear even more ghoulish as it bathed her in a sea of red. Violet waved smelling salts under Gemma's nose and took her pulse. "Faint but steady," she said. Gemma's eyelids fluttered but remained shut. In the distance, I heard the wail of the ambulance siren. When I was a child, my mother taught me to always say a prayer when the ambulance sped by. Now that bit of advice seemed particularly apropos.

Help is coming. Hold on, Gemma. Help is coming."

"So much blood," Mandy whispered. Her voice quivered, but she managed to contain her emotions even as she clutched her daughter's hand.

Gideon did his best to console her. "Head wounds bleed like crazy, Mandy. Don't read too much into it. We'll know soon enough."

Soto was a silent sentinel glued to Gemma's side. There were signs of anguish on his face that surprised me. Perhaps he really cared about my friend. On the other hand, perhaps he worried that the assailant was someone very close to him.

I kept a firm grip on Fantasia for her sake as much as my own. The miscreant might still be roaming the park for all we knew. Gideon isolated the crime scene with yellow police tape. When the EMTs arrived, they scooped Gemma up and into the ambulance with Mandy at her side and sped away. Despite my desire to dash over to the hospital to sit with Gemma, Gideon advised me to go home.

"You 'll only be in the way right now," he said. "Don't worry about Mandy either. I'll stop over there as soon as we secure this area."

I was too exhausted to argue and agreed to wait until nine am before making a formal statement. That was barely six hours away, but any amount of rest would be helpful. As Violet and I drove back to my parents' home, one question consumed me. Was this a random attack, an assault on Gemma in particular, or something meant for me or my aunt? That distinctive cloak belonged to Violet, but I had proudly worn it to the library. Using the violet cord was an in-your-face action that tied everything into the other murders and to Poppet. When the assailant saw that his victim was Gemma, that may have saved her life. I shuddered, picturing that piece of purple fastened around Gemma's neck like the other two victims. Each scenario was chilling, and I gladly accepted my aunt's suggestion to spend what remained of the night with her. The distinction between bravery and cowardice eluded me, and I wasn't about to quibble.

* * *

Against all odds, I immediately fell into a deep, dreamless sleep until five hours later when the tantalizing aroma of espresso awakened me. I dragged myself into the kitchen, opened the back door for Fantasia, and faced my aunt. Naturally, she was perfectly composed and attired. I expected no less, even though I very much doubted that she had slept at all. Weariness wasn't

210

evident in her face, voice, or manner. Too bad she couldn't bottle and sell her secret. We'd make a fortune at Poppet.

"Have some breakfast," she said. "We have a long day ahead of us."

I broke off a crusty hunk of baguette and spread honey on it. Starvation wouldn't help either me or Gemma. Violet had already spoken to Mandy and assured me that Gemma was awake, out of danger, and resting comfortably, that old saw that probably was quite meaningless but nevertheless helped to allay fears.

"Take your time getting ready," Violet said. "You want to project courage and calm to the outside world. For Gemma's sake and as a message to the killer."

My response was flippant, far too snarky after her kindness. "Maybe I should wear a sign—-don't mess with the Davis dames if you value your life."

"Very amusing, dear, now scoot." Apparently, nothing fazed my aunt, even violent assault, or insolence from her favorite and only godchild.

I felt a bit shaky recounting last evening's events to Gideon. It wasn't his fault. His manner was subdued, and his inquiries were kind, but a combination of guilt and fear welled up within me, almost driving me to tears. Almost. When Violet leaned over and squeezed my hand, that steadied me. I explained that nothing unpleasant had occurred at the library except for that strange note. Even that was innocuous, and neither Gemma nor I had felt threatened. The violet extension cord figured prominently in our discussion. I explained that I had rounded up my entire supply and locked it away. Those items were available at most big box home stores, so anyone could have accessed some. Gideon narrowed his eyes when he asked if I had done any more 'detective work'—his term, not mine. I'm not sure he believed me, but he let the issue rest for the time being. Benny Soto had been assigned to guard Gemma at the hospital, a task he probably relished. Gemma might well have a very different reaction.

"You don't think the killer would try again, do you?" Aunt Violet watched Gideon's face very carefully. He waited a while before answering.

"Probably not. I think Gemma's attack was a case of mistaken identity. Her assailant was after either you or Marky. That I'm sure of. One or both of you pose a danger to this predator, and he—or she—is willing to kill to stop you."

Violet shrugged. "I can't think why, Gideon. As you know, I just returned to Harbor Bay. Same for Marky. It's hard to believe either one of us could stir someone up that fast."

He smiled for the first time that morning. "What's that saying. "Old sins cast long shadows"? Think about it. Seriously. Something you either did a while back or know is worth killing for."

"But I left after high school, for heaven's sake. Nothing big happened then. Just kid stuff. Fooling around, having fun. Going to parties and dances. Kid stuff." I recalled my high school years fondly, particularly warm summer days playing tennis, swanning around Lake Michigan in Blaike's corvette with the wind whipping through my hair. My parents indulged my every whim—after all, I was going to be the next Berthe Morisette or Georgia O'Keefe. A life of unlimited possibilities stretched out before me until reality interceded.

Violet agreed. "I hardly ever came back here once I left. Frankly, I outgrew Harbor Bay or thought that I had."

"Maybe that's the point. Abandonment. Success. Someone wants retribution."

I wracked my brain, trying to picture people I knew, either friends or acquaintances, who might want me dead. Most everybody liked me. Voted Miss Congeniality in senior year and most likely to succeed. Marky Davis, good girl. Had I been blind or delusional? It was a sobering exercise that I don't recommend. Someone, some secret foe, wanted me dead. But why? Even if someone envied or hated me, I knew nothing that would endanger a soul, let alone spark two murders.

Gideon just wouldn't give up. "You might not even be aware of it, but it's important to this murderer. And I don't need to remind you just how ruthless this individual is." He planted his massive hands on the table and rose. "Promise me you'll think about it, and please, be careful."

We thanked him and agreed to consider what he'd said. Gideon Hall was no alarmist. He didn't exaggerate or overreact. If he advised caution, only a fool would ignore the warning. Violet and I were no fools.

* * *

Before heading to the hospital, we stopped at the bakery to get sustenance for Mandy and some treats for Gemma if she was up to eating. "Hospital food is dreadful almost everywhere," Violet lamented, "although, in France, it is quite good. The country really prides itself on food and fashion."

Knowing Mandy, she had probably refused to abandon her daughter's bedside for even a cup of coffee. When we arrived, we learned how true that was. Soto stood guard outside my friend's room, looking fierce and quite formidable. Initially, he refused to allow us inside, but he was a poor match for the combined will of two Davis women. Mandy sat on a straight-back chair, head lolling. When she heard us, she bolted upright as if an electric cattle prod had nudged her.

"Take this," Violet said, handing her a double latte and a spinach croissant. "Hot out of the oven. Brought one for Gemma, too, if she's up to it."

"Oh, I'm not sure...." Mandy glanced fondly at her daughter.

"Cool it, Mom. I'm starving!" That was Gemma, shaking off her stupor and asserting herself. "They're making me stay another night. Some stuff about more tests or something. I won't last if I don't get some decent food." She dove into the bag, not even waiting for a plate and fork.

After lunch, Gemma told her story. She'd taken the shortcut through the park, walking at a brisk pace just in case. Suddenly, she'd sensed something, a foreboding perhaps, and she wheeled around. "Out of nowhere, someone jumped out and grabbed me around the neck. I couldn't breathe but believe me, I fought back. Probably would have gotten away too, but he clobbered me."

"He? Are you certain it was a man?"

"Nope. Just someone with a strong grip. Could be a woman or man." She flashed a smile. "Hey, I'm no sexist. Plenty of strong women around these days. Before I passed out, that hood fell back, and I heard whoever it was say something like, "You ruined my life. Time to pay the piper." Gemma yawned. "Of course, I could be wrong about the words. I was feeling kind of woozy by then."

She was getting drowsy, slurring her words. Still, I had something else to ask her.

"Gideon thinks either my aunt or I were the real target. Any thoughts on that?"

Gemma closed her eyes and laid her head down on the pillow. "Dunno." Before I asked any follow-up questions, she had dozed off. Just then, an officious nurse barged into the room and glared at us. She wore traditional garb—starched white uniform and hose plus a frilly cap. Most of the other nurses had abandoned that look for comfortable pastel pantsuits. That told me that this woman was probably a stickler for rules.

"What's this? My patient needs rest, not a party. Please leave at once."

I had no energy to defy her, and in a tussle, that angel of mercy would have probably prevailed. Aunt Violet was far too sensible to argue with a hospital gatekeeper of any kind. We gave Mandy another hug and promised to return soon.

Deputy Soto was still at his post, surveying each passerby with suspicion. He gave us a brisk nod and resumed his mission. It was almost noon, and someone had to open and staff Poppet. Plus, Fantasia needed a comfort break and lunch. We decided to open the store despite the horrors of the previous evening. Gemma's attack would be an open secret in a town that functioned as a gossip mill. Besides, we would probably gain plenty of foot traffic as neighbors milled about seeking information. Who knew—perhaps the murderer might join the throng as well. I shivered at that thought and put it firmly at the back of my mind.

Chapter Twenty-Six

Violet dropped me at Poppet while she went home to collect Fantasia. Sure enough, before I had tidied up and drawn the shades, Tilda Egan flounced in. I restrained myself from smacking that smug, self-satisfied smirk off her face. I was in the customer service business and had to tolerate all types of people.

"I heard about your trouble last night," she said, feigning concern. "Poor Gemma. I hope she's recovering."

I downplayed the incident. "She's a real trooper. Already struggling to come back and take on the world." My brave words didn't fool Tilda one bit.

"You must be terrified," she purred. "Having that murderer on your trail. Using that violet extension cord too. Very troubling."

"I'm surprised you know about that. Chief Hall asked us not to mention it."

Tilda's response stopped one inch short of insolence. "Oh, Josephine Soto told me. By now, the whole town probably knows. You know what a close community Harbor Bay is."

I urged Tilda to browse while I readied the store for other customers. She left after purchasing eye cream and an upscale shampoo. Tilda was a major irritant, but I had to admit that she was a reliable customer who was willing to shell out the big bucks for products she desired. Another thought also occurred to me. Was Josephine Soto merely repeating what her son told her, or did she have firsthand knowledge of Gemma's attack? She had the physical strength to subdue Gemma, but not much of a motive. I'd had very little contact with her before returning to Harbor Bay, and my aunt barely knew her. Tilda was an unlikely suspect also. She was malicious and might swindle, lie, and cheat, but feats of physical strength just weren't her style. I doubted that she would risk spoiling her perfect manicure by choking someone or wielding an extension cord.

My next visitor was an unexpected one. Mayor Zach loped into the store, oozing sympathy and avuncular charm.

"Marky," he said. "How's Gemma? What a narrow escape, poor girl. You both looked so sweet last night too. Kind of like little red riding hood." He patted my hand. "I told you to be careful, didn't I? You never know when something bad can happen. She didn't see her attacker, I suppose. Must have been some fiend from the city."

Something about his manner made me wary. It felt sinister. More like a threat than a warning. Was I reading something that didn't exist into an innocent comment? Paranoia simply wasn't my style, so I shook off my suspicions.

I reassured Dr. Zach that Gemma was fine and would bounce back to full strength very soon. Before leaving, he made a purchase. In low tones, he asked what kind of perfume a professional lady might like. Since the lady in question was probably Virginia, I suggested an elegant but subtle scent by Creed. Mayor Zach never even flinched at the three-hundred-dollar price tag, a sure sign that the man was in love and loaded. Before he left, I posed this question to him. Had anything bad happened in Harbor Bay that might be linked to Violet or me? Zach looked puzzled and shook his head. Other than the murders, he cited the waterfront development project and Patrick Stevens' hit-and-run death.

"Course, like any other place, we've had our problems," he said. "Cheating scandals in school, shoplifting, mostly minor stuff, and lawsuits. Plenty of them. You know how contentious people can be even when they have no reason to be."

"Cheating scandals?" I asked. That was news to me, and it put Philippa Gordon squarely in the bullseye. "What happened? It's important that you tell me."

Zach blanched and tried unsuccessfully to backtrack. "We hushed it up. Never prosecuted anyone. No need to ruin a fine person's reputation over one mistake."

Math was never my strong suit, but I could add two and two like a champ. "That's when Principal Gordon resigned, isn't it?"

He nodded. "Retired, actually. It wasn't her fault, but she took full responsibility. See, she was close to the man behind it. He was a slick one, too, I must admit. He moved away, and she resigned." He shook his head. "Funny how that worked out. He got a promotion, and she got a bellyful of guilt."

Once again, I almost—almost—felt compassion for Philippa. I recalled Mandy's description of the woman who took Philippa's place. She looked a lot like me. Was that the link to the hideous crimes afflicting Harbor Bay? It seemed improbable, but as the Great Detective observed, once you eliminate the impossible, what remains, however improbable, must be the answer. I thought of Lionel Stevens and allegations of financial mismanagement. I already knew of Kim's shoplifting problem. None of that involved me or my aunt. Perhaps Gemma was the intended victim after all. I decided to quiz her about that topic when she recovered. Between Gemma and Mandy, every town peccadillo was an open secret. Had either of them uncovered something too incriminating to ignore?

My tangled web of thoughts, coupled with a lack of sleep, gave me a whopping migraine. Still, I managed to hold the fort and present a reasonably professional façade to the customers who straggled in. When Violet arrived around four p.m., my stiff upper lip began to quiver. She immediately recognized the signs and urged me to leave Poppet to her. Only one thing deterred me. Fantasia was not with her.

Aunt Violet quickly explained. Blaike had stopped by looking for me and took Fantasia home with him. His dad was visiting from Chicago, and Mitchell had to see his favorite girl. "He said he'd bring her back to your place, Marky. Don't worry. I doubt that Mitchell is equipped to give Fantasia the attention she needs."

I was suddenly gripped by a crippling fear that the dog I had grown to love might be snatched away by her rightful owner. Blaike knew how I felt about Fantasia, and the two of us had hardly parted on good terms. Would he be cruel enough to punish me that way?

Immediate action was called for. I slipped away to my apartment, changed into something comfortable, and rang Blaike's number. He answered right away in the warm, friendly manner that had me hooked so long ago.

"Hey, I tried to see you earlier. How's Gemma doing? Have they caught the guy yet?"

I explained the situation before broaching the topic of Fantasia. "Mitchell doesn't plan to take her back, does he? I love that dog, Blaike, and she loves me. Please convince your dad that she's better off with me." Normally I hate begging, but this was no time for pride. When he hesitated, I felt the sour taste of defeat.

"Look, Marky. My dad's lonely in Chicago, and he misses Fantasia. She helped him through some tough times after my mom died."

I clutched the side table waiting for the final blow, but by some quirk of fate, I got a reprieve. "He's always liked you. Wanted you to be part of our family. Expected it. Maybe if you talk to him, you can convince him to leave her with you. He'll be here until tomorrow morning. Can you drop by tonight? We could have pizza just like in the old days."

I caught a whiff of nostalgia in his voice. Before I left for Chicago, we'd celebrated Pizza night every Thursday with Blaike's mom and dad. None of this fast-food stuff, either. Mitchell Harrington made his own sauce while his wife rolled the pizza dough. We ended the evening with a fierce session of Scrabble, where competition was keen and contentious. Those were good times. I couldn't help wondering if I had sacrificed simple pleasures such as those for a failed attempt at fame in the big city.

"Bring your aunt if she's available," Blaike said. "Dad thinks a lot of her."

I caught Violet just as she was closing the store and explained the situation. She was reluctant. I could see that, but my aunt was also a good sport.

"Oh, why not," she said. "I haven't seen Mitchell in ages. Just don't blame me if I doze off. The past few days have been rough."

Before we left, Violet told me to bring my trusty police baton. "That thing is a lethal weapon, and with all that's happened, we can't be too careful." We clambered into her Mercedes and sped toward the Harrington home.

* * *

The house was a spacious, imposing colonial with stone pillars and a massive three-car garage. The backyard included a large patio with brick pavers, an outdoor kitchen with a pizza oven, and an Olympic size swimming pool. The vast size of that cement pond intimidated me. My swimming skills were limited, so I hadn't used the pool much despite Blaike's relentless teasing. He called it cowardice. I labeled it caution.

At first, no one answered the doorbell, although I could hear Fantasia barking. That made me wonder if I had confused the time or if the Harringtons were using the pool and couldn't hear us. Violet circled around to the back yard. while I peered into the garage. Both Blaike and his dad enjoyed tinkering with cars and often holed up there. The side door was unlocked, so I entered and called Blaike's name.

That's when I saw it. At first, it didn't register. Blaike's Range Rover was parked in the first stall, and his motorcycle in the second. But nestled in the third garage space was a vehicle I hadn't seen since high school—his beloved Corvette Convertible. He'd babied that car and kept it in pristine condition. I'd always teased him about that because he treated it like his firstborn child. It was custom painted—Cadillac bronze with gold flecks and a black rag top. But now, its shiny surface was marred by a crushed front end that had succumbed to rust.

"I'm sorry you saw that," his voice said. "But I guess it doesn't really matter now."

"What's going on, Blaike? I thought you sold that car ages ago."

"I wanted to, but it wasn't possible." I turned to face him, noting that his appearance hadn't changed, but something else had. He wore a fixed grin that was very unlike anything I had seen before.

"I don't understand. Where's your dad? Did you find Aunt Violet?"

He walked toward me with the same moronic grin on his face. This wasn't the man I knew. The man who offered me his ring. The man I'd thought I knew. I didn't panic, but I felt very close to it. I edged toward the front of the garage, searching for a weapon or a means of escape.

He didn't seem worried at all. "My dad's not here."

"Oh. Did he leave already? I heard Fantasia barking."

He took another step closer. "He never was here. I lied."

"Why? I don't understand." Where oh where was my aunt? We needed to grab Fantasia and make tracks.

"You never did understand, Marky. That's your trouble. You plow through life on your own terms no matter who you destroy. Always trying to be like that aunt of yours. As if nothing in Harbor Bay was good enough for you."

"That's not true." My hands felt clammy, and a drop of sweat trickled down my back.

His grin had been replaced by a sneer. How could someone so handsome morph into such a sinister figure? "You ruined my life," he said. "You destroyed everything I cared about."

Those were the very words that Gemma's assailant had uttered.

"Let's discuss it. But first, where's Aunt Violet?" I prayed that she was unhurt. No purple cord around her neck.

"Violet's fine. For now. But she won't be interfering. This is the final scene in our little passion play, Marky. Your aunt will be our audience."

He motioned toward the side door. I evaluated my chances of making a bid for freedom but thought better of it when I saw the large wrench he brandished. Blaike must have read my mind. "I wouldn't advise it, Marky. This makes a terrible dent in the skull. Prentis found that out. Crane too. Now be a good little girl and follow orders."

He grabbed my arm and dragged me around the side of the house to the pool area. Aunt Violet was there tethered to the chaise with one of those absurd purple cords. That monster must have bought out the entire stock of them. In a touch of irony, he had used one of her Hermès scarves as a gag. Fashionable to the end, my aunt. I knew she would appreciate the distinction. Her eyes were alert, and despite the situation, she seemed relaxed.

I knew that I had to subdue my panic if I expected to survive. Violet's life and Fantasia's welfare were at stake. Blaike was twice my size and totally self-possessed. Eerily so. He was also a double murderer.

"Okay. What's your game plan?" I asked. Admittedly that sounded odd, but Blaike, the super-jock and MBA, routinely used that type of language. To beat him at his own game, I had to think like he did.

Once again, he read my mind. "Game plan? How civilized. Before I kill you, I want to explain things. Just so you know."

I saw Aunt Violet nod. That buoyed my spirits and spurred me on. Maybe we would survive this after all.

"Okay. I'm listening."

His face contorted as he listed every snub and heartache I had inflicted on him. "When you discarded me, that's what you did. Don't deny it, you destroyed me." He described a downward spiral of drugs and drink that threatened his sanity. "I thought of suicide, believe it or not. That's how bad things got. Then early one morning after a night of alcohol, it happened."

He didn't have to say it because I already knew. Blaike Harrington, local hero, and respected citizen, had taken the life of young Patrick Stevens. The proof was there right on the front end of his precious Corvette.

"How could you? You killed that boy!"

He shrugged. "I didn't even realize it until I got home and saw the damage to my car. My dad took care of things. He pretended to discover the body and called the cops. Nobody ever suspected a thing, and that next week I left for college. We told everyone I needed a more reliable car, and nobody questioned us. The Harringtons are respected in this town. I drove off with a brand-new Jeep and a clean record. My dad phonied up a receipt, but Gideon Hall never even asked to see it."

He saw the look of horror on my face and frowned. "It was an accident. That kid was dead before he knew what hit him. Why ruin my life over that?"

I recalled the cruel set of his mouth when he discussed the waterfront project. Perhaps I never really knew Blaike Harrington after all.

"What about Paul and Jonathon Crane? Were those accidents too?"

I was mesmerized by his calm recitation of facts, so like the Harvard Case

Studies, he'd read in graduate school.

"Prentis must have been nosing around here when he saw the 'Vette. Your little secret wouldn't have bothered him one bit. He was as amoral as you, Blaike." The truth of those words sickened me. Prentis and Blaike were more alike than I'd ever realized.

"You got it, Marky. Such a smart girl. He figured out what it meant and used it to blackmail me. I knew where it would end, and your little party was the perfect opportunity to eliminate him and implicate you." He preened. "Two for the price of one. Pretty slick, huh? Paul was groggy from drugs and liquor. That made him an easy target. I counted on your incredible naïveté to spare me from suspicion. Bad things just don't happen in Marky-land, do they?"

I felt sickened by the cavalier attitude of this murderer, a man I'd considered a friend and a bit more. "I suppose Crane figured it out, too," I said.

Blaike laughed. "That guy and his damn podcast. He was arrogant, I'll grant him that. He previewed the thing for me. Asked if I had any comments to make before he called Gideon Hall. Can you believe it? What a dope."

In retrospect, Crane's actions were foolhardy. Some would even say stupid. I knew all about that kind of mistake. At least for now, I was living proof of it.

Blaike continued his narrative, chuckling as he did so. Clearly, he was enjoying the show. "I had a comment to make, alright. That fool was down for the count before he even knew what hit him."

"But you spared Gemma."

He glared at me. "Naturally. She had nothing to do with it. I'm no monster. Once I saw my mistake, I just left her there. You really shouldn't loan your clothes to other people you know."

Control. I willed myself to maintain control. "Untie my aunt's hands and remove that gag. No one will hear her, and we both promise to behave."

Suddenly he morphed into the perfect host. He untied Violet, poured two glasses of lemonade, and handed one to each of us. That was more disquieting than his earlier show of malice.

Violet shook her head and swallowed her drink. "Thanks," she said. "I see only problems for you, Blaike. How do you dispose of two more bodies? After all, people will search for us."

MBAs from the University of Michigan are coveted in the business world. Graduates require keen minds and superior analytical skills. Blaike displayed both of those qualities as he explained his plan. "I anticipated that already. The roads are dark here at night. Treacherous. So easy to miss a curve and have an accident. The cops won't even question it, especially when I tell them how upset you got."

"Upset?" I couldn't help protesting.

Naturally, that merely fed his enormous ego. "Yeah. Everyone knows how you love Fantasia. When you found out that you couldn't get her back, you freaked out. Naturally, I tried to stop you, but you are so headstrong."

Violet sipped her drink and studied him. "Very clever. How will you work it? Forensics are so accurate these days. If you drug us, they'll find out. Ruin your perfect plan."

That perplexed him. Blaike thought about it for a minute, furrowing his brow as he did so. At one time, I'd thought that deep-thinker pose was sexy. Now it seemed contrived and silly.

"I'll just have to risk it. Besides, when your car crashes and burns, there won't be much left of either one of you. Gideon Hall won't spend the money for sophisticated tests." That goofy grin again. "And you know just how convincing I can be. The bereaved lover mourning the woman he adored... being consoled by Gemma and Mandy." He rolled his eyes. "I can just see it now. You'll have a grand wake. That I promise you. Maybe I'll fill the hall with your paintings. Yes. That's the perfect artistic touch."

The sun had set, and as evening skies darkened, so did our prospects. Any notions I had about reasoning with him were long gone. Bottom line, Blaike intended to add us to his list of victims. I wasn't fearful, just saddened by the loss of my future and that of my aunt. I couldn't bear to look at her knowing that because of me, she had to suffer.

Finally, Blaike stretched and leapt up from his chair. "Time's up, ladies. Let the show begin." He grabbed my arm and dragged me toward the gate.

"Ow! That hurt!"

He'd never raised a hand to me before, but this time he cuffed me hard on the side of my head, making my ears ring.

"Hurt? I know all about that, Ms. Marky Davis. Your pain is only beginning."

Violet uttered a faint cry and charged toward him. "Stop this nonsense, Blaike. What would your mother say?" She aimed a kick at his tender parts but missed.

He didn't respond. Instead, he stunned my aunt with a glancing blow from that wretched wrench. Not enough to kill but enough to daze her and blunt any further attacks.

"Feisty, isn't she?" He hooked his other arm around Violet and propelled both of us toward her car. He was strong and muscular, two things I had always admired and lusted after. Now I wished I had chosen that geeky nerd who chaired the chess club and couldn't bench press a toddler's weight. I could have handled him.

Blaike pushed Violet into the driver's seat and tossed me into the back. "Don't try anything," he growled. "If you do, I'll clobber your aunt with this wrench and end things here." Before we started the engine, he taunted us. "Make sure to fasten your seatbelts, ladies. Safety first."

Violet backed down the circular driveway, but she didn't stop there. Instead, she gunned that mighty Mercedes engine, shifted into drive, and headed directly for the back yard and the Olympic swimming pool.

He roared when he realized her plan, hurling language at us that no gentleman should know, let alone use in mixed company.

Meanwhile, I retrieved that little item I had placed under the seat. My trusty Pelican tactical torch crunched down on Blaike Harrington's well-shaped head with a resounding thunk.

That sent him into slumberland.

People always ask, could you really hurt someone if your life was threatened? My answer was a resounding yes!

Meanwhile, Violet stomped on the brakes just at the edge of the swimming pool. She flung open the car door and screamed at me, "Come on! Let's get out of here while we can." After a second, she glanced at Blaike and said, "Better clobber him again in case he starts to revive. No sense taking chances."

I followed her instructions and gave my former love another tap on the noggin. Not enough to kill him. I checked that. Just enough to knock him out. Violet found one of the extension cords and bound his hands. How appropriate that the tool he had used to discredit us was now restraining him.

I slipped into the house to free Fantasia while Aunt Violet called Gideon Hall. The beautiful collie instantly jumped into my arms and covered my face with doggie kisses. She was mine and always would be. We belonged together.

Police sirens, flashing lights, and the convergence of the news media created quite a circus at the Harrington manse. Before Blaike was carted off in an ambulance, he concocted a wild tale about an unprovoked attack by the Davis duo. One look at the mangled corvette in his garage put paid to that lie. Traces of Patrick Stevens' blood still clung to the front bumper of that car. In his arrogance, Blaike hadn't bothered to hose it off.

Epilogue

The aftermath of that horrific encounter will never leave me. Sirens, flashing lights, and the inevitable media spotlight consumed my life for longer than I would ever have imagined. With it came the inevitable nightmares featuring a wrench-wielding Blaike Harrington. Aunt Violet told me it would all pass, and as usual, she was right. New customers crowded into our store, eager to glean salacious details of what became known as the Hometown Hero Homicides. I kept my head down, focused on our business, and refused all requests for interviews. The entire experience was so appalling that it left me feeling empty. Had my rejection of Blaike triggered that malevolent spree, or had he merely unleashed the evil already within him?

A poignant scene with Kim and Lionel Stevens made everything worthwhile. Dredging up the details of Patrick's death was painful, but it freed them to finally move on with their lives, knowing that their son's killer had been found. I was proud of that.

Blaike's legal team won a change of venue to Grand Rapids. Despite their attempt to portray me as a heartless femme fatale and sell a diminished capacity defense, he was found guilty of two murders, vehicular manslaughter, and false imprisonment. A sentence of life without parole was pronounced. Mitchell Harrington's part in the coverup was handled more compassionately. Due to declining health, he was given probation and assigned community service.

"Do you feel guilty?" Gemma asked me after the trial ended. "After all, you dumped him, and that started everything."

Luckily for her, as my friend and business partner, she got a pass on questions like that. Gideon Hall discovered that Blaike had committed a few less serious crimes around Harbor Bay while he was still in high school. Unsolved burglaries, car thefts, and the like were subsequently attributed to that hometown hero I thought I knew.

The Harbor Bay town council needed an infusion of talent after Tilda's resignation and Blaike's removal. Mayor Zach, newly married to Virginia Lanter, vowed to invigorate that august body; Tongues wagged after the mayor's whirlwind courtship, but most people applauded Zach's new lease on life. He was less successful with Disraeli, although he vowed to woo the Corgi until they reached detente.

Two new faces now graced the town council. Aunt Violet, our landlord and invaluable consultant, agreed to permanently relocate to Harbor Bay, despite Thomas Wolfe's warning that you can never go home again. And with the encouragement of all who knew her, Mandy Watts found her voice and became a forceful advocate for the forgotten workers of the town.

When my parents returned from their sabbatical, they were stunned by the changes in our sleepy little town and horrified by my brush with death. My mom clutched me so hard I could barely breathe, but dad was far more philosophical. "Never a dull moment around Marky," he said with a shrug.

Gemma and I knuckled down and devoted ourselves to making Poppet a roaring success. We had the help of an engaging mascot to aid in that effort. Fantasia became our official greeter and my treasured companion. I'd learned a lot since leaving Chicago. Glitz and glamour were less meaningful than the bonds of friendship and community that I'd forged in Harbor Bay. That lesson was well worth learning.

A Note from the Author

I have always loved the transformative power of cosmetics and the thrill of solving mysteries. This series combines both elements in a heady concoction designed to intrigue readers.

Acknowledgements

Belcastro Literary Agency, Ella Marie Shupe agent

About the Author

Former Federal Executive Arlene Kay was an unconventional public servant who renounced her bureaucratic ways to pen mystery novels that are sly, slightly snarky, and filled with clever clues. She is the published author of three stand-alone mysteries, and two series featuring smart, sassy heroines with a yen for justice and an eye for adventure.

SOCIAL MEDIA HANDLES:
   https://twitter.com/Arlenekay1
   https://www.facebook.com/Arlene.Kay.author

AUTHOR WEBSITE:
   https://arlenekay.com/

Also by Arlene Kay

Intrusion (Mainly Murder Press)

Die Laughing (Mainly Murder Press)

The Abacus Prize (Mainly Murder Press)

The Boston Uncommon Series (Bellebridge Books)
    Swann Dive
    Mantrap
    Gilt Trip
    Swann Songs

The Creature Comfort Series (Kensington Lyrical)
    Death by Dog Show
    Homicide by Horseshow
    Murder at The Falls